Andy Barnett

&

Forgetfulness

Abolfazl Hajimohammadi

Title: Andy Barnett and Forgetfulness

Author: Abolfazl Hajimohammadi

Publisher: Supreme Century, USA

ISBN: 978-1939123817

Date of Publishing: March 2019

Andy Barnett

Magical Rain

William Barnett was a tall man with black hair and brown eyes. He owned a home appliances store in Butterbahn. His friends and acquaintances all knew that he would use any opportunity to travel around. This time he decided to explore the dark jungle that lay close to an ancient village called Tourin. At times the jungle would get so dark that even a ray of moonlight could not penetrate it. Having heard about overnight screams of strangers in the jungle, William was so excited to visit the mysterious place but once he stepped into the jungle, he realized he was not so gutsy he had thought he was.

At sunset in the fall when William was taking a stroll in the dark jungle to get back to the village inn, he suddenly heard a horrendous sound. He recalled the time when he had told his friends that if he heard such a thing, he'd summon the person who was the source of the sound and take a snapshot with him but now that he was running away among the woods, he sneered at his stupid assumptions blaming himself for going a long way from the village. For a while, William ran through the trees that started to look scarier any moment. He was unable to find the way back. Unlike his claims, he'd never been a courageous man. He was trembling with fear. William was frightened at the sound of feet being dragged on dry leaves of the jungle but once he realized it was a village girl from Turin, he was relieved. She was a beautiful girl with unibrow and eyes the color of the stars. She was walking in the jungle so contentedly as if she was not scared of anything horrible in the world. William blamed himself for being a coward again. At first sight, the girl realized that William was lost.

'Are you OK mister?'

'Er…I…yes,' he replied agitatedly.

'But you don't look OK. Are you lost? I'm going back to the village,'

'Who me? I never get lost,' said William trying to show off his bravery.

'So, go back to the village because the dark jungle gets into a bad mood at night. Even now you can hear it if you pay attention. Good night.'

She had only taken a few steps away, 'Where are you going?' I lied. I'm lost.' William asked her with a beseeching tone.

Bewildered, the girl stopped and asked, 'So, why do you make believe you are a hero? Come on! Get a move on!'

On the way, William came to learn that she was Tom Jackson's daughter, the village headman. Williams was so envious of his chivalry. Fear was meaningless for him.

Her name was Telma. She told such things about the jungle that William thought to himself he would never have set foot there had he already knew them. Savoring the sweet taste of love for the first time, William tried hard to prove to Telma that he came from a reputable family but Telma loathed narcissistic men.

In the following weeks, William returned to the village under different excuses. One day he said he was taking photos of the kids and monuments; another day he would say he was attending the nuptials of one of the many people he had made friends with. One day Mr. Jackson, Telma's father, pushed him to a corner.

'What about building a house here and joining us as an honorary member of the village? Pull yourself together, selfish boy! My girl doesn't like you. If you go on like that, I'll have my dogs chase you. Get a life, man!' said Mr. Jackson.

For a while, William tried to suppress his feelings for her but he didn't allow himself to be disappointed. Preferring his heart to his brain he forced his wisdom to follow his passion. He used to make fun of lovers but now he had become one. He promised himself not to judge others anymore. William insisted so much that finally one of the villages known as the wise elderly mediated for him. He first told William to pledge he would stop misdemeanors and stop being arrogant. When looking at himself from outside, William thought the old man was right to give him such advice. He went away and confined himself to a corner. Yes, the wise elderly was right. A girl like Telma would never marry an egoistic man who just cared about his own whims. He made up his mind to face the facts and fight himself. Truly fighting oneself is the greatest battle of all times.

Several months later the wise elderly who was badly ill made good on his word and got Telma's consent. The fruit of the marriage was a boy called Andy. After he was born, Telma uncovered a secret that she had kept from everyone. She gave William her memoir but got his word not to read it until after her death. Telma spoke as though she was expecting to die any moment soon. For days and even months afterward they lived a happy life but finally, after three years of married life, Telma died in an accident.

William could not believe his eyes when her body was being taken to the Tourin cemetery. He couldn't believe it was over. He kept moving around expecting to see Telma among the crowd. William got so depressed that he would shed tears in an abandoned house at the cemetery every day. The house that villagers said was haunted by wandering ". William was not afraid of these rumors and even he would sit near Telma's grave overnight and read he memoir which started with this prelude,

7

"I'm Telma. The girl born to hear and see. My body is on the ground and my mind in the sky. It's me Telma. I hear the cries of the universe. The galaxy whispers in my ears. I'm brimmed with things people have never been able to see. I'm full of memories that if hears, I'll be called insane. It's me Telma. The daughter of the galaxy, the daughter of the sun and the rain, the daughter of thunder and wind."

Four years later when William managed to overcome the bitter memory of Telma's death, on fall night he felt he was burning with an intriguing feeling. He felt like visiting the cemetery again. He was so adamant as though he had no other choice or as if the haunted house at the cemetery was calling him for a rendezvous with Telma. He was filled with the sweet feeling. At dawn, he got in the car with Andy and headed for the Tourin cemetery. He was cognizant of the fact that staying at a cemetery would not suit a six-year-old boy, still, he couldn't help going there. He felt he was not in control and being pushed by a metaphysical force.

Williams reached the cemetery but he still felt something extraordinary which he was not able to resist. After two days of stay at the cemetery, he was still doubtful. That day when he started his walk through the woods, he mostly talked to the people about his recent equatorial journey. He replied all the questions properly and helped a lady bearing a heavy backpack. As he reached the remote parts of the jungle, he came across strangers. Some of them were wearing suits and some other had long robes on. First William thought he had entered an old movie shooting location but he was wrong.

Among those strangers, some of them were pointing at the sky and saying things that William could not accept. 'Rain pour down and wash'. How on earth would it possible to await rain while the sun was shining and there were no clouds? They left. William noticed the last group walking up the jungle path. There were three poor men with worn clothes on. One of them was wearing a big beard covering his square shoulders with a tread-bear and faded coat. The second one had a blonde mustache and a short neck. He was so short that his long and gray robe touched the ground. The third man was down in the dumps. He was frowning in such a way as if it was the end of the world. The heavily-built man was called Howard. That's what the frowning man called him.

'…Howard, my friend, since the cursing wolf has found his way to the jungle we have lost our permit,'

'By thinking about the permit you just get upset. There's nothing we can do about it,' said Howard.

'How can I stop thinking about it? How are we supposed to make a living? Look at these clothes. They are supposed to belong to defenders of the spell but they have proven useless since long ago. If the poor magicians' committee had not reached out to us, God knows what would've become of us.'

With a soothing tone, Howard said, 'We'd better wait so the magical rain washes away all the spells and that goddamn wolf shows up.'

William who had made enough observations today stepped forward with hesitation and said, 'Good day gentlemen! Nice weather!'

'Good day mister. That's right. Great weather. It's gonna rain tonight. So, if you have nothing important to do, do not leave your house,' replied the big man.

With a smile on his face, William replied, 'It's impossible. There is not even a patch of cloud in the sky. I'm sorry but were you talking about a wolf?'

'Yes, we were discussing to see how likely that'd be for us to see a beast,'

'You may hear strange sounds around here but there's no wolf.'

'Thank you, sir! Are you from the village?' asked Howard with a smile.

'Since the day I've lost my wife, I hardly ever go to the village,' said William sadly.

'Oh, sounds like you've been through a big loss. Good-bye, pal!'

William bade farewell and headed for the village. This was his daily routine. At sunset, he would go Mr. Jackson's house to take Andy back to the cemetery. On the way William had on multiple occasions turned toward a sound from tree branches. Once after a scarecrow moved his eyelashes, he immediately turned but the scarecrow was standing still. William was coming to believe that everything is weird.

That night when it started to rain, he remembered the poorly-dressed men and the weather forecast that had promised of no rain till next week. Tonight it was raining cats and dogs. William visualized the men's faces who looked as though they whispered in his ears warning him of that night. William stopped those thoughts when he stood behind the window facing the cemetery. The night was falling over the jungle. William was not surprised as the dark jungle was known to be so dark but the sound of a wolf howling was not an accident. Oh, by the way, the poor men also mentioned the wolf. First William tried to calm down but he started feeling scared when unpleasant thoughts filled his mind like floodwater. Frightened, William picked up his gun and flashlight and set off. He told himself several times that he is just scared of an imaginary incident. He could hear the howls getting closer and closer. What had happened? Why did everything look so weird? Suddenly he recalled his first encounter with Telma. Tears and rain trickled down his face. He remembered how scared he was then when Telma came to his aid. William gulped down his saliva at the sound of a horrendous sound from a tree overhead. He was wondering if the people's tales of " could be true. He thought he heard the sound which felt good as it would make the mysterious wolf get away from the cemetery.

It rained all night. William who spent the night with strange dreams woke up to Andy's voice. He was talking to someone.

'Thank you! You saved my toys. I'll make it up to you. I will give you a big fat rat.'

Yawning William got out of the room and said with surprise, 'what's up to Andy?'

'These cats are really good at forecasting the weather. Had he not told me to pick up my toys yesterday, all of them would be drenched now,' said Andy pointing at a kitten.

After the cat mewed, Andy added, 'You are welcome Pico. Don't mention it!'

'Who is Pico?' asked William surprisingly.

This kitty. His mom calls him Pico but his dad says he must be called Jerine but I don't care about his dad. Pico sounds better. They have stopped talking to each other over picking a name for him. They are cross now but Miss Venice says ….'

'Who the hell is Venice?'

'Pico's mom. She says Polouk…oh, Polouk is Pico's daddy. She says Polouk always starts a fight and then comes for conciliation. He is afraid of his wife but he is a kind man. Mrs. Venice is bad-tempered. She wouldn't let anyone comment. But we agree over the choice of Pico as a name,'

Smiling, William said, 'But cats cannot talk!'

Andy looked at William in great surprise. He thought he knew nothing.

'So, how come they talk to me? Don't know why nobody believes me except mommy Telma. Of course, her friends also believe me but sometimes I cannot sleep 'coz the poor Yurgen sits on her grave and sings. Once I cried out of the window and asked her to stop. I told her I didn't like her voice. The tall woman laughed and said no one likes my voice. They treat me so nicely, especially the tall lady.'

Thinking that kids like making strange stories, William pretended that he believed what he had heard.

Leaning on the door William cast a look at Andy who was following the cats out of the house. Andy would wave his hands happily as he was passing the graves and would say something. William smirked and went back in. Andy kept walking. When he reached an old oak tree in the middle of the cemetery, he came to an abrupt stop. He looked as if he was petrified. A branch moved, a head came out. It belonged to a midget with a woolen hat and white beard. The midget asked with admiration, 'so, I'm glad I visited my father's cemetery.'

The midget who had kept aloof for a while was doubtful but he eventually said, 'Yes, it may be harmful but would save him.'

The midgets were murmuring something when a horse of smoke jumped out of the branches and started galloping around the cemetery. Andy was still standing still staring at the ground. The midget consulted himself one more time and finally made up his mind and uttered strange words. In the end, he pointed at Andy and said, 'Mood Boora Karbias!' Then he smiled proudly and said, there you go! That's the strongest spell for midgets' forgetfulness. It's better this way. I should be going now. The parallel world, I'm coming back. Bye, little Andy. Take care! You must be very important.'

Andy made a move all of a sudden. He felt pain all over his body feeling his feet were numb. Now after that strange spell who would believe Andy understood the cats' language? He had lost his power and didn't even remember having that power before.

At ten in the morning when William was holding Telma's memoir he was walking through the graves. When he reached the grave of the wise elderly, he stopped for a moment. He must do this. William had learned to act that way toward anyone who'd been kind to him. The wise elderly had helped William marry Telma. On his tombstone, it was written, "Oh, you, the passer-by! Like you I was also passing this way but when you are reading my tombstone, I've already started a better life." William muttered some good wishes for the old man and kept going. He stopped at a grave on which Telma's famous saying could be read. "It's me Telma, the daughter of the galaxy," taking a sigh, William sat there and opened Telma's memoir,

"After a warm sunny day now that the heat is gone and the night has fallen, heralding the arrival of the stars, it's such a pity that black holes, deep and dark, swallow everything. What does this deadly newcomer want of the sky? What is this sound from its black throat? Why is it fighting the creation? It may harm the graceful face of the moon with its claws. It's the moon that makes life possible in the dark of the night. Its rays shine over everything lovingly. It shines over the mountains and the seas, the plains, and deserts. It shines over a white butterfly that's sitting on a flower, over the ant carrying a grain toward home overnight.

It's a strange night tonight as the sound of the sky can be heard so clearly. Is it my sense of hearing that has come to its peak or am I dreaming? Mars is stormy with a pounding scream in the air. Jupiter's calm. The sound of water boiling…"

Hearing a familiar voice William stopped suddenly. It was the same poor men about whom he had thought all night and day…It's hard to believe that a wandering midget is able to force the hateful wolf to flee. I like these pig-headed midgets so much.

The short man who was called Mathew said, 'How on earth can a creepy creature from the horror world come to the dark jungle? How could a midget emerge from the parallel world? Interesting, isn't it?'

'What the hell does this cemetery have to attract so much attention?' asked Frank, the drowning man.

Hurriedly William arrived.

'Greetings! You are great at forecasting the weather,' said William.

The three men turned to him surprisingly.

'Good day pal! I just expressed my hunch and looks like it has come true,' said Howard.

I was hoping to see you again so I could hear more of it,' said William excitedly.

'To be honest, we don't know much either likes you,' said Howard.

'I guess you are hiding something gentlemen,' said William doubtfully.

Looking at William, Howard tried to find the right words.

'Sometimes curiosity brings nothing but fear and pessimism.'

William thought he was being threatened. He looked as though he was analyzing the recent events.

'Don't worry. I didn't mean anything. Be optimistic like us,' said Howard.

'How can I be optimistic? Everything is weird. Strange sounds, the howling of a beast, the rain which I never expected. I feel the world has changed. Even my son is daydreaming. He thinks he can speak to cats and he is very serious.' Howard looked as though he had found the answer to the mysteries inside himself. He turned to his friends then feeling anxious he turned to William and said, 'Take your son out of here right now. Do you understand? Right now!'

William had just realized that whatever worries the poor men should worry him too.

'Excuse me sir, but can you tell me why?'

Howard was staring at the jungle fearfully as if he something had him concerned.

'Just listen to me! Alright? Please!'

He then left hurriedly and once again asked William to run away from the cemetery before it was too late. William felt he had gained an insight after the brief conversation. He ran toward home. Quickly he picked up his stuff. As he was leaving the cemetery he knew that this would be his last stay in that haunted house.

The Familiar Corpse

One could hear the voice of a woman in number 7, Mailman Street who was reminding others of their duties in the absence of William during the last month of the summer. William had gone to the North Pole that was his biggest wish ever. Flora Cooper who had married William after Telma's death had two daughters named Dianna and Dennis. With her small and round glasses, she looked pretty serious. She was tall and thin. The only thing she shared with William was the fact that they both preferred a house with a classic design.

Andy was 12 and despite the passage of years since the mysterious incident at the cemetery, he still didn't realize the wonderful power he possessed. Like William, Andy had black hair and brown eyes but he looked innocent with unibrow like his mom. He shared many characteristics with her mom but his face didn't show all of them. His bravery, lengthy contemplation, and self-sacrifice reminded William of Telma. Andy was neither thin nor heavily built. He imagined he had a special sign; the sign did not actually exist. He would only see that in his dream. Something like a book was being written out of his left hand's lines.

Andy didn't realize what had become of him during childhood. He didn't realize how he had survived dangers miraculously. He even didn't realize the wonderful power within himself. Still many didn't know there is a boy living in house number 7 that is a wonder boy even if he didn't realize that.

The nights of the Mailman Street were the weirdest nights for Andy. Every night he would hear whispers but as he would look out of the window, he wouldn't see anybody out there. In daylight, he would hear strange screams. No matter how hard he concentrated, he couldn't get to identify the source of the noise. This happened at least once a week. One day when Andy had gotten home in a hurry to tell them about an invisible woman crying, his step-sister Dianna was sitting on the couch watching Andy with her mischievous eyes. Dianna was three years older, she was rude and selfish. The characteristics that anyone in the first encounter would agree she had. Excitedly Andy entered the house and said, 'Hey Dianna. Where's the mom?'

My mom or yours? If you are looking for your mom, look for her elsewhere.'

'You have no right to insult my mom.'

'Mom? Better call her a wanderer in the woods.'

Angrily Andy cast a look at Dianna. It had become a routine of the day for Dianna to insult Andy's mother. Andy kept looking at her with eyes full of hatred. He felt like crushing her under his feet like a cockroach but he tried to calm down. Andy reserved the right to complain to Flora but it was difficult for him to tell Flora what ugly words Dianna had used to describe his mom. Those days everyone kept accusing Andy of delirium.

Andy climbed the stairs and slammed the door shut. Sitting on the bed he stared at the ground angrily. He was so mad but he didn't get the chance to feel that way as he heard somebody from the alley but as usual, it wasn't clear who the voice belonged to. When Flora and Dennis got home, Andy did not feel like telling them about the invisible woman. Anyway, such stories were repeated many times and nobody cared to listen to them anymore.

At the dining table that night, Andy was still mad at Dianna. His younger brother, Dennis was jumping out of his skin for being able to join the school's scientific group. He explained for several times how difficult it'd been for him to achieve that. Dennis was 9 with big, black eyes. He was so skinny, they had difficulty to find clothes that'd fit him. He regarded Andy as his hero and had told the bullies that beat him up he had a brother who could beat ten people at a time.

While eating fish and chips impatiently, Andy raised his head at the sound of the door and asked, 'Are you expecting anyone? Somebody is knocking at the door.'

'Yes, we are waiting for invisible people.' said Dianna with a smirk on her face.

Madly, Andy looked at Flora. Had she not heard the knock at the door either?

'There's nobody there my son. Have your meal,' said Flora sympathetically.

Knock, knock, knock. There was a happy woman at the door…

'Hello…anybody home?'

'Somebody is at the door,' said Andy surprisingly.

This time he looked at Dennis. He hadn't heard anything either. Scared, Andy ran to the door. There was no one there but Andy could still hear her.

'…thanks, good boy. Ok, let's see what's going on here.'

Andy was sure someone had gone in. Dianna was shooting with her small camera to entertain her friends. Flora did nothing as instructed by the psychologist. She took as sigh as she was standing there with her hands crossed trying to hide tears in her eyes. No one believed Andy as Dennis did. When Andy was pointing to different corners of the house, talking to the invisible person, Dennis would start trembling with fear.

'…look here. What a nice lampshade!' An invisible man said, 'Yes, that's too old. I like classic homes. Ok, let's go, sweetie. This boy is making too much noise…let's go. Why should he be able to hear us? He is a strange boy…'

In the eyes of others, Andy behaved strangely but the presence of ghosts in the house where they lived was so frightening that he wasn't able to stay calm. it was a strange night. When he went to his room after Dianna made fun of him, again he heard the steps of an invisible person who didn't want to leave Andy's room. Despite all the fingers of blame pointed at him, Andy sat there patiently and bore them all. He could still hear Dianna who was nagging about his behavior. He wanted to go to her and say as she is blaming him, he can hear someone in the house which scares him to his death but he tried to stay calm.

After calm returned, Andy stood behind the window thoughtfully. He told himself those who live around him cannot be seen. They must have come back, so Andy thought he could talk to them without others noticing them. Maybe this would work. He taught he had the guts to do that. To go to school Andy had to pass the Kalagan market. It was a wide and stone-paved street for electric buses only. All the alleyways of Kalagan were busy, just like the main marketplace. On the way back home, Andy noticed a little boy who was pulling his mom to a toy store. There was a man with some cloth in his hands asking people to buy 'the world's best material' from him. He could hear the bicycle bells. 'Newspaper, newspaper, latest news, the secret of the fiery Morris is out'. Andy reached the bookstore called the 'house of fantasy'. Standing at the window, he didn't notice the people who had to mind their steps not to bump into him. The 'Lazy Pumpkin', the week's best-seller, was in the window. While he was checking out the books, he heard someone say,' I've read it. It was fun.'

Turning around, Andy noticed an old and poor peddler who was looking at him with a nice smile. He could hardly agree the old man was a book worm. The stranger had his gray eyes fixed on Andy. He seemed so satisfied with the encounter as if he had expected it for such a long time. He was holding a book under his shoulder so tightly as though the book would run away. He had salt and pepper beard, before talking, he looked at Andy for a while.

'Can I ask your name?'

'Andy Barnett,'

'I'm Edwardo Butterfield. One thing I like to do is to give books to people as a gift. If you don't mind, I can get you the Lazy Pumpkin,'

Andy was thinking if the poorly-dressed peddler had any money to buy him a book. Anyone else would have thought that way.

'Oh, I didn't realize I'm not dressed properly for a friendly meeting,' said the peddler who had guessed what Andy was thinking about. 'Not always do I look so bad! Actually…actually, I had gone somewhere and I had to dress like this but I have enough money to buy a book. Here, let me prove it to you,'

Edwardo stepped into the bookstore quickly. The bell atop the door started to sound. 'ding, ding.' The bookseller, with his shining mustache, welcomed them. Andy knew Mr. Jackeline who always had a big smile while sitting on a chair at the counter. Casting a look at Andy with his green eyes, Mr. Jackeline turned to Andy,' look who's here! William's son! Your dad is a customer of mine; did you know that? Now, which book do you want?' said the bookseller with his funny tone.

'Lazy Pumpkin,'

'Lucky boy you are! This is the last copy in the window. Good books are rare. They sell like hot cake. You have to wait till the next copy comes out if you don't hurry. He was still looking at the book eagerly when he was handing it to Andy.

'I know your dad has traveled to the North Pole. He told me that. We are friends.' At that moment the kind part of Andy's brain started functioning. He thanked him and left the store. Andy thought Mr. Butterfield was not normal. Why should a total stranger buy him a book during their first meeting?

'I may look like a strange man. Well, to be honest, I am. I will explain why I am so should we meet again. Good-bye!' said Edwardo before Andy said anything.

Andy didn't figure out what the peddler meant by being strange but he had liked him. Now he felt he was starving. He headed home smiling while recalling the bookstore saga.

That night Andy was waiting for a regular guest with his face stuck to the window. Little by little when the sky was filled with stars, somebody stepped out. Andy recognized the round and fat face of Mrs. Clara Davis who was approaching. She was Mrs. Cooper's closest friend. Andy preferred to sit close to the window before going downstairs so he could gaze at the sky and find some comets. All of a sudden he got away from the window. What's become of the world? The sky and the earth were both sinking in darkness. A horrendous silence had prevailed. There was only one voice whispering in Andy's ears quietly, 'the dark jungle is not safe anymore,'

Be quiet! Someone is coming this way,'

'I know him, run away. Runaway,'

'We should remain behind this tree.

'No, he is merciless. We should go. We should inform others too,'

'We have no time pal. We gotta do something.'

'Nooo! You killed him an idiot! I will take revenge,'

'Don't go! Don't get close to him. Stay away! No! nooo!'

Andy looked pale. He felt some extra mass is leaving his body, something like a spirit. His feel could hardly bear his body. He fainted and fell off.

Andy's body was lying on the floor motionless but his head was full of nightmares. It was midnight and he was standing near the Tourin cemetery. The cemetery's abandoned homes could be seen. The strange mumble could also be heard from the dark jungle, like always. Shaking with fear, Andy noticed a dead body. Oh, my god! That was his own body! The thought of dying and looking at his body from another world as a soul scared him to death. He could feel his heart in his mouth. Just then a howl could be heard and then the shadow of a big man fell on the trees. One more time Andy looked at the corpse. What should he have done? Should he have left his body there? He was not able to make a choice. Andy took a sigh of relief as he heard the howl from farther and farther away. What had happened? He could not fancy the idea of having a twin brother. He stepped forward and bent over the body to cast a look.

'Get up! We must go! He'll be back any minute.'

This was the last nightmare Andy had. He came to at that moment. He had a splitting headache but no trace of the nightmare in his head.

Burning Cups

Later Andy asked himself many times what had happened on the night when Miss Davis was their guest. He knew that he had fainted, he recalled having heard someone whisper something but he did not remember anything else. He could still feel the terrible moments of that night like a cold and biting wind in his ears. Just as he was about to remember everything, he would face a world devoid of any mishap. That memory lingered on but it wouldn't be refreshed but Andy could feel phantoms and discomforting details. Andy was so deeply immersed in his thoughts that he didn't realize he had turned around the Kalagan market three times. In an uncrowded part of the marketplace, he heard something.

'...I'll wait for it to return. I'll get my mouse back! That's my right!

Surprised, Andy stared at the cat's mouth. Can cats speak he waited there for five minutes so he could hear the cat speak again but it seems as though he was wrong and he could just hear the cat meow? So, he called himself a mental and set out on the road feeling frustrated and sad.

The following days, Andy spent most of his time in a library close to the home looking for some sort of cure to his ailment. On Saturday he would read a book, on Sunday two more books but gradually he was coming to the conclusion that he is suffering from an unknown disease which has to be registered by himself. The thought of that made him laugh. Andy's Disease!

It wasn't that only! It wasn't only Andy who called himself a lunatic; others shared the idea, too. Since Andy had said in the classroom that he is distracted by an invisible man, he started to feel lonelier day after day with everyone distancing themselves from him. Nobody was willing to see a mind around. Since the word was out at school that Andy is haunted by ghosts he started to feel more isolated and forsaken. Some parents would go to school and insult him warning him against having anything to do with their children or else they'd call the cops. Every day the school sends Flora an unfair note. Andy laughed at all those ludicrous letters. He had never said he had anything with two-headed Jinn. He had never threatened he would hurt them with the help of the ghosts if they didn't listen to him. Mr. Hafling, the school principal, seemed willing to get rid of Andy in any way possible. He tended to listen to the pupils' parents and would do anything they'd asked him to. Finally, he did what he thought he had to do. He sent Flora a letter filled with lies about Andy.

'Ms. Cooper, I'd already informed you of some facts about Andy hoping to see some change, but I'm afraid to announce that not only your son's attitude has not improved, but it's also even worsened with him calling himself a member of the ghosts' association and urging others to join them by committing suicide. We will no longer put the safety of our children at risk. Many families are concerned about their children. We will have to have Andy leave school for a month so he could receive medical treatment. In case he is not treated, then I'm afraid you will have to look for another school.'

At the top of his voice, Andy told Flora that he has not done such a thing. Flora tried to calm him down. As a matter of fact, she believed what she had read.

That night Andy couldn't sleep a wink. He was thinking about his strange ailment and Diana's hateful smirks. He even dreamed of objects in the room opening their mouths murmuring about Andy calling him abnormal.

After that disgusting letter, Andy felt even more lonely. He was not even allowed to go to school. Talking about strange subjects was not permitted at home even if invisible people started marching in his room. He was in a bad situation. Most of the time he would take refuge at the Kalagan market. At least there he could attribute the invisible people's voices to the shopping crowd, something he was unable to do at home. Everything happened very clearly. Just last night he heard the sound of high-heels walking on a wooden panel depriving him of a good night's sleep.

The Kalagan Market was crowded as usual. Frustrated, Andy was deep in his thoughts on a store step at a corner. Sounds of whispers mutter and screams were getting louder and louder every day. Where was this going to go? What was expecting him? Among that hue and cry, Andy even heard Edwardo's voice. Was he also able to become invisible? When he raised his head, he just realized that Eduardo was standing there with nice green clothes on smiling at him.

'Good day, Andy! How're things? How do I look?'

'I thought you'd gone for good,' said Andy bored.

'Why should I leave when I have got a good friend like you?'

'Thanks! But not everyone agrees with you,'

'They shouldn't as I come from a place that's weird for normal people,' said Eduardo while rubbing his hands together.

'You mean somewhere like mars? Only there is it possible for people not to call me weird,'

'You look pale! You don't feel very well but let me tell you something....,' just then the market bus passed by making it impossible for Andy to hear the end of the statement.

'What did you say?'

'I said we may just as well end up in Mars too! Everything's possible in our world!' Eduardo behaved in a way as if he had some mysterious news to give.

'What are you talking about?'

'You need a little time to get to believe my words. But someone should tell you after all! I know certain things about you, Andy. That's why I don't think like others. In fact, nobody gossips about people like you in the world I belong to. Well, you have the right to be agitated but should you know why... then maybe you'll suffer that much,' said Eduardo while looking at Andy lovingly.

'What is it that I must know? Who are you, sir?' asked Andy scared.

'I'm one of the thousands of magicians in the world,'

'What? A magician?' retorted Andy in a way as if he was hit with a knife.

He then looked at Eduardo with doubt. He was expecting something to go wrong at any minute.

'What is it? Are you scared? To be honest, I don't want you to worry but it's been long I've been watching you. My job's to find people who are talented to become magicians. You may have realized some of that talent too,' Said Eduardo.

'Like what?' asked Andy while looking around worriedly.

'Like hearing strange sounds,'

All the pessimism was removed like dust getting up to the air! Happily, and with a mouth that was not going to stop talking, Andy turned to Eduardo. You could tell easily that he had fallen for magic.

'I wish we had met much sooner! Can you do something so I would stop hearing those strange sounds?' asked Andy excitedly!

'Can you tell me exactly what's happened?'

'I can hear voices and sounds; they're everywhere but cannot be seen. I have nightmares. I even saw a cat speak!'

'I was expecting this but not so soon!' said Eduardo who was thinking to himself.

'Oh, my god! Well, in the world of magic these are commonplace. Nothing to worry about! I should get going. By the way, welcome to the world of magicians!' said Eduardo trying hard to smile.

'But I haven't accepted that yet,'

'You have, you just haven't uttered it yet. Here's the address,'

The address was written on a piece of fur reading Publishers' Street, Password.

'Where's this?'

'This is where you need to be. I'd be happy if you could make up your mind soon. Of course, if you want to get rid of the voices of those invisible people. Just… just one more thing… doesn't tell your family about this. You know… they are not like you and me. It's hard for them to believe such things! Good-bye!'

Andy looked at Eduardo leave. This meeting was even stranger than the one with invisible people. Magic? Did he belong to the magicians' world all the time he was looking for a name for his ailment in books? Wow! How amazing! What a bizarre meeting! He stood there for a while until a trolley brought him back to himself.

'Hey young man! What are you doing? Stand back!'

'I'm sorry mister!'

While going back home, Andy was busy thinking. So, that's what he is! A magician! A magician? He had no idea about magicians; neither good nor bad. His mind was totally blank. He was sure he would not be able to find anything about magicians in the library either. He had hundreds of questions in his mind but he mostly wanted to know how Eduardo had gotten to know him. He was grateful to him as he had saved him from all that maddening insanity.

Nothing had changed at home. The only difference was that Andy was no longer trying to tolerate the incessant agony anymore. While leaving home today, he would not imagine he would go back home in such a mood. Eduardo had rocked his world by uttering those few sentences reluctantly. Now there was light shining over the dark side of his mind making him an optimistic view of things around him. He was no longer frightened unless something really scary would come his way like the moment he stepped into his room. Like all others, Andy went mad at the sight of his room first! Who had done this to his room? When he went downstairs angrily, he could think of only one person, Dianna! As he reached the last step, he found Flora standing there.

'Your room looks like a warehouse, Andy!'

'No, that wasn't me. Someone has gone in without my permission and made a mess of things,' said Andy while giving Diana the daggers' eyes.

'What the hell! Perhaps those invisible ghosts have done that!' said Diana mockingly!

Flora frowned at Diana.

'When I was your age, my room was not that tidy, either, darling! Please go to your room now and clean it up!' said Flora kindly.

Andy knew Diana was usually behind such stupid things; yet, he thought to himself it could also be the invisible people. No, it wasn't possible i.e. it couldn't be possible! They had already put him to too much trouble. They couldn't have gone that far! He was not ready to accept that audacity. Yet, when night fell, scary thoughts came back to him again! Several times he put his head out of the blanket to look around the room. Everything was in order but what if he saw something moves? He put the blanket over his head again and told himself while painting,' No! Impossible! It's all a dream! Didn't you see what Eduardo had said? When will morning come?'

Next morning Andy jumped out of the bed hurriedly and went to the window. He could hear those voices again. Once again he imagined a horrible prospect for his life but he couldn't sit idle. He should have done something. On such occasions, he would usually remember an address he had hidden under the bed.

After a few nights of nightmares, Andy finally made up his mind. He said he was going to the library. When he got to the Kalagan bus stop, he was still dubious. The sun was going up and some buses came and left the stop but Andy was still sitting there thinking about different eventualities. Finally, he mustered up some courage and took the next bus.

Andy was being more surprised as he was walking down the Publishers' Street. He thought 'Password' must be the name of a famous place as they'd usually shorten the address to famous locations like that. No one had heard of it! It was all in vain! Andy sat on a bench in a corner staring at the ground but when he looked up; his eyes were shining with delight. Password was the name of a long dead-end. Why couldn't he think of that sooner? Password alley was empty. It looked like an abandoned alleyway without any inhabitants. It was paved with brick-red stones that would make you feel weary and the lamp posts were so old as if the city had been unaware of that part of the town. Looking for the alley sign, he reached a wooden door at the end of the dead-end. He knocked three times but got to reply. Then he sat on the small wall on the sidewalk. He never felt so good despite the fact that there was no one there and it was so empty! Eduardo may arrive at any moment! He was so excited! Finally, after twenty minutes, somebody arrived. A middle-aged woman with big glasses and a dress??? on her shoulder.

She was approaching with a smile.

'Hello, young man! This workshop has been closed for long,' said the woman.

'What workshop? I'm here to see 'Password',

'Oh, so, you're one of us!'

One of us! That means that Andy was standing by a magician.

'But you're mistaken, madam! It says Password on the sign,' said Andy.

'Oh, my god! You must be a newcomer! It's written with hidden words. Only magicians are able to read that. Ordinary people only recognize it as a workshop. In due time you will also be able to read both words like me,'

Andy was proud he was able to read the hidden word.

'I'm Julia Roberts. What's your name?'

'Andy Barnett,'

'Welcome Andy!'

When Ms. Roberts tingled the wooden door, Andy asked with surprise, 'What are you doing?'

'You gotta tingle it to open it. Of course, you must be one of us to be able to do that.'

First Andy thought that was a joke but when the wooden door was opened, he grinned and took two steps back and while his heart was thumping, he stared at Ms. Roberts and told her about those exciting moments and praised magicians for that. Ms. Roberts set off before Andy would faint with joy and excitement.

The wooden door opened to an alleyway both sides of which had tall stone walls. Andy's heart thumped harder and harder as he reached the end of the alley. He was excited at the thought of the kind of place he was about to visit. He reached a dead-end with an empty circular space. He could hear something there. Ms. Roberts would not Andy to go beyond a certain limit and Andy did not utter a single word until facing a signal. He could still hear things. It sounded as if some people were busy stamping something. Ms. Roberts was losing her patience.

'Come on! Why are you taking so long?' said Ms. Roberts impatiently.

Andy expected someone to throw a ladder to the other side but at the sight of objects there were gradually being obvious, he started wondering what's going on. First, he saw two counters with people sitting at them. Then several long doorways appeared on the wall. A short man was moving the packages between the two counters.

'Sorry, Ms. Roberts! There was an important move that had to be made.'

Andy could not believe his eyes. He had to come to terms with all these unexpected things as part of his new life. Those sitting behind the counter were either stamping papers or writing on them. Ms. Roberts bade him farewell and took the third doorway out. Just then a man in a dark brown jacket and a brown top hat called Andy.

He was sitting in the section with burning cups on the other side of the western counter on a high chair and looked to have little to do.

'Identification paper please!'

'What paper?'

'The same paper with which you were led to this place. Don't you have one?' said the man in a bad temper. Andy handed him the paper hurriedly. The man who looked calmer at the sight of the paper flashed blue light on it and inspected it with a magnifying glass. He then brought a notebook and started writing. He finished the first page but he was still writing on the second page. Andy thought how could so many things be written on that little piece of paper or maybe the man was dragging his feet to make believe he was doing something important. He kept writing up to page four. Then he took four burning cups from among a lot of them at this side and put them on the counter.

Andy was waiting to see what would happen next. The man put the fur leaf in the first cup that had no signs on. Andy realized the importance of the note every minute. After the note sank in the flame, Andy could hear an old. The man listened to the whisper and moved his head.

'Andy Barnett. So, you are Andy Barnett,' said the man.

'He's gotten old. He doesn't do things like he used to,' said the man pointing at the cup.

As soon as Andy put his hand in the fire to pick up the note, Andy extended his head out of a natural reaction to stop him but he changed his mind as he could not notice any sign of burn on the man's face. It seemed as though the fire burning in the cup was cold and harmless.

'We call this cold fire. You'll deal with it after the fourth year. Let's move to the next stage!' said the man.

He did the same thing with the second cup. It was a golden cup with a bright, yellow flame. Upon listening to the whisper from the second cup, the man said with surprise, 'the house on the side street!'

All of a sudden, the men stopped stamping the leaflets and started looking at Andy. They acted as if they had no trust in him. Andy freaked out under the burden of those unfriendly eyes gazing at him. With a pale face, he looked at them. They had all stopped working. Andy could hardly look them in the eyes. He realized the importance of the third cup when an old man from behind the eastern counter asked Barack to hurry.

So, the man was called Barrack! Andy didn't have a good feeling. They had raised their stamps but they were not going to bring them down until after hearing Barack's response. Barack put the leaflet into the third cup and started listening to the whisper.

'Nothing to worry about men. It's only a new conjurer, who's arrived with a delay,'

They didn't care about the rest of the story, so they resumed stamping the leaflets. With his shining green eyes, Barack winked at Andy and pulled out the note.

'Looks like you are being honest but based on the law the last cup must be checked too,' said the man.

There were close to a hundred little paintings moving on the body of the fourth cup. The painted figures were speaking to each other with no voice. Some of them were sitting; some of them were standing and pointing at somewhere. One was smiling and the other one was crying under a tree. Barack left the note in the fourth cup happily. A flame as high as one meter gushed out and depicted Andy's face.

Nodding his head, Barack pushed a button under his hand. Ding! It sounded as though someone hit a steel glass with a spoon. He then pointed to doorway number one.

'Have a good day!' said Barack.

The House on the Side Street

Doorway number one took Andy to a big yard with giant trees. Andy looked around worriedly. The only inhabitable point in the big yard was an old mansion in the northern flank. The house had a very old tiled roof. Andy took slow steps with hesitation. He had lost his determination. Just until a few moments ago he expected to step into a crowded place so, he was taken aback by silence. He could hear nothing but the crows. He hesitated for a moment but he started heading for the old house again. Hardly had he arrived at the mansion than a man with a gray suit on stepped out and waited for him in the shade. He had short gray hair and sounded quite formal and strict when he started to speak.

'Hello, Mr. Barnett! I'm Nicolas Falker,'

'Good day Mr. Falker!' said Andy in a formal tone.

'Leave all your doubt aside and follow me,' said the man.

He went inside while Andy was still trying to overcome his hesitation. What was expecting him there? It was only a few steps away! He could hear the people inside the mansion speak. There was only one more step to the entrance. He could've gone back home before it was too late. He was deeply thinking when he heard an invisible woman whispering. She was talking to herself about some personal issue and changed her mind several times. That exactly when Andy badly needed to stay calm. Invisible people had picked such a bad time for the disturbance. That was exactly when Andy needed to focus. Luckily, it didn't take long and the lady let Andy go by telling herself, 'So, that's what I'd do.' This reminded Andy of the fact that if he returns now, he has got to tolerate those disturbing creatures for the rest of his life and bear the nickname abnormal. He stopped behind the door and stared at a point. He could see some grass grown at the side of the wall under the tall windows. Out of distrust, he wanted to cast a look inside from behind the window before entering the place but the window was covered with a long curtain. Andy told himself any moment someone may get out and curse him for keeping people inside waiting for him and blame him for being discourteous. He pulled himself together, opened the door and took an inquisitive look inside. It was exactly the same way he'd imagined it to be. An old mansion, weird with some mysterious emotion that bugged him furtively. With the first glance, he was unable to see all the details. He then heard somebody get up and walk but a moment later; three people his age showed up and looked at him in such a way as though they were invited to a ceremony unveiling a new discovery. The three were standing in a line, yet Andy's eyes fell on a beautiful girl first. Her name was Lisa Brighton. She had blue eyes, big teeth, and blonde hair. She was very attractive but Andy realized soon he could not like her as she was so jealous and narcissistic. Beside her stood a cute girl with very black hair and a friendly voice calling herself Emily Henderson. She seemed to be so edgy. That shrill voice also befitted her.

On the left side of the three-person wall was a big boy with blonde hair and rabbit?? Teeth that was waiting to speak. He cast a mischievous look at Andy.

'Not bad! Eduardo is good at picking apprentices. Just like myself. I'm Eric Parsons. Welcome Andy!' said the big boy smiling.

'Thanks, Eric!'

Elsewhere in the mansion which had escaped Andy's eyes, there was a flabby woman with hazel eyes who was standing there like a shadow staring at Andy with great enthusiasm. Ms. Lili Wagner was the housemaid. She looked fascinated by checking Andy out several times.

Mr. Falker was sitting in a corner in silence. Andy was aware of his phantom-like presence all the time. He had a poker face! Once he got up, he rubbed his hands together.

'Well, if you are done with the introduction, I would like to make a few statements please,' said Mr. Falker.

Mr. Falker had started with a formal tone since they met and Andy felt kind of embarrassed -without showing it- as he had always assumed himself to be a magician but seemingly he was a mere conjurer without any magical skills. Conjurers had to undergo a special course under a trainer to be able to enter schools of magic. 'The conjuring course, despite the fact that it is looked down on among magicians, is of the essence on its own right. You are advised not to heed of others' making fun of you. You may stay away from performing magic, yet, you will have to be trained so that your mind would be prepared and you could enter the school of magic. You must be prepared to embark on a rough course at the end of which you will be put to the test. In case you are not found qualified, then I'm afraid you will have to go back home.' Said Nicolas.

Andy was afraid Nicolas may say something and make him more hopeless. How easily they could put an end to everything! If they expel him, he will have to stand those invisible people for the rest of his life! For a second, he was brimmed with despair. Then he was so thoughtful that he did not notice Nicolas talk about numerous other subjects. Only when Nicolas extended his hand toward him to say good-bye did Andy get back to his senses.

'I trust you boy! You will definitely make it!'

Feeling shy, Andy shook his hand but did not give him a reply. He heard himself say I really hope so.

The formal air abandoned the mansion as soon as Mr. Falker left. He was truly serious! Ms. Wagner led everyone to the wooden table by the window. The furniture looked unusual. Andy could not figure out what most of them were used for. The doors were tall as the ceiling keeping that bizarre feeling inside Andy alive.

'Andy Barnett, so, that's what you're called,' said Ms. Wagner happily.

Chairs started to make noise still everybody heard Andy reply.

'Yes, Ms. Wagner,'

'I used to have a little brother your age,'

'Where is he now?'

'He is not alive. I miss him!'

'My mom's also dead. My stepmother is very kind though,' said Andy.

Emily took a sigh with her shrill voice and plunged into sorrowful daydreaming. She dreamed a lot and was able to make a mountain out of a molehill. Now she was thinking about the horrible life of a lonely boy who was brutalized by his stepmother.

'Oh, dear! Your mom must have prayed for you,' said Wagner sympathetically.

'Thanks, Ms. Wagner! By the way, what does Password mean?'

Lisa smirked. It was rude but Andy did not complain.

'Password is a security building run by the council of magic. It's been coded by the spell,' replied Ms. Wagner.

'Why is there a spell?'

'You don't know much, do you? So, it must be interesting for you to hear about such things. There's a spell on Password so that others like rioters would not be able to enter it. They are not magicians but they are inclined toward treacherous deeds. They serve mischievous magicians,'

Ms. Wagner realized that's she's gone too far after looking at Andy's face.

'Forgive me, dear! It's not the right time to speak about this. Are you hungry? Do you care for some chocolate cake?' said Wagner while trying to compensate.

'No, thanks! Ms. Wagner,'

Emily was still thinking about Andy's mother. She was imagining a strange story. She pictured Andy kissing his mom's picture while shedding tears.

Among all the strange furniture in the mansion, Andy noticed a slender stick Ms. Wagner was holding. It was fifteen centimeters long with cone-shaped charcoal at the tip.

'What's that?'

'Magical pen,'

'Where can I buy one?'

'When you buy books, you can get that too. Don't worry! I'll go with you. Each pen is identified based on the tree it's made of like the lemon pen. The cheapest pen is known as the branch pen that's made from extra branches and sticks. Pens from certain trees like blue beech pen have the best quality and are much more smooth. Of course, conjurers are allowed to use branch pens only, just like the one I'm holding,'

Lisa could not remain silent anymore. She immediately showed off her blue beech pen.

'Of course, not all conjurers! It's unpleasant for our family to write with a low-quality pen. I took my mother's pen,' said Lisa.

Lisa expected a politer reaction from Andy that's the same reaction she always expected of everyone but Andy was indifferent. He kept looking at Ms. Wagner's mouth.

'Look Andy! You gotta study hard to pass the test. It's got nothing to do with pens and all that jazz. It's true that most of the conjurers make it to the school but if you get a score higher than 100, then you can pick one of the top five schools.' Said Eric sarcastically.

It was great to see someone like Eric there to make up for Lisa's bitter comments. With the arrival of Eduardo, the situation changed for better for Andy.

'Oh my God! Look who's here! Welcome! Most welcome! I have no doubt you will be a great magician one day,'

'But he still doesn't know what a magic pen is.' Said Lisa with a humiliating tone.

'It's because he doesn't come from a magician family...oh, by the way, Andy, you haven't told your family anything, and have you?'

'You mean he doesn't have his parents' permission?' asked Ms. Wagner surprisingly.

'What? A lookalike? I also wanted one but nobody cared!' said Lisa in disbelief.

'Don't be sad! She can't help feeling jealous.' Whispered Eric in Andy's ears.

'But you were not qualified, good girl!'

Andy realized that lookalike must be something of great worth.

'Could you tell me what a lookalike is?'

'It's a unique invention! A magical twin who's created from the blood of the original person to fight the families who are against magic or those who should not be informed of magic for certain reasons. When you are not home, there must be somebody to fill the vacancy and do your job in such a way that others won't realize your absence. That's terrific, isn't it?'

"That's impossible!' said Andy in disbelief.

It looked as if Lisa had a tantrum.

'So what? It's too bad for a family not to have any magical skills and to be forced to use a lookalike. It's embarrassing!' said Lisa nervously.

'But I know a girl who cried one whole day to have a lookalike,' said Eric mischievously.

'You be quiet, nosy boy!' said Lisa while venting her anger with a loud scream.

Eduardo cast a happy look at Andy once again.

'There are still more interesting things for you to see,'

Eduardo was the happiest of them all. He had ideas he could not utter. He felt as if a heavy burden had been lifted off his shoulder. Now that he saw Andy by his side, he couldn't believe how easy everything had happened. Till a few days ago he was busy thinking of ways to convince Andy to go the Password. Of course, making a mess of his room was also effective. Andy was happy but he looked sad.

'What's wrong?' asked Eduardo surprisingly.

'I feel sorry for my family. I wish I could tell them about it. At least Flora could know. School writes her all the time…,'

'No, no, no! if you really care about them, you'd better keep quiet!' Eduardo then looked at others.

'OK, kids, Andy joined us a bit late. Help him make up for it,' Emily said she was happy to help. Just then a tall man entered the mansion. Mr. Henric Blind was in charge of training at the Council of Magic.

'Good day everyone! Good to see you at home Eduardo!'

'Good day Henric! What do you have for us?'

'The letter on Linker's return,'

'Oh, my god! I'm delighted to see him! Definitely, his presence can of great help to the Lost and Found Section. He can smell better than dogs!'

'We need him or else I would have told him what you said' said Mr. Blind as he looked at Andy with interest.

'Good day young man! Are you a newcomer?' asked Mr. Blind.

'Yes!'

'I'll get you the conjuring books,'

'Can you also get me a blue beech pen too?' asked Andy shyly.

'Ok. Be my guest!'

'But that's not the conjuring pen!' retorted Lisa immediately.

'I want to give him my pen. It's brand new! What's wrong with that?'

'Well, it's not right! It's against the law!'

'I'd realize that if it's against the law, right?'

'Just wanted to remind you. It's none of my business,' said Lisa as she was biting her lips out of jealousy.

Mr. Blind cast a meaningful at Eduardo. Eduardo smirked.

'I know; she is a Brighton after all! Jealous, narcissistic and crazy!' said Eduardo quietly.

Andy heard Eric say to Emily quietly that if it goes on like this, Lisa will commit suicide.

Mr. Blind and Eduardo went to a corner of the mansion to speak together.

'When will Andy reach the peak of talent?' asked Mr. Blind.

'No need for that! Get him the books on the black hole talent. I don't want him to know about it though. For now,' Said Eduardo after a pause.

The tall man looked confused.

'Are you sure Eduardo?' so, what on earth is he doing here? He doesn't need to be a conjurer,'

'There are certain issues you are unaware of. He needs to be close to me,'

'What if you are wrong? You'll lose your job then,'

Eduardo approved of his pick with a contented smile.

'The council is aware of everything. Can you do me a favor?'

'I'd be glad to do anything for you!' said Mr. Blind anxiously.

'Go to the talent castle. If you find Andy's name in the black hole section, remove it. The council knows about it but some may have done something willfully,'

Mr. Blind was already thinking of troubling issues.

'Alright! But can you tell me why?' he asked.

'It's not the right time for that. I will explain later. The permit has been issued. I can show it to you.'

Mr. Blind believed the honesty in Eduardo's words but was not able to conceal his confusion while he was leaving the mansion.

Dias, a Book to Begin with

After the departure of Mr. Blind, Eduardo took Andy to a big library at the other end of the mansion. He came across the book that was one meter in height and required strong men to move them. Inside metal stores were filled with books. Once you picked one, another one would fill the gap. From the dust collected at the side of the window, it seems that the library was not being used much.

Eduardo left Andy among the long lines of books for a while and headed for an old shelf on the other side of the library. Andy didn't dare open magical books. He just enjoyed reading their names. From their names, he concluded that he was standing at the section related to magical novels…the giant of the dark plains… the daring goats… as he was checking the book out with enthusiasm; he reached the depth of the salon. He had never seen a speaking book and would not believe such a thing ever existed. With his eyes wide open, Andy stood in front of a book that spoke with a woman's voice.

'… we have of care for wandering goblets so they wouldn't dive into magicians' meals. We shouldn't trust the equatorial snails. They have been traitors all the time! Everyone knows that even if we keep equatorial snails in special perspiration absorption machines, they still hide amounts of venom under their skin that can make you unconscious. We all know that they are really keen on poisoning us…'

Andy could not still believe his eyes! One more time he looked at the book's protruding lips. It was speaking so fact as of it had been deprived of speaking in long years. With its bizarre eyes, it also watched Andy while uttering words. Eduardo returned.

'It is called the chef," said Eduardo with a smile.

'It's known to be a torturer always looking for someone to lend it their ears. let's get out of here before we go crazy,'

Before Andy reached the table at the end of the library, he looked at the azure blue book Eduardo was holding. It had no name on it. When they got to the table who asked him about it quickly.

'Were you looking for this book? What is it?'

'That's what you are here for. Many like to have it but like to have it is not enough! I hope you can communicate with it. It's important that you do that. It's a great guide,'

'What exactly should I do?'

'Think of your memories well. Think of war, evil, all human virtues. You need to fully focus to be able to present yourself as a good magician. Can you do that? I'm sure you can. You just need to be yourself,'

Andy found out there was nothing written in the book so he turned to Eduardo and looked at him in surprise.

'Yes, that's right. Nothing is written there. That's the problem!'

'It even doesn't have a name,'

'You must ask for it,'

'Don't you know fewer and fewer people read books every day?' asked Eduardo while laughing quietly.

'I'll leave the rest to you. You have to be alone!'

As Andy watched Eduardo leave, he told himself Eduardo should not have trusted him as he found himself a loser already! He sat by the window for a while. There was some dust from old books. On every table lay many books abandoned half finished. Andy took a look at the azure blue book. He wanted to start but he didn't know how.

'How are you doing buddy? How've things?' said Andy with despair.

He received no reaction from the book as he expected.

'Look! We can be friends. I don't know what you are good for but I'm told to talk to you. How old are you?' continued Andy.

The book still had nothing to be read.

'Are you not a guide book? Say something for god's sake!'

For a long time, Andy stared at the book in silence.

'You know nothing about how many people read books every year. What a ridiculous question that was! If you were aware, you wouldn't do this to me. You know these days you have to pay some people to read a few pages of books. I don't like you at all. You are so selfish! I'm not one of those magicians that would beg to you. Give me a break!'

He then left the book on the table angrily and went to the other sections of the library. He had mustered some courage so he started checking inside some of the books. A few moments later when he passed by the window again, he was filled with hope as he found a golden name shining on the cover of the book," Dias, a book to begin with"

That sentence was not there before. Before checking the book, Andy rose his head as he felt for a second that a man with magician's gown was standing before him but there was no one there so he put his head down looking at the book again. Now he could find sentences written on the first page.

"Dias, a book to begin with; the beginning of a life entwined with mystery, menace, and excitement! What you see will not last forever and you will have to do what you read. Beware of what you have no knowledge of and avoid uttering words you are unfamiliar with. Shadows and dark corridors are lying in ambush to take you down to the abyss of horror. So, beware! This is the mysterious world of magicians...Dias"

Andy was frightened a bit. If the writer of the book were there, he would look angry when uttering these threatening words. He was so scared he didn't dare touch the book. Once he extended his hand, picked it up and left the library.

Silence prevailed the house, which frightened Andy. He ran quickly and calmed down once he found Emily standing at the window as if she was petrified.

'Where are others?'

'They're out shopping. They'll be back soon,'
I really want to know how Dias works but it sounded scary. I couldn't get along with it,'
Emily's smile froze once she noticed the azure blue book. She put her hands on her cheeks and opened her mouth wide. She thought Eduardo may have shown the book to Andy. Then she recalled that even Eduardo is not able to read that book. So, how was this possible?
'That's impossible! Oh, my god!' said Emily in disbelief.
She then started thinking loudly.
'You'll be famous Andy, I promise. I would be standing by your side when people whisper to each other saying, 'look at Ms. Henderson, the cute girl. See? She's standing by that wonder boy, the one who has read Dias. Let's go get his autograph. Oh, Andy. I promise your fame will even reach the parallel world,'
'Where the hell is the parallel world?'
'Don't you know about it? Didn't Eduardo tell you about it?' asked Emily with wide eyes.
Andy thought that must be really important as Emily looked quite surprised and envious.
'The parallel world is a secret world that cannot be seen with the naked eye. You definitely don't know what the horror world is, either. Right?'
'The World of Horror?'
'A beastly world that is inimical to magicians,'
'Let me tell you something. Until this morning I had no idea what magic is all about,' said Andy in an embarrassed tone.
Emily realized that she had used an improper tone that was kind of reprehensive so she tried to tone it down a bit.
'Well, I was not aware of the parallel world and was told by others about it. Sit here and I'll tell you about it,'
They sat at the table opposite each other. Emily looked at Andy in amazement.

'The parallel world was discovered accidentally by a magician called Jupiter. I don't know when exactly. It was almost a thousand years ago! He was supposed to invent the magic for being lost but all of a sudden he ended up in the parallel world. When he got back, he lived like crazy people for a while. He could not believe he had made such a discovery but later he got to learn that that mysterious magic only worked for him,' explained Emily excitedly.

'So, how did he prove the parallel world?'

'Wait! Jupiter didn't sit idly by. With the help of a mythical bird called Phoenix, he found a way that's called the gate of fame transfer. He made fourteen gates to go to the parallel world each of them in one part of the world. For the time being, they only use the public gate and the other thirteen are secret and used only in emergency cases. The center of magic is in charge of monitoring the 14 gates. The center is based in the parallel world and supervises the council of magic in different countries,'

Andy tried to make believe that he's comprehended it all.

'Magicians even have their own radio and television. After you pass the test, you'll be able to get yourself a Walsh. You know conjurers are not allowed to buy magical stuff,'

'What's a Walsh?'

'A magical broadcasting machine. Among the papers, Poor code and Celebrity are the most reliable. Among radio channels, you shouldn't miss "Nuts without borders",

'What's Dias? Where is it published?'

Emily got excited again!

'Dias is a different thing. It's a book that's alive and has senses and logic. No one is familiar with its workings. Nobody knows how many copies of it are available. It belongs to a great magician called Dias who has fought the horror world. Those who are able to read Dias are rare and try for unknown reasons not to publicize it, which I believe is insane. You should take advantage of this to become famous,'

Then she got up.

'Let's look around the mansion,' said Emily passionately.

To begin with, Emily took Andy to the section of the mansion that she regarded was the most important.

'See, Andy, this is called the communication wall. It is high security and installed in administrative areas. It does formal correspondence. Conjurers are not permitted to use magical ways to communicate. Our only way of communication is the one that you see here. Luckily they have fitted one system here for the sake of Eduardo. Each wall has its own identification code. Inside the city, there are communications channels with which you can link with other walls. There is one on Kalagan Street,'

Andy was realizing how insignificant conjurers were in the world of magicians. They were deprived of almost everything. The communication wall was a sand panel stuck to the wall but the sands would not fall down.

'What are you waiting for? Try it. Put your finger on this part,' said Emily proudly.

Andy placed his finger in a spot that looked like the fingerprint. In a jiffy, the name Andy Barnett appeared on the sands

'Wow! What happened?' said Andy surprisingly.

'Nothing. You were identified. This way no one can correspond with others using someone else's name. Now you should think of the destination wall, for instance, the one in the training office. When the sands turn white, communication has been established and you can use your finger to write on the sand. The wall here is old but it works perfectly. When you're done, you just put a big cross on the sand and that's it,'

After the communication wall came the boys' and girls' dormitories. It was a spacious room but had no bed for Andy yet. Next, they visited the science workshop and the living room. They also checked a stairway which led to the Password. Andy did away with visiting the library and went upstairs instead where conjurers' classes were held. There were five classrooms and a banned room from which voices could be heard. Emily explained that the voices came from a store of magical words that are used in emergency situations but she was not aware what those situations looked like exactly. The room's door squeaked and wouldn't open.

Emily did her job right and left no question unanswered. Now there was only one more thing left. She was waiting for the inhabitants to return to the mansion so she could tell them about Dias. Andy in the meantime demonstrated the book several times and got rewarded by Emily's poetic and graceful thoughts. Andy realized there are years of distance between his thoughts and those of Emily but something made this difference look insignificant, Emily's genuine emotions and honesty.

Emily had an eye to the window all the time. Suddenly she ran out and seconds later Eric entered while looking as though he had seen a ghost! He was petrified. The rest didn't look much different either but Eduardo tried to look normal.

'Thanks, good boy! I'm so happy! Let's see what you've done. You must have spent tons of energy,'

Andy laughed to himself at the thought of the amount of energy he had spent to start communicating with the book. Ms. Wagner pushed everyone aside as wanted to see the scene before anyone else did. Now Andy knew what to do now. He just had to touch the book and ask it to show itself. It seemed he didn't even need to do this either. He was only thinking about this when suddenly the book started to shine. Ms. Wagner who was so fascinated by seeing that, pulled Andy and hugged him tightly. Then she pulled out her yellow magical camera and took photos. In the end, she held the camera upside down and transferred the images to a photo paper like colorful dust. Andy looked to be under pressure in all the photos.

'I am feeding you so, why should others take all the credit? Do you promise to pick me like your program manager?' she said in a satisfactory tone.

'Definitely! I don't have a better candidate,'

Andy felt proud. Even Lisa with all her jealousy could not take her eyes off the book and uttered words of praise.

The advice the book had given was exactly what Eduardo wished to see. He was delighted as the book had not uttered anything to be a source of concern. Apparently, things went ahead just as Eduardo wished them to. While everyone was speaking about press and reporters enthusiastically, he was nurturing furtive thoughts. He didn't want to see Andy's name in the headlines. He felt the danger in his soul. He asked Andy to get ready to return home. Then he left while looking thoughtful.

The Tyrannical Sphere

The first day as a magician was kind of strange for Andy. On the way back home he still didn't believe it was true. He thought maybe it's been one of those weird dreams that cross his mind. Something like those things that he's able to see but others aren't. Maybe he was asleep but why doesn't he wake up?

During the day Andy was expecting to wake up any moment and go back to the real world but as night fell, everything looked to be back in order. What wonderful day! He had to register it as one of the most memorable says of his life especially the book which he could not put out of his mind for a second. Even while sleeping he could recall Dias flying in his room like a bird. It would also appear as a human and seemed kind and good-tempered despite Andy's assumption.

'Knock, knock, knock,'

'Wake up jungle boy!'

Frightened, Andy woke up. It was terrible to have to wake up with Dianna insulting him after all those sweet dreams. He craved to be a great magician one day and turn Dianna to an ugly creature. He took a deep breath and urged himself to only think of the Password and good memories there.

That day when he got to the side?? House, he first hears Eduardo had banned using Dias so that Andy could do his assignments. Andy had a bitter taste in the mouth. He had never heard anything worse than this. Even Mr. Hafling's letter from school had not been so terrible. The news even put his friends to pain especially for Lisa who wanted to see her photo next to Andy on the front page of a magical newspaper.

When the children were sitting at the table feeling down in the dumps, Ms. Wagner put a parcel with Andy Barnett's name on it on the table which included some petty conjuring tools.

'Enough! Eduardo never said you don't have the right to use it at all. He said you'd better focus on your lessons for a while. That's it! I will also mediate if necessary.' Said Ms. Wagner.

'After Ms. Wagner left, Eric opened the parcel.

'It smells new!' said Eric after taking a deep breath.

He then quickly reviewed the list of book.

- What conjurers need to know about themselves, compiled by the Council of Magicians?

- Elementary spells and ways to treat them by Professor Brian Berkov

- The history of magic by Antoine Henderson

- Stories to learn from by Margaret Holem

- Good and evil in the eyes of a magician by Professor Kevin Pickford

- Poisonous plants and useful poisons by Alfred Vittel

After the book list, Eric picked a metal panel.

'Oh, my God! "Expandable notebook, up to 500 pages", they have sent you the latest version. Mr. Blind is being so generous!' said Eric in disbelief.

'What's it good for?' said Andy.

'To take notes in classes. Once it's full, you can empty it in a normal notebook,'

Once again Eric took a sigh.

'It's five hundred pages! It won't finish so soon,' said Eric.

The expandable notebook was a thick blank sheet of paper stuck on a metal pad. The paper wouldn't get wet nor would it burn. Once full, with the tip of a magical pen, you could tap the bottom of the page so the page would disappear and a blank one would emerge. Emily put her hand inside the parcel.

'The blue beech pen, the combination model. How open-handed! The invoice is not there so we could figure out its combination. It'd be great if it is a mix of fig and pomegranate,' said Emily with admiration.

Lisa was unable to stop herself so, she was thinking loudly about Mr. Blind.

'So, where are you wishing papers? This Mr. Blind doesn't know how to do his job right.' Said Lisa.

'What's wish paper?'

Once again Lisa was wearing one of those hateful smirks on her face.

'A black and shining paper on which you write your magical wishes so they'd come true. No matter what pen or color you use, things will appear in white. Most conjurers wish to enter the magic school but I wouldn't waste paper for such things because I will definitely pass the test. I wish to be working at the center of magic,' said Lisa.

'It cannot realize impossible wishes! You should've wished like me to become a magical chef. I want to invent all kinds of magical dishes,' said Eric cunningly.

'I wish one day I will be able to teach magicians' etiology. I have another wish that is personal' said Emily enthusiastically.

'You must have wished the apple you bite to turn to a princess of wishes whose white horse you'd ride and go after your destiny!' said Eric.

'No, that wasn't it!'

She then started thinking and before she sank in daydreaming, Eric found the wishing paper.

'No, now we should help Andy. Where are you going? To the wonderland?' asked Eric.

All the three of them wanted to help Andy to make a good wish as if they believed the paper would grant any wish written on it. Andy was wondering if the change of Dianna's behavior could be regarded as a magical wish. Getting rid of invisible creatures could also be a good wish but he didn't know if it was considered to be a magical wish. Until an hour later, Andy was still unable to think of a good wish. The suggestions were not that good either. So, he decided to do that at a proper time.

The first class was about good and evil as viewed by magicians. Nicolas was a strict lecturer and showed little cordiality. At the beginning of the class, after a formal welcome, the opened the topics page and started with mistakes made by ancient magicians. After finishing a lesson, Nicolas would immediately start a new lesson and he would never be satisfied with his students' performance. They had not been able to figure out what exactly would satisfy him.

On day one, the classes finished at one o'clock. Andy had taken so many notes that her fingers took the writing position even on the way back home. This tiring trend continued even after a few days which were when Andy just realized why Eduardo had banned Dias. When he got back home, he would keep writing until night and was under so much stress that he would panic any time someone knocked at the door. He was concerned they may send him on errands and he'd be unable to do his assignments but gradually things were starting to go smoothly and he was getting used to his new life. The conjuring giant no more looked horrible. The conjuring books shared so much information which facilitated learning despite Nicolas still behaving too formally.

Andy would follow up every day since he gave some blood to Eduardo for creating a lookalike. After a fortnight, while returning home, he heard some good news from Eduardo.

'Your lookalike is ready. Take what your necessary stuff tonight. It's not clear when you would go back home,'

Andy was delighted.

'When can I see it?'

'You're not supposed to see him. I mean for now. You may be shocked and face some problems. Give your clothes to Ms. Wagner tomorrow. Your lookalike will go back with the same clothes on.

Andy's smile froze. He insisted more but to no avail. When he got home, he started thinking about something which had slipped his mind for a while. How long was he supposed to stay away from home? Thinking about it made him miss home.

Next morning Andy felt he was about to leave his family for good. He looked at Denis's big and bright eyes. At least he was sure he would miss him. Like always Denis made fun of Andy to make him laugh. Andy was silent during the breakfast. The grandfather clock showed 8 o'clock. At times Andy would glance at Flora with embarrassment and felt guilty for not informing her about an important issue like that. He held a court in his mind in which he played the plaintiff, the defendant, and judge. At the end of all the question and answers, he was proved not guilty due to the fact that there were only a few days left until the one-month school suspension period. If his lookalike went to school instead of him, then nobody could hurt Flora with disheartening letters anymore. The invisible people's saga would come to an end. Even he would get rid of Diana's sarcastic comments. Anyway, this situation had its own advantages that helped Andy exonerate himself of any guilt. When leaving home, he promised Flora when he returns from the library; all the weird events will also come to an end.

'Thanks, son! It will, definitely! You must go back to school. They have no right to mistreat you. My son is great!' said Flora happily.

Andy took a sigh of relief and set off for Password contentedly. The alleyway was quiet as always. The wooden door would open with a little tingling and smirk and be regarded as routine fun for Andy. Andy's expectation of entrance counters to be invisible was useless but still, he was glad he had the one-time opportunity to experience it.

Ms. Wagner was expecting him impatiently.

'Are you here, Andy? Why are you late today? Change quickly. I have to send your clothes to the council,' said Ms. Wagner.

'Can you please call me when he arrives so I could meet him?' deplored Andy.

'Sorry, Andy! He is not supposed to come here but if you are really looking forward to him, you can go to the mirror and talk to yourself!' said Ms. Wagner while heading for the kitchen.

Her last remark made Andy feel even more wistful. Is this how they resembled each other? He took a glimpse at the magical paper on the table. It was the first time he saw a magical newspaper. That paper reflected magical incidents. In a place called The Castle of Talent, a man called John Strode had been killed. Ms. Wagner got out of the kitchen.

'What are you doing there, Andy? Come on!' said Ms. Wagner.

Andy could not take his eyes off the newspaper.

'Where's the Castle of Talent?'

Ms. Wagner who was supposed to explain things clearly approached Andy.

'It's where you should go soon,'

Then she folded the newspaper.

'That's where the intrinsic talent of conjurers comes to the fore. Most of the children have general talents but if you are placed among those with a special talent, then you'll be able to find your way into the school without undergoing conjuring courses,'

'What's meant by special talent?'

'That means a person who has special and unusual characteristics, for instance being able to move objects without touching them. If they had the right to choose, everyone would go for the black hole talent,'

'What the hell is the black hole?'

'A certain talent which if genuine and powerful can hear the sounds from galaxies and events happening in the world above, even the sounds from the world beyond the black hole, that is the World of Horror!'

'What do you mean by genuine and powerful?'

'That means he should be able to understand the language of cats. Of course, most of the black holes are only called black holes but they do nothing special. The most they're able to do is they can hear the neighbors whispering and poke their nose into their affairs! It's been a while I've not heard of a genuine talent. Now, give me your clothes. Then attend your class on the one-hundred branch spell. It's a tough course.

The spell course resembled a rock cave. Andy never liked the sigh of skulls on the wall. With their hollow and horrendous eyes, they look at Andy in a way as though they are conspiring against him. Nicolas stopped speaking as Andy arrived. Andy greeted them quickly and sat between Emily and Eric after greeting them briefly.

In a corner of the classroom, on a round stone table, along with a large number of tools related to spells and astrology. There was a glass sphere that looked like the full moon. Inside it flew a milky haze that would look like an eerie eye and at times it moved to the other side like an explosion. A number of marbles were turning around the sphere as though they had no way to get away from it. Andy knew that Nicolas doesn't like to get on a tangent in his class.

'Excuse me, Mr. Falker! What's the use of that sphere?' he asked.

Nicolas became speechless suddenly and turned to the sphere.

'So, you like it too, right? That's how it has taken the marbles hostage and wouldn't let them get away. It's called the tyrannical sphere. It's designed for third-graders but if you remove the spell, you can have the marbles,'

Andy got hold of the tyrannical sphere after class and saying good-bye to Mr. Faker. He wished to take off the marbles and run away but he was afraid. The milky haze caused horror. Once or twice he was about to extend his hand but he changed his mind. Every time he heard Eric encouraging him to do it. Upon hearing a strange sound, he turned his head and the world plunged into darkness. Frightened, Andy turned around himself regretting what he had done. He shouldn't have meddled in the sphere's affairs. This dark world was the result of an unwise interference but he came to realize that it had nothing to do with that. It was a terrifying nightmare, a familiar one. Once again he turned around. He was standing in a dark jungle near the Tourin cemetery. He turned back upon hearing the resonant voice of a man who was talking to some people.

'…he can't return to himself. There's nothing we can do.'

The mysterious silence prevailing the place felt like the air around a dying patient. Andy stepped forward with hesitation.

'Excuse me, sir! What's up?'

Nobody replied. They seemed to be invisible. Andy called them several times when he suddenly stopped and gazed at something lying on the gourd. They were standing at the grave of a corpse. The corpse belonged to Andy.

'Anybody can hear me? It's me. The one lying on the ground,' said Andy with fear.

Nobody replied. After a howl was heard in the woods, Andy stopped speaking. The man with the resonant voice started to speak.

'We must save him. They mustn't find him,'

Andy was happy. He thought he is still alive. They took the corpse and ran toward the cemetery.

Andy was running hard but he couldn't reach them. All of a sudden, everything vanished and he found himself standing in the middle of the class on spells hearing the surprised voice of Eric.

'How did you do this, boy?'

Andy realized he's holding a marble and the Tyrannical Sphere is torn apart.

'Maybe it's been expired. It's not possible for the sphere to be destroyed by a conjurer,' said Lisa in disbelief.

As usual, she uttered the word conjurer with disdain.

Fear was evident in Andy's face. He bent over his knees and remembered that this was the forgotten nightmare he had during Ms. Clara Davis' party. When he held his head up anxiously, he was trying to come up with an excuse to deny everything but that was true and something told him on the back of his mind that this is for the second time and maybe more than Andy has forgotten things like the first time. Was he still thinking that it had to do with the fact that he was a novice?

Andy uttered the last thought loud unwillingly.

'Did anyone mention you as a newcomer?' asked Lisa surprised.

Andy started thinking again. Eduardo had told him all the time that this strange feeling happens to any magicians but why hadn't any of his friends experienced such a thing?

'Are you OK, Andy?'

'Yes, Emily. No big deal!'

Suddenly Emily turned back and ran out of the classroom without saying anything. When she returned, she was cautious and her voice was trembling.

'Strange situation, guys. Mr. Blind is checking all the nooks and cranny in the mansion,'

'After the Talent Castle incident, we must be more careful,'

'But what has that got to do with Mr. Blind being here?'

'It has something to do with it, Ms. Wagner especially now that kid is here,'

'You mean Andy?'

'I didn't expect you to be so careless Ms. Wagner!'

'I didn't expect you not to notice those nosy children, either,'

When Henric Blind turned his head, the children greeted him instantly and fled. Mr. Blind thanked Ms. Wagner for informing him about the kids' presence there.

'Eduardo is only wasting his time. We'll be in trouble soon,'

'Mr. Blind can you speak clearly?' said Wagner while standing still.

'I just don't want to catch you by surprise,'

'But you're frightening me,'

'Andy can speak to cats!' said Mr. Blind after looking around.

'You must be mistaken,' said Ms. Wagner smirking.

'No, that boy has the strongest spell on oblivion,'

'But, why must be under spell?' she said worriedly.

'Because the World of Horror is after him. It's not only that.'

'Please speak out Mr. Blind' said Ms. Wagner as she was trying to overcome her fear.

'I cannot talk if you cannot control yourself,'

Ms. Wagner promised to be put herself together.

'That boy carries the signs of life after death! Talking to the dead!'

Ms. Wagner was filled with terror.

'For thousands of years, magicians have waited for someone to be found to prove this fact. That child is already one of the most unique magicians on earth,' continued Mr. Blind with agitation.

The dusting cloth slipped out of Ms. Wagner's hand. She looked pale and spoke so softly that Mr. Blind could only understand half of what she said by staring at her lips.

'You mean the Castle of Talent…'

'That's right. No trace of it must remain. They mustn't find it,'

'How can Eduardo be so sure?'

'He's known this since long ago. He heard a midget talk about it. You know what I'm talking about, don't you?'

'No, I really don't. I have no clue!'

'A few years ago word was out about the dark jungle that three poor magicians were hunted by the hateful wolf. It may be hard to believe that the attack was aimed at getting to Andy.

'With all this threat, why didn't they send the poor child to the parallel world then? He cannot be traced there so easily' asked Ms. Wagner worriedly.

Mr. Blind cast an eye on Ms. Wagner in silence. Wagner realized what that meant very soon.

'Is there anything else?'

'After that incident, the dark jungle had another bizarre guest too, a deadly rider who had wreaked havoc with the parallel world,'

'Oh, poor boy! The Dourin Rider? The salvage rider of the parallel world?' asked Wagner in pain.

'Of course, it's still unclear if the Dourin Rider had to do with Andy. It makes the council members not to allow Andy to step into the parallel world anyway…'

Andy wished to tell his friends about the corpse and the nightmare but he thought he could wait until Eduardo returns. After hearing about the nightmare, Eduardo looked pale. The children who heard the corpse story for the first time kept looking at each other with great surprise. Why hadn't Andy told them about it? Eduardo was thinking deeply. He was afraid of possible dangers. All his plans had got disrupted. He had to do something and he knew very well that he didn't have much time. All the things he feared may happen were happening one after another. After a while in silence, Eduardo got up and sat in front of Andy.

'Tell me what you've seen one more time,'

'I saw a corpse. It was mine and a cemetery which I know. Did you not say that nothing threatens me?'

'I still say that.'

Andy was smart enough to make a reverse interpretation of what he was hearing.

With all the evidence at hand to be worried, Eduardo didn't want to be merciless so he didn't utter the truth.

'When the spell of the Tyrannical Sphere enters your body, it's natural to have bizarre nightmares I'm worried about you Andy. I don't really know how many malignant spells have nested in your body,'

Then he went to his office worriedly and came back with a bottle of an elixir.

'Drink it,' he ordered seriously.

Andy cast a look at the bottle. Two litters of a grayish liquid to drink! The elixir was stinking. With the first sip, Andy could feel his blood moving faster in his veins. He didn't want to drink anymore but Eduardo frowned at him and pushed him to finish the job.

Andy gulped it down with a lot of difficulties. He felt weak. He cursed himself why he had talked about the nightmare. His eyes were closing. In the first glance, he saw a vague image of Eduardo who was hugging and carrying him to the bedroom.

Eduardo was anxious. Before leaving the mansion, he pulled Ms. Wagner to a side.

'Perhaps if Hendrik Blind was able to keep secrets, I could have asked you to behave naturally. I know it's hard but please pull yourself together Lili. I want to go somewhere that has to do with this child. I will be away for several days. Don't worry about Andy. I had to cast a spell on him again. Good day Lili.'

That night Andy had bad dreams. Sometimes he dreamed he was in the middle of a turbulent sea and at times in a dark jungle. All of his dreams shared the element of terror. Andy dreamed that the sky gets dark and black-clad men covering their faces, move him in the middle of an ancient graveyard at the foot of a rocky and hot mountain. When he woke up, he found nobody around. Then behind the window and the prevailing silence, he thought of a horrifying song he had heard while dreaming. Suddenly, the black-clad men surrounded him from all directions. Frightened, he turned but he calmed down again as Andy's internal adviser had asked him to be brave.

The Invisible Midget

Andy was thinking of all possibilities. He had questions he had found no chance to ask. He was walking in the mansion with clenched fists. It was hard for him to accept that even after getting acquainted with Eduardo, his problems still persisted. What could he have done? It was unfair to blame Eduardo who had been gone for two days. Andy was almost certain that his leave had something to do with him. With an angry face, he sat by the window and listened to a feeble voice in his ears. There was no more nightmare. Things were getting farther and farther. He knew that there was something surprising in him and that there was some scary knowledge behind this negligence but if he were able to dream of those facts without any fear, he would definitely go for it, yet, dreams had brought him nothing but horror.

The air in the mansion was burdensome and bizarre. Nicolas who was quite punctual had canceled his class. Ms. Wagner treated Andy with caution and sympathy. His friends also kept being kind to him in the past two couple of days. He was thinking about the trio when they showed up.

'That's enough Andy! Aren't you tired? You just happened to see something that we weren't lucky enough to see,' said Emily.

'Lucky?'

'Yes, lucky. Aren't you lucky to be able to see something wonderful? You are different! Even Lisa cannot help deny this despite all her jealousy, can she?' said Emily bravely.

Lisa looked as if she had swallowed something sour.

'Yes!' said Lisa who had no other choice.

Nicolas finally showed up on that day. He started with cracking jokes, something he hardly ever did. He didn't mention the reason for his absence. First, Eric complained about the class cancellation which could harm his scholastic progress.

'So, we'll have a make-up class over the weakened,' said Nicolas.

Eric hit his forehead regretfully.

'I was kidding!' said Nicolas with a smile.

For a while Nicolas talked about the Tyrannical Sphere and its weird uses; he spoke of the people who had faced issues with the sphere as well. He concluded that the sphere's curse had changed Andy psychologically. In fact, he tried to convince Andy that it's been nothing to worry about. After he succeeded in doing so, he started to teach the new lesson. It was difficult for him to let go of his emotional tone even while teaching.

'I'm glad we're studying this interesting lesson at last! It's true that people have varying tastes, but I think everybody will enjoy the lesson today. I'm going to talk about a wonderful creature that has opened new windows to the magic science. A creature called 'the invisible midget'.

'What? Invisible midget? asked Eric seriously.

'It seems you haven't even taken a glimpse of the book 'Stories to Learn from'. Invisible midgets unlike the midgets in the Parallel World had no magical skills. In fact, they lack magic, pain, ability to speak to humans and senses. Even at the time of death, they feel no pain and die with a smile!'

'What useless midgets we have around!' said Lisa hatefully.

'Where are they then?' asked Emily.

Nicolas turned around the classroom.

'That's a good point. They are invisible,' replied Nicolas.

'Are you putting us on?' asked Eric with greater surprise.

Nicolas moved his notes.

'They can't be seen with the naked eyes. The only way to see these eerie creatures is to drink an elixir called offer. They also share a point of weakness, carrots! They love carrots.'

He then placed a cylindrical bottle on the table with some yellow elixir boiling inside it. At times bubbles went up the corkscrew.

'This is safer,'

'They are not wise creatures, so why shouldn't they be seen?' asked Eric sarcastically.

Nicolas took his admiring eyes from the bottle and took a side.

'First off, you must know that the invisible midget is very funny and that reasons enough for me to like it. Even at old age, it looks and acts like a kid. It never gets old! Burning its hair removes the black curse. Its tears prevent elixirs from going off. Boiling and drinking a glass of its pure, odorless and germ-free sweat makes the worst ailments tolerable, making us hopeful that probably there are other unknown creatures in the world,'

Emily was looking at the boiling liquid.

'Where do they live?'

Nicolas hit the bottle in such a way as though the midgets were there.

'It can be anywhere. Timothy Brox was the first magician who discovered invisible midgets. By making another he intended to fight weak eyesight but he came up with the invisible midget instead. Read his book. It's fascinating!'

'I sometimes drop by them. They're not very far,' said Nicolas furtively.

'You mean they are also found in the Password?' asked Lisa surprisingly.

Nicolas gave a negative response with a smile.

'Not at the Password but there's a place like it which is supervised by the Council of Magic. I know a secret route but it's crowded in the daytime so, I go there at night. It's illegal but it's worth it!'

Lisa's efforts to figure out the midgets' whereabouts were in vain. Emily was daydreaming, as usual, telling the midgets stories. They had their hands under their chins, nodding their heads at the end of each statement. After Nicolas explained different views regarding the emergence of the invisible midgets, Ms. Wagner arrived at the classroom out of breath.

'We have an urgent message from the communication wall, Mr. Falker,'

Mr. Falker was seemingly expecting the note, so he left the classroom hurriedly and when he got back, he was extremely happy.

'Sorry, kids! I have an important mission. Won't be around for a week. Good-bye!'

He didn't even wait for a reply.

'He just proved how sorry he was!' said Eric unhappily.

After Mr. Falker left, they kept reading the book. It was explained that invisible midgets had nothing to do with the Parallel World. Andy was curious about the midgets in the parallel world as the book put it, they were extraordinary creatures.

'Have you even seem the midgets of the parallel world?' turning to Eric,

'I haven't seen them but I hear they don't care much about magicians' rules,'

'Why?'

'They find our rules ridiculous. For instance, the elixir of wish is dangerous for us and impacts the nervous system but the midgets use it as a regular drink,'

'What's the wish elixir?'

'It realizes dreams while asleep. This would suit Emily the best,'

Emily smiled sweetly. Eric continued with his speculations about invisible midgets. He thought the abandoned houses of the Password neighborhood could be a place for the midgets but based on accurate information Lisa had, none of them were magical.

'They must be somewhere around here. Nicolas doesn't lie,' said Eric uncertainly.

Then he gazed at the yellow and lucid bubble that was going up the desk at the end of the classroom. He went there quickly.

'He's forgotten to take the elixir. You may not believe this but it's not hot at all despite all the boiling inside. I must give it to Ms. Wagner,' said Eric in disbelief.

'Mr. Eric Parsons, don't be an idiot! Do you really want to hand it in? didn't Nicolas say that visiting the midgets is worth ignoring the law? Take a bit of it and then return them the bottle. No one will realize anything.' Said Lisa blameful.

'I'm such a good boy! I won't make any infringement. I never even thought of it,' said Eric with a sigh.

'So, let them have it, good boy!' said Lisa with a big frown.

'No way! I was just' kidding! But how are we gonna find a midget now?'

First Lisa thought they could drink safer and midgets will appear but Eric thought that was a stupid idea.

'Do you think another will last till we find the midgets? We can use it only once, not several times. It'll finish!' said Eric as the objection.

Andy was uneasy with the plan.

'Why don't we ask Ms. Wagner about it?' said Andy.

"She wouldn't know!' said Eric.

'No, you're wrong. She knows a lot! She is a magician after all!' retorted Lisa.

'Now, wait and see!'

As they were climbing down the stairs, Ms. Wagner got out of the kitchen. She told them excitedly to try her strawberry cake.

'Believe me. I've not used magic,' she said.

Then she invited everyone to sit down. She acted in such a way as if she had nothing to do but to make them happy. She came back with her source of pride, the strawberry cake! She had never baked a cake without using magic. Lisa took a slice.

'Excuse me, Ms. Wagner, but do you think there's a place around here that is run by the Council, like the Password?' asked Lisa.

'I thought you've already found out!' said Ms. Wagner in disbelief.

'Well, you know…'

'Don' gimme that bull, girl! You may not have noticed it but behind the abandoned storehouse in the year, behind that tall wall, there must be something. That's why the wall there is taller. That's Mr. Radiche's farm. He died years ago and as he had no heirs, the Council inherited the farm. This must be an exam question by Nicolas, right? Don't let him know I told you about it,'

Eric turned away so Ms. Wagner wouldn't realize he had a plan.

'Have you been there?'

'Just once! That's when Mr. Rediche was alive. There were nice things there. Oh, good old days!' answered Ms. Wagner.

'Nice stuff? Like what?'

'You can ask Nicolas about the rest. I'm not supposed to reveal the Council's secrets,'

They had the cake quickly and went back to the classroom.

'I see! There are nine kinds of stuff over there,' said Eric mysteriously.

"And we will be the first conjurers to ever see those things! I will record everything with Ms. Wagner's camera. We'll need that in the future!' said Lisa whose blue eyes were shining.

Andy looked at her. He wanted to tell her not to put herself to trouble and stay away from Ms. Wagner's stuff.

After dinner, each had a portion of the elixir as determined by Eric. Andy believed that little amount of another that tasted like ginger was enough for adventurism but an unknown feeling was making his head warm. The warmth was reaching other parts of his body as well. It was not time for Eric to hand in the bottle to Ms. Wagner. He made believe he had found the bottle just a minute ago. He was surprised to realize that Ms. Wagner knew nothing about another.

So, what on earth had she seen on the farm? He told everyone else about it.

'Snofer must have been discovered recently then,' said Emily.

'So, what has she seen on the farm that she calls interesting?'

'Maybe she just wanted to pretend she is important,'

'Let's go!' insisted on Lisa.

'Not as long as she is awake,' said Eric.

They left the mansion at eleven sharp. Like always, the yard was dark. Huge trees showed the signs of fall with different colors. Tree leaves could be heard as a cool breeze was blowing gently. When they reached the abandoned storehouse, Andy got disappointed.

'It looks as if it's been abandoned for such a long time!'

'Magical storehouses have a guardian spell. Don't touch anything!' warned Eric.

'With all these crowded rooms and halls, I don't think we'll be able to find the secret route till morning,' said Lisa hopelessly.

Andy thought that was the only logical statement Lisa had made that day.

The search took half an hour. Andy asked several times what exactly should they be looking for but he was happy to see others didn't know the answer, either. He thought he was a fool but he was relieved now. At last, Eric was lucky to find some clue. He explained that his father had taught him about doors that looked like walls. The wall at the end of the storehouse could be one such door. After staring at the wall for a minute, they could hear something and the door that looked like a wall opened. Proudly Eric went to the door but once he saw the farm, he got startled! The Rediche farm was a magical one! Comparing Eric's body with the farm produce was like comparing hazelnuts with watermelons. Lisa stood under a ceiling of giant ivy.

'Maybe Nicolas referred to human visitors as midgets,'

Eric was leaning on a two-meter pumpkin.

'I didn't know I can become invisible!' he said sarcastically.

'What kind of cucumber is this? It must weigh fifty kilos! I'm sure Ms. Wagner has neither seen these nor the midgets,' said Emily.

She then pointed at a house in the middle of the farm excitedly.

'That must be Mr. Rediche's house. Let's go in!',

Just then they heard a scream.

'Hellooo! Anybody there? I'll inform the Council.'

They ran to seek shelter immediately. The guard repeated the same statements as he was distancing as if he was following his instincts. Andy was hiding under giant mushrooms. He noticed a bottle that had been blown out of proportion by magicians. Then he started having sweet dreams. Was this real? He was sure he was awake but it seemed like a dream. There were so many strange things in the world which required him to get out of the mansion to see. He had to defeat fear. He had to cease agitation to be able to get out and see the world outside.

Andy thought walking under tomato plants that might throw a several-kilo juicy tomato down was not wise. Soon, they took a path that took them to Mr. Rediche's house directly from below huge sunflowers.

Emily missed ordinary life so much in that short period of time. When they reached the house, she ran inside as though she had been deprived of something for a long time and hugged a small glass. The furniture was mostly old but some of them not that old.

Those ones were related to the last years of Mr. Rediche's life. Andy looked around the house and checked out the paintings on the wall with admiration. What he spoke of a strange man. Perhaps in their lifetime human beings never get the chance of being recognized but death is brave enough to unveil various hidden aspects of man's characteristics. The paintings clearly depicted Mr. Rediche's various life periods. Andy was standing in front of a painting that showed a young Rediche next to a beautiful woman. Most of the paintings dealt with training students mostly in the wilderness suffering thirst and hunger. Mr. Rediche, however, had a rosy face, brown hair and bright eyes smiling in most of the paintings. They were not ordinary paintings. Mr. Rediche had transferred his emotions to them with the help of magic so that the visitor would closely feel the psychological air depicted. The first thing that crossed Andy's mind was the fact that there was a wonderful world flowing in Mr. Rediche's soul. Turning to the window, he noticed a rocky mountain that was shining like a golden egg. Then he thought about the sorrowful yet lovely paintings of Mr. Rediche. All of those were gone and most probably most of the people who were smiling in those paintings were no more there. What had replaced all that joy? That zeal that was flowing in Mr. Rediche's meaningful look. Where was he resting in peace?

Hearing something at the window, Andy came to. The midgets were there. Andy was about to cry out of happiness and scare them away. Each midget was biting on a potato greedily making a funny noise. Their fresh faces showed they were not older than 13 and what was said about them was not true as they were always young!

Andy's mouth was wide open! Eric realized from his looks that it must be the midgets. He nudged Andy with his big body and stood by the window. He showed two thumbs up.

'Here I am, pals!' said Eric happily.

Then, he ran out. He had hidden some carrots under his shirt. He made friends with the midgets in no time. They gathered around him jumping up and down happily like little kids. Eric could not overcome his emotions. He hugged three of them and rolled on the grass.

Andy was standing outside the house in disbelief when he realized a midget was poking him with his little finger. He seemed to be the smallest one and wanted to play. Andy wondered if it was a child. Maybe he looked that way because of his special genes. Maybe he was 20 years old or even more but from his innocent look and manners Andy thought he couldn't be older than 6. His clothes were too big for him. Andy looked at his friends for a moment. Most of the midgets had gathered around Eric for the carrots. Lisa was taking a photo with some of them with the help of Emily asking them to imitate her pose. It seemed there was only one midget left for Andy who was poking him innocently and wouldn't take his big eyes off him for a second. At last, Andy took his hands and started strolling under the shrubs. What a night! Was that real? He wouldn't be surprised if he was told that he was asleep. How on earth did they end up in such a place? Now he was certain that if time went back, he wouldn't change his choice as this strange life was in full harmony with his idiosyncrasy. There was nobody to blame him anymore. Here they even had greater respect for unusual people. As he was thinking,

The midget yawned, lay on the ground and went to sleep.

Before long, another midget jumped on his stomach and woke the poor child up with a cry. He was weeping, yet, he was happy. Andy stared at them surprisingly and thought what kind of life the midgets lived. Then he started walking under the shrubs alone and entered a gigantic bottle. Were all of these Mr. Rediche's work? What a wonderful man! He was thinking deeply when some midgets turned the bottle and pushed it down a slope. Andy turned and turned and eventually stopped in a dried brook. He got out of the bottle nauseated. He sat there. It was serene all over the place. He felt dizzy. He had no idea which part of the farm it was. When he heard Eric's laughter from far away, he realized he had to take the path behind him. He was holding his head when he heard a horrific echo. His whole body froze upon hearing the devilish sound. He then noticed the specter of a woman standing in among the shrubs silently. Andy ran away. When he reached Eric, he was out of breath. A sound of laughter was heard. It was so horrific that Eric jumped up like a spring. Lisa and Emily also joined them fearfully.

'What was that sound?' asked Emily.

'I have no idea! I thought it was you!' said Eric.

'No, it wasn't us. We are not crazy! Was it you Andy?'

'Me? No. it was a woman's voice. I saw her,'

The wind started to blow unusually. When they heard the laughter again, the midgets started running away.

'These idiot creatures escaped. Why should we stay here?' asked Lisa.

Emily pointed to a spot behind them fearfully and was unable to utter a word.

'Rioter! Run away!' cried Emily after a few seconds.

Before they could get away, Eric was heard saying ouch and holding his side as if someone had hit him with a stone or punched him there. He was so scared; he forgot the pain for a moment and started to run away.

The Inventions Museum

While Andy was running to the mansion through the yard, he looked behind him several times. Eric was nauseating and as they got home, he was no longer able to stand on his feet. Lisa looked as if she was being kind to Eric.

'We promise not to let anyone know what's happened to you,'

'It wasn't only me!' said Eric angrily.

'That was a rioter! A rioter with an insignia! I saw that around its neck. It was the famous coffin,' said Emily worriedly.

'What the hell could he do to us? They aren't' magicians!' said Lisa contentedly.

'No, that wasn't an ordinary rioter. To bear an insignia, they have to kill an innocent and powerful magician and drink his blood to be able to perform magic,'

'Makes no difference again! They can never be as powerful as a real magician,'

'But it has turned to a devil that has no respect for anything!'

The rioter's story did not manage to disturb Lisa but Ms. Wagner's camera did have such a power. Lisa blushed all of a sudden.

'Hell! There's no midget in the photos,'

Eric's pain couldn't stop him from being satisfied with that fact.

'You know the camera cannot drink Snofer after all!' said Eric mockingly.

Just then, Ms. Wagner showed up like a furious executioner.

'You were not in the room. You weren't in the mansion. I looked for you everywhere,' said her instantly.

Lisa hid the camera under the table nervously.

'We were in the yard,' said Lisa.

Ms. Wagner was angry yet sympathetic.

'Why should you be in the yard at midnight? I thought you've performed some banned magic and put yourself to trouble. Or maybe you've done something to disappear.' She then looked at Andy and tried to sound kinder.

'Or maybe someone forced you to go with him!'

'There could be better hypotheses,' said Eric sarcastically.

'No, there couldn't! Cried Ms. Wagner nervously.

Hearing the scream, Emily gulped down her saliva and turned to Eric.

'She's right! There couldn't!'

For a minute, silence prevailed. Then Ms. Wagner left them angrily.

Eric spends the whole night with dreadful nightmares. In the morning when he heard hear his chest wheezing, he jumped out of the bed. He looked so ill that Andy could distinguish it in a jiffy.

'Hey, are you OK?'

With no reply, Eric bent over his knee as if he was vomiting. Andy ran away and returned with Ms. Wagner who was surprised to see Eric that way.

'Nothing wrong with him,' she said.

'It's only a simple stomachache,' said Eric with sweat drops on his forehead.

'Maybe you're hungry. Let's go have to breakfast!'

Ms. Wagner prepared the breakfast rapidly.

'We've got mushroom and beef meal. Hurry up!'

The doorbell rang. The new mailman was not familiar with his duties very well yet. Ms. Wagner explained to him he could leave the letters at the door or drop them in a special box at the side house. After a big apology, the mailman left the mansion. Ms. Wagner opened the letter and started muttering.

'Wow! The Council wants me to deliver a speech to graduate students today!' she exclaimed gladly.

Then she showed them the memo and the official seal of the Council proudly. Everybody was surprised. Ms. Wagner was so busy cleaning and doing household chores all the time, it was hard to believe she had other skills too.

After breakfast, they would sit and watch Ms. Wagner. She had spread all of her notes on the table so she could put together a decent speech.

'Stop looking at me like that! Of course, you still don't understand what fame can do to you as you are not famous like me yet,'

Emily laughed quietly and turned around so Ms. Wagner couldn't see her.

'How famous have you become exactly?' asked Lisa.

'Such a big dummy you are, girl! I'm about to lecture a large number of students. As of tomorrow, newspapers will rush to interview me.

'Yes, sure! Numerous students!' said Lisa sarcastically.

Before Andy looked at Lisa with hatred, Ms. Wagner sprang up.

'I have to go now. The world of science needs me. Please wish me success.' she said.

Upon making the final statement, she left the mansion.

Eric was complaining of his pain. Emily went to the library and got back with a book called "invisible guards".

'Listen to this! Invisible guards or wandering magicians are responsible to protect secret locations. As soon as strangers arrive, they deal blows that are not deadly but harmful. They can end up in long weeping, nightmares or bedwetting,'

Everybody looked at Eric. He seriously rejected having nocturnal enuresis. He got up and sat in a corner alone.

Emily kept reading the book but as she realized Eric was unwilling to listen, she put it away and answered Andy's questions about rioters. Emily knew much about them. Andy just realized that everything started out of stupid jealousy. Non-magicians found their way into the realm of magic out of jealousy. The saga was entertaining for Andy until before they ran into a rioter with insignia.

Lisa who had disappeared for the past half an hour came back with an old photo and an angry look. There was a middle-aged man in the old photo with deep eyes and bony cheeks standing proudly next to something that resembled a piano.

'I won't let him be forgotten,' said Lisa.

'Did you remember your grandfather again? You can't find that chest,' said Eric.

'Which chest?' asked Andy.

'The recreation chest. It's said to turn everything to its original form. You give it to paper, it gives you wood,'

Lisa blew her top.

'Why are you speaking in a way as if it's a lie? If Eduardo had let me last time, I'd have proved it to you,' said Lisa furiously pressing her teeth together.

'I will go to the inventions museum right now and find it.'

'It's not the first time you're bluffing. I'll go with you to prove there's no such a thing,' said Eric.

Lisa got up angrily.

'You don't have the guts to go with me,' said Lisa.

Eric blushed.

'I'm just beginning to understand why your family was so happy to see you go. When I told them I'd protect you like my sister, they gave me a dirty look. They had exactly the same feeling that my mother had when my sister got married. She felt relieved!'

'I bet your sister is also as crazy as you are!' retorted Lisa with a scream.

'OK. Enough Eric! You've promised to treat her like your sister,' reminded Andy.

'Do you have any idea how I treated my sister?' asked Eric hatefully.

'You are a coward! You're saying this because you don't dare to follow me,' said Lisa.

At this point, they both looked at each other nervously and then headed for the abandoned section of the mansion suddenly.

'Do you know what's happened?' asked Andy.

'I do very well. We'll be in trouble. Let's follow them. Let me put this back in the library first.'

This was the first time Andy was visiting that part of the mansion where all doors were always shut. When he was climbing down the spiraling stairs, he was wondering what was expecting him down there. He turned around ten times and finally got to a long passageway where some noise could be heard. With long steps, Andy went to the end of the passage. As he crossed a door, he first thought he had stepped into an arcade. He didn't believe seeing so many magicians in one place. He looked around. There were more doors like the one he had used but nobody was coming that way. Everyone was arriving from the western part of that long and wide corridor. They ended up in the eastern corridor. Andy thought how it was possible for that big crowd to have gone through Password alley. That was not possible! The alleyway was always deserted. There must be some other way.

Emily was checking the crowd.

'No sign of them here, we must find them before Garry Watson finds them,'

'Who's Garry Watson?'

'The most violent guard at the Password, he's bet he'll punish a conjurer with his special whip. If he does so, he'll have elixir served to a hundred people for free,'

'With special whip?'

'It's a magical whip that locates the guilty like radar and ties their hands and legs so tightly that they would scream,'

Andy tried to look worried to keep Emily happy but he was paying full attention to a large area where people were moving in all directions. He doubted if he could ask her about that place as she seemed to have lost her tolerance. Anyone who arrived there would look up first. So did Andy. The Password building was constructed around a tall dome that lay under the ground. There was no way you could access upstairs. Andy looked at the people surprisingly. They were walking in the air to go upstairs without there being any stairway. He then looked at Emily in disbelief. She was overwhelmed with joy.

'It's called the invisible stairway. If you don't have a permit, you'll fall down,' said Emily proudly.

Andy checked out the area once again. It seemed many of them didn't have a permit to go upstairs. He wished one of them would be daring enough to try and go upstairs so Andy would be able to see them fall. Then he noticed another stairway. It was visible but the steps would disappear and then reappear elsewhere.

'That's called the guiding stairway. Those who don't know which direction they have to go, use that to be led to their destination. You ought to have a permit for that too or you'll fall,'

'What's the function of the Password?'

'Well, it's got different sections, the criminal section for instance that's deal with pursuing offenders and sabotage,'

Just then an old man stood in front of them.

'Is Eduardo back yet?' asked Emily excitedly.

'Yes, he's coming. He said he would join us later,'

'OK. Good to see him back. I'll wait for him.'

After the old man left, Emily saw Gary Watson who was walking among the crowd with his famous whip. As usual, he was wearing his maroon jacket. Emily pulled Andy behind a statue swiftly.

'Look Andy! This is no joke! If he knows there's a conjurer here, he'll give you the hell!'

Andy's eyes were filled with terror staring at Emily.

'What are we gonna do now?'

Emily was panting as though she had been running for hours.

'We have to go to that corridor quickly. The one with a few people,'

'The darker one? OK, let's,'

'One, two, three!'

They ran to the corridor and took shelter in the shade of a wall. It was so eerie! Fainting yellow light, walls with damp patches looked nothing like they jubilant air outside.

'Is the museum here? Where's Eric then?' asked Andy worriedly.

'No, it's not here. Follow me,'

Emily stopped right after she moved. She almost hit Andy.

'Wait a sec! Are you just worried about Eric? What about Lisa?

'I'm also worried about her but I just don' wanna mention it,'

'You'd better not to hate her. She's is kinda selfish but she has a kind heart,'

She paused a little.

'She's also a bit too demanding,'

She didn't know what else to say.

'You know, everyone is jealous!'

'You forgot to mention being nervous,' added Andy.

'Leave it! Let's go!'

Andy ran after Emily hurriedly.

'Where are we?'

'Among all banned section at the Password, this is the most banned!'

Andy stopped.

'Seriously?'

'Eduardo said so when we last came here with him. Also, he said if they catch anyone here, they will be tried in court…By the way, he also said any moment an eerie creature like a mummy may get out of these corridors,'

Andy swallowed his saliva.

'Do you really hafta tell me all of this?'

'Yeah, we wouldn't fancy taking adventures,'

'I bet you made up the mummy story!'

'Yes, but fearing a mummy if better than being caught by Watson,'

Emily passed a number of corridors none of which were as dull as the main one. Then she stepped into a corridor where Lisa and Eric were sitting contentedly on a dirty and old chair by an old door.

'Enough is enough! Let's go back. I saw Garry Watson,' said Emily.

'I think Lisa is right. We'd better have some fun,' said Eric unexpectedly.

Andy knew Lisa well or else he would've thought she's cast a spell on Eric.

'What fun are you talking about? They are just some magical stuff you don't know how to use. Don't you understand the situation? We were about to be spotted

'Leave him alone Emily! No one asked you to come here,' said Lisa.

She then turned to the door on which it was written, "speak into my ears and go in". Lisa put her mouth close to the door.

"Nobody has seen the end of you and nobody will!"

Andy felt the old door was pleased to hear that. It opened. Behind it, there were some one hundred steps that were lit by winged lanterns suspending in the air like bees.

'Where are we? The end of the world?' asked Andy surprisingly.

'Don' worry! We've been here once, but this time Eduardo is not following us,'

Said Lisa.

Eduardo's absence was the greatest source of concern for Andy.

'This is stupid! We need to be highly intelligent to comprehend it,' said Emily.

Lisa smirked and together with Eric went through the door.

'Do you still insist I should like Lisa?' asked Andy.

'Shut your mouth, Andy!'

Emily explained to Andy that there's a light place down the stairs that is where the museum equipment is kept. The storage was detached from the museum with a short wall. Andy tried his best but did not manage to see the dark world on the other side of the wall.

There were so many objects piled in the storage that Andy would simply accept it's the very museum. He checked out the stuff used to go to the museum. Emily who had gone to the other side of the storage got back with some chocolate.

'Here's chocolate to raise your voice. Have one of these so when you find the chest anywhere in the storage, you would give a yell so everyone could hear you,'

'Hey wait! Are we not supposed to go together?'

'We won't have much chance of finding the chest that way,'

Just then, Lisa arrived with a speaking book.

'Leave me alone mean girl! I shall not victimize wisdom for ignorance! I shall only utter the words of justice and I shall only tread the path of truth. Leave me alone before I lead you to the butcher house of the museum,' said the book angrily.

'These idiots only respond to the Magical Entertainment Administration but it should speak out today,' said Lisa.

'What you have in your mind started from your dark heart. Take your filthy hand off me devilish girl!' cried the book furiously.

'Couldn't you find a politer one? Asked Emily.

'No. He was lying to his friends, who called him teacher when I got it from behind,'

Andy who was still stuck with thoughts before Lisa arrived felt worried.

'You said we should be alone. Is it possible in this darkness...' inquired Andy.

Emily looked at the part of the storage where some winged lanterns had gathered and asked somebody to follow her.

Andy was happy to see one of the lanterns was trying to make its way to reach Emily. Wherever the lantern went, it created a path of light that would stay. Eric and Lisa called their own lanterns immediately and went through the doorway.

Andy looked at the ceiling hanging over his head like a dark cloud. Then he imagined what could be found behind the wall recalling what Lisa had uttered, "Nobody has ever seen your end and nobody will". What a bitter statement! How was possible for this faraway dark world not to have any beaches? He wished it had another name. He liked to hear someone say you will soon approach the end of the way but more bitter than the entrance words was the fact that he was standing in the museum storage all alone. Andy was eying the group of lantern worriedly.

'One of you follows me,' commanded Andy.

He was pleased to see two lanterns fighting each other to go to his help. Eventually, after some noisy brawl, fat and bright lantern came as the other two were still fighting each other and passed through the wall with Andy. The big lantern seemed to have realized that Andy was scared so he had stopped his siesta to offer him abundant light.

For a while, Andy moved forward on empty stone-covered space with the help of the lantern while he felt both scared and daring. He reached a city of magical tools. There were so many things there you could pick the word city to describe it. If possible, Andy would change its name to the city of inventions. He left behind packed alleyways one after another hitting some of the stuff with signs on them reading danger or don't approach. Shop windows were full of magical instruments and the counters displayed things the like of which Andy had never seen. Andy was losing his determination gradually. Now he was passing by things one of which could be the recreative chest. He checked the lantern over his head several times. What if it left him alone? What if it would turn off and stop shedding light on the way behind them? He came to the conclusion that he's dealing with a cowardly Andy. At last, the only thing that could distract him from his unpleasant thoughts was the hazard sign on a big metal chest. The chest door was ajar exposing a gray robe. The hazard sign bore a red circle around it for further emphasis. Andy was curious to take a look at the writing on the chest.

"What do you know about the Blanca transformation robe? If you have no idea, it may cost you dearly! Many analysts of the magic world have written about the hazards of this ruthless robe. They all agree that it's made from a mix of fatal curses. So, bring your freaking mind under control. In case you are unable to do so, maybe it'd help to know that the Blanca transformation robe does not take your orders, it rather decides what you will be transformed to. Maybe you'll turn to a giant, a huge spider or you may even acquire wonderful skills.

By wearing the robe for two days, you will not be able to keep your original look. The only magician who was able to order the robe to take action was Ms. Blanca who's passed away, so stay as far away as you can."

The instructions were so clear that something crossed Andy's mind warning him against trying the stupid robe.

'It's only curiosity,' the reply slipped out of his mouth.

Andy set off again. Did all the magical instruments belong to magicians? Will he also be able to have something kept in the museum in his name in the future when he's a great magician? He was savoring the sweet dreams when he reached an alleyway on whose giant counters was written skulls, human skeleton, black spheres…it seemed he was in clairvoyants' area. As he raised his head, a wooden sign endorsed his assumption, "clairvoyance and its joys". Andy first sat on a basket chair and took a straw hat. On the hat it was written in shining words," the hat responds to your emotions". Soon, Andy got to learn what that meant. It was a musical hat that would pick the tune on the basis of what was crossing Andy's mind. After thinking about a soccer match, Andy got an exhilarating piece of music from the hat and resumed walking happily.

A few minutes later, he was skillfully combing through the objects to find the recreative chest but once he got to the paintings section, he stopped with fear as he was suffering an unpleasant feeling. The thought of having a nightmare of corpses again was so dreadful that he tried to get rid of that situation soon. He knew well that the forgotten memory was trying to return to him but all doors were closed and that memory, which took orders from the disobedient part of his brain, had stopped behind the castle of his compliant mind. Still, he was able to hear a silent cry which said, "Open the door. We have brought you the truth."

Eric raised a cry after taking the voice boosting chocolate. Lisa thought he has found the recreative chest. She had run so fast that she was panting when she reached Eric.

Eric was standing at the entrance to a village with wooden huts with a sign reading, "Death expects those who approach the graveyard."

'I found this interesting, so I thought you'd like to see it too,'

'Is there a graveyard?' asked Emily.

'I don't know. It should have one,' said Eric.

Nobody realized that Eric is acting abnormally. Lisa was running to one of the houses.

'I've found it. That's it! I don't need that stupid book anymore,' said Lisa.

'History must weep for your parents who have raised such an impolite child' said the speaking book hatefully.

Lisa threw the book on the ground nonchalantly. With its thick cover, the book was dragged on the ground to take itself to the museum storage.

'Yes, move along! You'll arrive at the museum tomorrow at this pace. You took a taxi here but you gotta go back on foot,' said Lisa mockingly.

The book that was sick of arguing with Lisa, said nothing in response and kept going.

The recreative chest resembled a half black half white chest standing under a wooden shed.

"The recreative chest. Made by Albert Brighton." That's what appeared on the sign.

"Everything in the world has a central core that constitutes most of its components. For instance, a paper is made from tree bark. Now, would you like to know where the objects around you originated from? Try it!"

'Let those who were saying this is a lie come forward and watch it,' said Lisa.

Eric was sitting on the ground in a mysterious silence.

'That's wonderful! Why didn't they allow it to be produced?' asked Emily admirable.

'Because the Object Evaluation Committee finds it dangerous,' said Lisa frowning.

Andy was wondering why the chest was made. He wanted to know if it will adjust itself to be large enough so he could push Diana in it. The chest would probably feel bad and throw up. More interestingly, Lisa was not familiar with the way the chest worked.

'Well, you should perhaps put something inside it,' said Emily with the objection.

Andy felt like playing a hero, so without anybody asking his idea, he opened his belt and threw it inside the chest.

The chest was filled with black dust making Andy pull back. A hissing sound could be heard.

'What the hell! Get away, everyone!' shouted Emily fearfully.

Andy was staring at a cobra snake that was getting out of the chest in a menacing way.

'Those who are familiar with the cobra know that it's no joke!' said Emily.

Andy had something else in his mind. If the snake hid somewhere in the dark museum, what would happen to future visitors? Then he thought if he plunges into the realm of nightmares again and loses the ability to recognize his surrounding, then he may extend his hand toward the snake involuntarily, just the same way he had reacted to the Tyrannical Sphere. He was the worst off.

Everybody had run away but Eric remained motionless. It looked as if he cannot move his legs due to a snake bite. Andy looked behind when he heard Lisa scream and noticed Eric. Then he moved toward him bravely. The snake's hissing sound had filled the mysterious air of the museum.

'Don't come this way, Andy! Looks like it prefers you to others,' cried Eric.

This at least indicated that Eric felt good. Andy took a shiny boomerang from inside a box and threw it at the snake with all he had in his power. The boomerang turned and turned and surprisingly lifted the snake off the ground and took it to the depth of darkness at the museum. Before they took a sigh of relief Lisa warned it was going back in their direction.

The boomerang turned around the hall several times. The snake's hissing sound helped the children locate it in different positions. Eventually, after it shone brightly one last time, it tossed the snake into the chest and fell off. Andy's belt was then thrown out.

'What happened?' asked Emily.

'I think the boomerang takes orders from the person who throws it. When I was imagining the snake's return to the chest, it just did so.

'I have tons of respect for the Object Evaluation Committee. Anybody who's against this had better take their family chest with them before some people get killed. And I'll throw anyone who tells me about my attitude toward my sister into the chest!' shouted Eric angrily while leaving the village.

The Hidden Castle

Eric bent over outside the village that was considered to be cursed. He was out of breath. Nothing could be seen in his eyes and he looked so pale as if he's seen a ghost. He had a devilish smile on his face. He told himself he had to go as soon as possible. It would be amazing to see bloody eyes and the black body. Yes, he had to go.

'Are you OK?' asked Emily surprisingly.

Then she pointed at his horrible looking eyes.

'Your eyes! What's happened to your eyes?'

'None of your business!'

'Of course, you can! You're a strong boy!' muttered Emily.

She then started running.

Andy was wondering if Eric has gone mad. Eric's lantern found its way to the middle of the museum. Eric was murmuring something while running toward an unknown destination.

'He's not gone mad. He is under a spell. Hey, where are you going? Said Emily.

Eric wouldn't listen to them. He stepped into places that were frightening for the children. Eric went past ancient statues and mummified bodies. He got to a half-burnt camping area. Gradually, more and more warning signs could be seen as it got darker and darker. The lanterns were also losing their brilliance. He finally stopped running and stood by a clay jar with nothing painted on it. It was standing on a stone platform. Andy arrived sooner looking around fearfully. He felt he had arrived at a hazy cellar from a cloudy and starless night. He was wondering how horrible the end part of the museum could be!

Eric still looked pale and was panting. Emily went ahead cautiously.

'Are you alright Eric?'

Eric did not answer any question for a minute. At last, some blood ran over his face. He looked normal but he panicked by what he saw around him. He was flabbergasted. Before uttering a word, a ray of light like the polar twilight got out of the jar and turned into a man with a greenish blue body the lower part of whose body resembled a snake. The man had black eyes and mustache and his greenish blue body was so transparent you could see inside.

'Good day! Let me introduce myself to you lovers of magicians. It's me the Young Bellinger. Lasting at all times, with endless thoughts, I offer flawless gifts,' said the strange man joyfully.

'Who has summoned me?' he asked with a smile.

Nobody was willing to introduce Eric as a culprit.

'Hey, I didn't do that. I was just looking. Please go back to your jar…excuse me to your home,' said Eric nervously.

'No worries young pal! Bellinger jar is powerful. It offers great gifts. Don't you want to get one?'

'I sure do. Now that I've summoned you, I'm your master, right? Asked Eric gladly.

The greenish-blue man looked at Eric loathfully but he smiled again.

'No need to fight. There may have been some flaw in your training course that's why you've mistaken me with the magic lamp's giant. Let's deal with it! Whatever comes out of the jar accidentally will be your gift. Based on law seven and nineteen of the Bellinger jars, I'm responsible to make arrangements for that.

He then repeated his words and went back inside the jar.

'It's me the Young Bellinger. Lasting at all times with endless thoughts. I offer flawless gifts.'

For a while, silence prevailed but the greenish blue man got out of the jar soon afterward. At the same time, a paper sprang out like a butterfly. Emily snatched the paper in the air, which made the man angry.

'No, you are not allowed to read it. No one is allowed to read it,' said the colorful man angrily.

Emily quickly returned the paper. The man got more and more surprised as he read the paper, but before making any reaction he consulted himself first.

'Err…it's hard and kind of impossible. How many kids may ask for this? What brings you here? Black and dark but unwanted!'

He then looked them pessimistically and stretched his body encircling them like a snake so that they couldn't get away. Then he stuck his flush face to their faces one by one smelling them and looking in their horrified eyes curiously.

'You neither have dark hearts nor vicious intentions. I must admit sometimes Belingers make mistakes too. I apologize for mistreating you. You are unusual and confusing. I cannot judge this leaf but I will surely raise the issue at the Bellinger's society. Farewell, unusual little ones! Have fun!'

The greenish-blue man got back to the jar like a beastly whirlwind sending out a black mass surrounding them like a wall. The wall seemed to be brimmed with treacherous spells shining so luminously that nobody dared to approach it. Inside that cloud-looking wall was a door with some poetry shining on its framework.

Our hidden castle is filled with fire

Breaths are held from its flames

Cold, dark and deserted

Harpoons are wailing in mourning

Eric was about to faint when he saw the poems. It was not because of the curse this time but thanks to the knowledge that was invading his mind like a horrendous monster.

'I had seen this place in my dream last night,'

'Try to remember what you saw then,' said Lisa fearfully.

Eric shut his eyes to recall whatever he'd put out of his mind, but it was in vain. Then he mustered some courage and poked the jar.

'Hey, we don't want gifts. Just let us go,' beseeched Eric.

This time an ugly man from the smoke came out of the jar. He couldn't be liked in any imaginable way. He had a coarse voice.

'Nobody has the right to return their gifts or else they have to deal with me!'

'But he didn't tell us how to use it,' said Eric with fear.

'None of my business,' said the man furiously.

Lisa was truly frightened. She opened the door slowly and said, 'I don't think it's dangerous. It's only a room,'

The smoky man examined the magical wall. Eric ran to the room.

'Let's go. This guy is mad!' shouted Eric.

They all took refuge in the room. Eric slammed the door shut with a bang. The sound was not scary compared to the door being locked quietly. No sooner had Andy forgotten the dull body and dreadful eyes of the smoky man than he another fear came his way. Again, he could hear the voices of invisible people in his ears. No, it couldn't be them! He examined the room carefully. It was a small room with no windows. The only thing is seen there was a sundial that was so luminous that an image of a city could be seen on it. Andy touched the door handles involuntarily and heard Eric's voice.

'Don't try! It's no good! The door is locked.'

Now that the troubling sounds had subsided, Andy got the chance to think what to do.

'What are we gonna do now?' asked Andy worriedly.

'I know nothing,' replied Emily disturbingly.

Just then church bells started to sound. Everybody stared at the sundial. The moving shadows of the sundial moved over the city map. Then they heard tic tac and all of a sudden the bells began sounding again. The sundial turned like a ferocious whirlwind taking in everything inside it. Andy who was screaming went inside the tornado while he was unable to open his eyes. He hardly noticed a bird flying over a dark road under black trees. In the end, the road was standing lifeless dummies whose horrendous looks which were devoid of any affection pulled Andy's heartstrings. Then things got dark and depressing with a discouraging whisper being heard. Andy could no longer stand the pressure. He got unconscious   moments   later.

The sound of church bell which could be heard more clearly this time helped Andy come to. He could see with weak eyesight that the world has changed and Eric is trying hard to help him come to.

'Enough, Eric! How many times do you slap me on the face?'

'No. that's not enough! You must see what's happened very soon,'

Andy just realized that they are under the shade of an ancient gate at the end of 1 7th Street. It was a stone city empty of any hustle and bustle. At the far end of the city on top of the hills stood a castle from whose tall tower a bell was heard. One more time Andy eyed the street which turned left a bit further ahead.

'Are we dead? Touch your body and see if your still warm, Andy,'

'Why don't you do that?'

'I'm warm. I thought you're dead and I'm dreaming of you,'

'Stop being funny! You are bigger than all of us. Go and see what's up out there,' commanded Lisa impatiently.

'I wish you would make your choice based on wisdom, not body size. Then, I wouldn't be picked for sure. Of course, I'm sure you wouldn't be either, Lisa,'

Andy was wondering how on earth Eric maintains his sense of humor even in that situation. No sooner had he taken a few steps than he stopped at the turn.

'I really think we're dead. You should go and figure that out on your own!' said Andy anxiously.

Cautiously Andy checked the street from beside the wall. In no time, he felt his heart in his mouth by what he saw and decided to flee even sooner than Eric. The city was occupied by stone humans who were walking inside the walls rather than in the streets. They were not able to leave the walls. Andy's mind couldn't take it all! He took his breath and pulled back. Emily leaned against the wall in horror. This time she had made her way into a world that seemed to be a greater fantasy than her daydreams. Lisa told Eric angrily that they were there just because of that bizarre dream. Eric pointed to the point where the street turned left.

'Miss, you'd better ask everyone for forgiveness before you die!'

One of the stone humans had reached there. It had a feminine voice.

'Hey!'

Any expected to see a large number of other stone humans to rush there any moment but no one showed up. The woman walked inside the wall toward them. Upon approaching them she sounded kind.

'Poor kids! What are you doing here?'

Eric was relieved by the warm tone and felt he could make some noise from his throat.

'Who on earth are you?'

'Don't worry! I'm a human being like you. This is the hidden castle that is the magicians' prison. Any prisoner who gets close to the wall gets a moving stone-made form of their body formed inside the wall, like the one that you can see. I'm not on the wall. I'm behind it. If you are magicians, you must know where you are. You are magicians, are you not?'

'We are conjurers,' said Emily shyly.

'What? Conjurers? I thought you are magicians,'

The woman's facial expression changed by hearing the word conjurer. That was even obvious in the stone form.

'Do you know how we should go back home?' asked Lisa.

The woman paused a little. Maybe she found it beneath her dignity to answer conjurers' questions. She turned to Emily.

'You must utter the magic of the room,'

'What magic?'

'Stupid conjurer! Do you want to get yourself killed? Do you think you can utter such deadly magic and survive?'

'So, what the hell should we do? Asked Eric hopelessly.

'Nothing! You have to wait for guards to save you. They show up once a week. They were here yesterday,' said the woman mockingly.

'We will starve to death by then!'

The woman sounded to be enjoying seeing them scared.

'Don' be a coward, big boy! Give me your hand. Maybe we could do something,'

'What?'

'I will utter the magic instead of you. Let's hope magic could pass the wall so the room could appear,

She then told him in a nonchalant tone to repeat whatever she said accurately.

'No. stay away from her!' said Andy involuntarily.

'So, stay there until you die!' said the woman hatefully.

'No, please don't go! He's wrong,' deplored Lisa.

The woman exhaled and stood where she was before. Then she took Eric's had and started uttering words.

'Soodoora, izaka numura!'

'Saroora izaka...' repeated Eric.

'It's not sadoora. Say soodoora. That's why you are a conjurer,' said the woman blame fully.

Eric looked at his friends. He was the most disappointed one of all.

'Soodoora Izaka numura!'

'Lizanteh heefaren!'

'Lizanteh Heefaren!'

The last words were really strange and the woman's voice was sounding ever more horrible!

'Dinasta Keragan!'

Eric found no chance to repeat those words as the woman instantly said at a louder voice, "and the body that gives away. Bonomooooos!"

The cold weather was biting but the coldness that was engulfing Eric's body had no outside source. The wall went into suction position and took in Eric's cold and lifeless body. Lisa screamed with fear which Andy never wanted to hear. Now Eric was also taken to the wall like a prisoner. He seemed to have fallen on the ground unconscious. There was no trace of the woman. They looked behind them upon hearing something. There was a person at the gate. Without uttering a word, they recognized him instantly. The hollow under his green eyes was colorless and cold. She the wind started moving his long robe, he was wearing a devilish smile on his face.

'You fooled us, rat!' shouted Andy angrily.

The woman was eying the castle atop the hill heedless of Andy. The wind was touching her face like a dream that had come true. After a long time behind bars, she looked pale but she was still beautiful. Had they encountered her elsewhere, they would never have been able to discover the devilish attributes she had hidden in her soul. The sound of the big bell was heard again but this time the woman held nothing against it. She seemed to be delighted, yet, there was still something missing for her to feel perfect joy. She was staring at the castle on top of the hill as if was awaiting something.

'What the hell have you done to him?' shouted Lisa.

The woman looked dissatisfied. She was angry at being distracted but she soon calmed down.

'Don't worry! He's not dead. He is just resting in my place. It's a pity that taking your life would only block my exit from here. I wouldn't mind that!'

This was nothing said to frighten anybody. That's what she really desired. A deafening silence prevailed. When the bell was heard again, they realized by looking at the woman's happy face that her dream had come true. A black deer started flying from the hilltop toward the gate. The black and angry deer was exhaling smoke from its nostrils dragging a carriage. It was adorned with precious gems all over shining brilliantly. The deer with its wonderful carriage turned around over the gate, dropped a bundle and disappeared. It seemed the bundle belonged to the woman. She opened it but she was disappointed as she did not find what she was seeking. She took the bundle angrily, put her hand on the gate and murmured something. The room's door with its luminous poems emerged.

'Where are you going murderer? What about him?' cried, Emily.

The woman acted as though they didn't deserve a reply. She entered the room and shut the door behind her. The room vanished into thin air.

'What is it?' asked Andy with a feeble voice.

'It may be a beast!' said Emily fearfully.

The strange sound was getting closer and closer. Eventually, an armor-clad guard with smoke rising from his helmet arrived staring at the trio who were screaming with fear. He didn't do anything. He went through a stone door to Eric. He raised Eric and carried him on his shoulder with the children following them along the wall until the guard put him down in a house and left. There the prisoners were watching it trying hard on top of each other not to miss anything. Emily was beating the wall hard while mourning.

'Do you have any idea where you are, idiot?' said, someone.

The sound of laughter was heard. Then a man raised his voice.

'What's up? An important person is gone and a big idiot is replacing her. He will regret it when he is conscious!'

Loud giggles were heard again.

'They could've brought this cutie instead!' said a voice greedily.

Unlike her usual mood, Lisa did not enjoy others praising her beauty this time.

'What about that boy? He could wash the dishes.' Said a coarse woman' voice.

Again giggles were heard even more loudly but all of a sudden, everybody stopped making noise as if death had arrived. Now the only thing heard was the sound of a walking stick a feeble old man with a hunchback was using. All the bodies inside the wall had plunged into silence. The old man paused a second and then started examining Eric. He then left and the people started making noise again. A woman sounded worried.

'Did you notice that too? Blood was dripping from his eyes. Mischief! That's what could happen any moment now,'

'Didn' you know that the death minstrel has fled?'

'What?'

The woman's voice turned into a scream. Just then the sound of a group of wicked men and women passing by faded the woman's voice away.

'Wow! Check that out! Little felons!' Said someone surprisingly.

'They don' look like felons. They look like loonies!'

'Who the hell dared insult the idiot?' shouted someone in protest.

'Shut up! I mean the idiots' band. I mean these guys. A bunch of idiot kids!'

'Oh, OK Wiki. I thought you were talking behind my back.'

A glass was broken. Then a woman started nagging at the top of her voice.

The voices of the prisoners were turning to a petty talk as he was attempting to find a way back home. Regrettably, he trusted the feeling of failure that he could sense.

In a quest that lasted till night time, Andy reached a street that led to the castle over the hill. Andy took his eyes off it immediately. It was only a few hours ago when he was standing at this very same point pinning hope that someone in the castle would look into prisoners' affairs. Then he had walked the way to the end of the street with a mixed feeling of hope and fear. It seems as if it was just a few minutes ago when things happened. He could remember every bit of clarification. When he got there, armored guards were standing all along the street. The fear boiling inside him out of recalling that moment was nothing compared to the time when the soldiers turned his way. Andy was ready to let those disturbing voices return to him in return for getting rid of the soldiers who were eying him while smoke was emanating from their helmets. For a while, he felt he was petrified when suddenly he heard Lisa's painful voice that sounded concerned and scared now asking him to run away. While fleeing he kept looking back for fear someone may chase him. Yet, that wasn't it! Just an hour ago when night fell, a loud cry was heard from atop the castle with a threatening tone. One more time Andy reviewed the horrible details of that moment. Nothing threatened them and the yelling may have been a signal for light since soon afterward street lanterns started to be lit one after another by a hand that emerged from the wall.

Andy was falling off his feet so he sat on a step on 19th Street. Lisa and Emily were speechless following a long brawl. Emily believed that Eric was not to blame for the dream. Andy was visualizing a moving black stain. First, he thought he is starving and hallucinating but the sound of footsteps could not be a hallucination. Even Lisa and Emily could hear it. The sound of footsteps came to a halt just a few steps away in the dark.

'Who is that?' shouted Andy.

No one replied. He was sure that his voice had been heard but they were not willing to respond for the unknown reason. A moment later, Eduardo together with a woman with long and strange fingers emerged from the darkness.

'It's them, right?' said the woman with a smirk.

'Yes, Dear Dr. Kitty. You cannot find conjurers more stupid than these guys,' said Eduardo.

Then he started looking at them as if he was examining a few crushed frogs.

'It was Eric's fault! He had a dream...' said Lisa suddenly.

Eduardo's reply was exactly what Emily liked to shout at Lisa.

'Enough! You are to blame the too selfish girl!'

Ms. Kitty Race seemed to have a satirical view of the saga.

'It's interesting to see the headlines of magical newspapers…the minstrel was released by four dummies,'

'Or to be exact, three dummies!' added Eduardo seriously.

Just then a prisoner who was passing the wall while whistling greeted Eduardo.

'Good night Cornelius! Good to see you, man! How come you collaborated with the rioters, man?' smiled Eduardo cordially.

'I'm innocent. My family put together a complaint with the help of the greatest attorneys. It's time they proved me not guilty,'

'Hope so pal! You used to lie a lot but I hope this time you haven't used this trick that's usually used by humans,'

'I hear the minstrel has fled. Who is gonna capture him now? I don't think anybody can. Farewell buddy!' said Cornelius.

Andy was so embarrassed to hear the news. He looked at Dr. Kitty's face. She was unusual and unlike Eduardo was flushing and had a smile on her face. Eduardo was uneasy and did not take heed of the prisoners who called his first name. Emily talked to Dr. Kitty quietly.

'I had never heard of this place,'

'I never expected you to either!' replied Dr. Kitty sarcastically.

'Why can't the prisoners escape?'

'Because becoming a prisoner with the "inclusion" magic you can never get away,'

Emily was ashamed of saying that she didn't have the slightest idea what inclusion magic was all about.

'Of course, an idiot like Eric may transfer that magic to himself and let a prisoner flee without the armored guard noticing it,' said Eduardo without looking back.

'What a stupid guard!' muttered Lisa.

'Yes, he's stupid 'coz he understands nothing. Just like you who have no clue about magic,'

Andy felt somehow relieved now that he realized even in such hard situations it was still possible to joke. When he reached 17th Street, the gate had turned to an exit point for agents who were getting out of the sundial. Dr. Kitty intended to go down the street so she uttered her final words.

'Don't worry about Eric! It's not possible to see him now though. Or let's say it's not wise for now. Farewell!'

Hiftoun's House

There were new faces frequenting the side House. Miss Kitty, the lady in charge of the hidden castle, known as Dr. Kitty with her cat eyes and unusual, long fingers was sitting by Eduardo. Mr. Mark Scot, a professor on the knowledge of spells and a member of the Council of Magic, was sitting farther away on the other side of Eduardo with his spiral stick that had a cat head grip. He was examining the documents pertaining to the Bellinger jar. Mr. Stringe was also there. His job had to do with rioters. They were all there on Eduardo's invitation in order to look into the evidence at hand.

'Nobody can force the Bellinger jar to do anything against its wish. As I already mentioned, this is impossible! No rioter is able to affect the jar,' said Mr. Scot.

But we all know it all started on the night when they encountered the rioter with insignia on Rediche's farm. The rioter must have cast a spell on them so they would go to the jar,' commented Mr. Stringe.

Marc Scot did not agree to it and found it beneath the Bellinger Jar's dignity.

'You are wrong Mr. Stringe. No rioter has such a fatal power. More importantly, the jars have no sense to take orders, so no magic works on them.

Dr. Kitty was wearing a cold smile.

'I agree with Mr. Scot. There's no report vindicating intervention by rioters. I have obtained results from the Council that go beyond imagination. We are facing a magician who is able to perform penetrating magic,' she said.

The impression on their faces changed dramatically.

'Don't be surprised, gentlemen. That's true. I believe you are all familiar with the penetrator story. That magic was created by James Harris in order to make disruptions in the administrative system of the Council of Magic. Out of vendetta against the Council of Magic, James manipulated the letters forcing the Council to apply higher security memos. James Harris was not dishonest at heart and never revealed his modus operandi. However, the magic has been used again. They have made a well-calculated move to get hold of the Bellinger jar. Anyone who is able to tamper with the writing on the jar is definitely powerful enough to convert the monthly letter of magical maids to an invitation letter asking Lili to deliver a lecture. Of course, the role of that fake mailman must not be neglected either.

'Ms. Wagner realized what'd happened only when she stood at the podium to deliver a speech,' said Eduardo sympathetically.

'At present, we have more important issues than that of Ms. Wagner to discuss. They led her away so that they could lead the children to the museum. They did it quite patiently,' said Mr. Stringe seriously.

'Who has performed the penetrating magic? Penetrating into the writing on the Bellinger jar! That's unbelievable! I swear by the foot of the Kolous the great that we are facing perilous magic,' said Mark Scot.

He then paused a little and then continued.

'But…but how can he do it without being present? The penetration magic needs to be performed in front of the writing otherwise it won't work,'

In the meantime, Dr. Kitty was trying to mention the documents in the right order and due consideration.

'There are clues that the Council has referred to. For instance, on the day of the incident, Lisa had an unusual wish to visit the inventions museum. Eric had a pain in his flank that had started from Rediche's farm and after he reached the Bellinger jar, it went away. The whiteness in his eyes had also gone. Now, what do you think has happened, distinguished scholars?'

It was getting complicated every minute as new players pitched in.

Dr. Kitty went on.

'You are all informed that the snofer elixir deactivates the body's defense system. It seems that on Rediche's farm something has infiltrated in Eric's body that's been with him even when he accessed the Bellinger jar but it could not have been with him in the sundial room as the room does not transfer any additional mass. They must have been waiting for a farm worker when they luckily ran into Eduardo's conjurers,'

Mark Scot was eyeing Miss Kitty in disbelief. He was thinking that her appointment as head of the hidden castle definitely had much to do with her unique talent. Just then, the door opened and Inspector Galidoun, who was an official at the Council of Magic's inspection team, stepped in.

'Oh, sorry! You'll forgive me for my delay but I'm sure the meeting has gone smoothly in my absence,'

Eduardo led Inspector Galidoun to a seat.

'All the guesswork is like a shot in the dark. We have no way but to resort to the old and failed method,'

After an hour they were all gone. Before leaving, Dr. Kitty turned to Eduardo.

'Without a doubt, this has something to do with that boy. Had it not been for your spells, they would have found him,'

Eduardo flushed and thanked her. He went to Ms. Wagner's room to find her wiping her tears.

'Oh, Lili, dear! I'm so sorry! It was terrible!'

'Thanks, Eduardo! I don't expect you to sympathize with me,' she said with a lump in her throat.

'I thought I hafta talk to you,'

She had wept so much her eyes were red.

'I didn't have many opportunities in my life to prove myself. I was always ridiculed for being fat. Nobody ever believed me! When I got to the podium, I thought that's the end of all humiliation…'

'Lili, laws of destiny are really brutal. They are written in such a way as though nobody should see their dreams come true. Maybe good and bad incidents are meant to be a means of progress for human beings. When you have the incentive, you make more efforts. For instance, you put together a great speech in a short time. This is what you said you had failed to do several times. For instance, the motive to prove yourself or to take revenge. Anyway, things may happen against our wishes at times, which is nothing bad. Speaking of wishes, I have to also mention the fact that you saw Jack Wagner among the crowd,'

Ms. Wagner looked embarrassed. She kept quiet.

'You saw him with his wife, right? Maybe that's why you are upset. You may have felt you were humiliated. Love during youth is fascinating and emotional, isn't that right Lili? Maybe your motive to prepare that great speech was because of the fact that you knew he would be among the crowd. I read your lecture. I have to admit it has been the best text ever written about the effect of removing spells in household appliances,'

'I hate making speeches from now on. Of course, I know no important speech will be proposed to me,' said Ms. Wagner sadly.

'I didn't know you'd be so upset. I was going to propose that you make a lecture at the 'enthusiastic families association','

'Where is it? When? Where?' asked Wagner happily.

Eduardo's eyes got rounded.

'Are you sure you've accepted my offer? They are only the magicians' families who are fond of getting acquainted with magic. Don't you think it's too unimportant for you?'

She left the room joyfully.

'Stop the baloney, Eduardo! The hell with the laughter of that selfish cousin! Hell with daddy long legs!'

For a moment Eduardo stopped in surprise.

The children who had heard Ms. Wagner's voice tried to look resentful once they noticed Eduardo.

'You are the weirdest conjurers of mine. This includes Eric too who's not here now, unfortunately. Be happy! Inspector Galidoun says he's fine. He also said you have to live with Ms. Hiftoun for a while,' said Eduardo.

'The foggy jungle?' asked Emily in disbelief.

'You have to learn ways of living a magician's life,'

'That's not fair!' said Lisa.

'But that's not unwise. The decision is not made by the Council. If you think the decision will change, you have to wait for the second decision,'

'Second decision?

Eduardo looked at her while buttoning up his coat.

'Eating the torture elixir,' said Eduardo.

'Ms. Hiftoun looks to be a good woman,' said Lisa confusedly.

Eduardo burst into laughter and got prepared to leave.

'Yes, she's a nice woman especially if the shared period stars soon. You'd better pick up your stuff. The driver will arrive in an hour.

The foggy jungle is desperately looking forward to the tree saboteurs!'

Eduardo was still laughing when he was leaving. Andy was happy to see him laugh.

'Is Ms. Hiftoun stricter than mummy flora?'

'You have no idea how terrible things are! You don't have the slightest idea! The Council has decided between eating the torture elixir and Ms. Hiftoun as punishment. Living in her house means living with "!'

As the old moped entered the yard, they found out they had a wrong image of the vehicle in their mind. The driver was an old man with big and yellow spectacles. He was feeble and weak and sounded so weak as if he'd die after hitting the first bump on the road. He was driving so slowly that Lisa got impatient.

'The punishment has already started. Was there no vehicle except this dilapidated moped? Complained Lisa.

'Be a quiet crazy girl! Insulting my moped is like performing banned magic. If you think it's no good for you, you can go on foot,' retorted the old man.

They got to the foggy jungle after four hours. They still didn't dare to complain. Andy was frightened to see shadows moving among the trees. He knew those shadows belong to " that were under Ms. Hiftoun's command. The old man had realized they were scared, so he moved in the shadows' direction on purpose and kept laughing. Andy did not feel upset as the old man was the only person who could infuriate Lisa he didn't have the guts to make an objection.

It was sunset when they arrived at Hiftoun's house. The dilapidated moped stopped outside the house.

'I hope she will bother you so much that you'd start crying with fear.' said the old man hatefully.

The children saw him distance from the house while singing happily. They then turned to the house. They could sense why the house was picked for their punishment. It was an old house with a ceramic roof that got wider as it went higher into the sky.

'I think we should have chosen the torture elixir,' said Emily hopelessly.

Emily rapped the knocker and then retreated. Andy felt he still hasn't felt the real terror standing at the door. Emily had said that Ms. Hiftoun's punishment would be leaving them alone with the " in the stable. She had said no student is able to shriek doing her assignments. Emily was looking at Andy fearfully.

'If we could go back, I'd never set foot in the museum again. Never!'

'That's too late! We can be a good lesson for others,'

They heard footsteps but their expectation to see someone appear at the door frame was in vain. When Ms. Hiftoun announced her presence by coughing from behind them, the trio turned around in fear. Emily was about to lose her voice.

'But the footstep was heard from inside the house...'

Ms. Hiftoun was a sixty-year-old and strong woman. She had salt and pepper hair, heart-shaped face and proud green eyes.

'The Council of Magic's introduction memo!' she said.

Emily handed in the sealed letters instantly. Ms. Hiftoun opened the letters.

'Go inside and wait,' she said seriously.

As they went in, they were looking at each other surprisingly for the house seemed to be a hundred times larger than what it looked to be from outside. The foyer was huge and long. Images of old magicians could be seen on its tall walls. Andy was confident he saw one of the paintings move his hand but it was motionless now. Maybe it was a hallucination. The corridors at the beginning of the foyer were known as eastern and western corridors. At the end of the foyer, there were numerous steps leading to the second floor and around space.

Maids and servants were on the move and you could hear from their conversation that a tough course was in the pipeline. Most amazing of all was the painted wall near the window which was three meters tall and wide. They heard a maid say it was called the jungle wall. The painting looked so real. Had Andy not heard it was a painting, he would leave the foyer through it in the future and hit the wall. The trees in the jungle were in real proportions moving in the wind. The closer he got to the painting, the more dimensions of the jungle could be seen. Andy pulled back when a group of ducks flew by. Ms. Hiftoun passed by from behind the window.

'The race between Iknar and Buknar " will be held tonight. Nobody is allowed to step outside,'

'We will never disobey your orders, dear Ms. Hiftoun,' said Lisa out of self-ingratiation.

Just then Ms. Hiftoun was standing behind her.

'Otherwise, you will have to experience being surrounded by dangerous "!'

Terrified, Lisa turned around. Ms. Hiftoun handed her an envelope.

'When you've climbed the stairs, you can open the envelope. I hope you will not prove to be an embarrassment,'

She then put her head outside of the window and cried.

'Get out of here disorderly "! At seven o'clock tonight everyone must be standing in front of the white line under the aspen tree. Any group that arrives late will be announced loser,'

Standing by the window, Lisa did not venture to turn around and take a glimpse of the escaping ".

'Why are you here?' said Ms. Hiftoun.

Andy pointed to the painted wall.

'Excuse me, Ms. Hiftoun! Is this a painting?' asked Andy.

Without any cordiality in her attitude Ms. Hiftoun replied.

'It's called the jungle wall,'

That's what they had heard the maid say. Perhaps it was so obvious in the eyes of the Hiftoun family that would consider explaining about it as ludicrous. With strong steps, Ms. Hiftoun entered the eastern corridor and asked them to think of a place for sleeping before night falls.

'Are they not going to give us a place to sleep overnight? OMG!'

The speaking Door

While climbing up the stairs at the end of the foyer, Andy was counting the steps. The fortieth step took him to a round space where a brass plate read "The Round Area". All around that space, there were nine long and dead-end corridors, each of them designated with a number.

The 1st corridor, the 2nd corridor…each corridor had eighteen colorful doors. On top of each door frame was a hole with a wooden jujube read head sticking out. Some of them had mustaches and some other had uncombed hair and a long beard. Some of them looked stern and some others kind. They were both men and women of different ages.

Lisa opened Ms. Hiftoun's envelope.

'It says here, "Answer the riddle the head asks you and find your room". Can a wooden head speak?' asked Lisa surprisingly.

When she pressed the handle of one of the doors at the first corridor, the wooden head atop the door got angry.

'Hey, crazy girl! You're breaking it!' said the door angrily.

Lisa's heart sank.

'Believe me. I didn't know that doors are able to speak, mister,'

The wooden head that was old and impatient took a sigh.

'A bunch of illiterate people again!'

Andy tried to make it up but he realized he just made a mess of it.

'You know, we're just conjurers. We still don't know much,'

The door cast such an angry look at Andy as though it had heard a four-letter word.

'What did you say? Conjurers? That's impossible! Get lost! There are so many other doors here. Why are you using this one?'

''but you haven't asked anything yet,'

''Being a conjurer is already more than enough! No need to ask anything,'

Andy was wondering if he had to frown or laugh at all this insult. So, he sounded in a state between the two feelings.

'Ms. Hiftoun said we have to answer a riddle,'

'Yes, Ms. Hiftoun! I'd like to ask her what she has brought for us but trouble. OK now, tell me what is the most important magic among wetting magic is called?'

A little pause was more than enough for the old door to tell them to get lost and not to show up there anymore.

Rudeness was a quality shared by all the doors. After waking up, most of them started with insulting instead of greeting and then asked why they were there. Knock, knock, knock! A wooden head atop a red door woke up and started speaking with a thick, sleepy voice.

'Which idiot is disturbing? Go somewhere else. I ain't got time to waste,'

Andy told him he had no right to treat them that way and that he had to ask them a question as instructed by Ms. Hiftoun. Now all the three of them knew that in this house mentioning Ms. Hiftoun's name was convincing. The wooden head had to do his duty.

'Name five fairies who got lost in the galaxy. I will take a nap until you find the answer. Just go somewhere else to think!'

Lisa went to the second corridor and stopped at a white door, a woman with uncombed hair. Lisa tried to stir her feminine emotions to encourage her not to take it too seriously.

'Here's a kind door. A lady who understands other ladies,'

'Wow! Such a pretty gal!' exclaimed the woman.

Thinking she had fascinated her, Lisa eyed Emily mysteriously.

'Raise a simple question. You are not a man to have problems with women,'

'Sure, honey! Tell me now. To nullify which magic must we use crystalline soil?'

'You said you'd ask a simple question,' complained Lisa.

The woman who was showing her true color now made a burst of devilish laughter.

'You cannot find any simple questions among my questions, idiot. Get lost, cunning and greedy girl!'

Lisa turned around feeling embarrassed. She couldn't keep looking at the speaking door anymore. She couldn't look at Andy and Emily, either. It seemed it was the end of the world, so feeling ashamed of herself, she left the second corridor. The woman could still be heard making repeated insults as though she had expected to do that in such a long time.

Andy touched one of the doors of the third corridor. Laughter filled the air.

'Don't do that! I'm sensitive to tingling. Hahaha! Take your hand off me!' said the door.

Andy was filled with hope.

'We should keep tingling this one so much to force it to ask simple questions,' said Andy.

'But this is cheating!' said the wooden head happily.

It burst into laughter again.

'What the hell are you doing? Stop it! Are you gonna kill me? You must be a conjurer, right?' asked the laughing door.

The tone was so humiliating that Andy was not sure if he had to tell the truth. Then, with a tone that sounded like he was admitting having done something wrong he continued.

'Yes, we are conjurers,'

The reaction of the speaking head was not that bad compared to other doors. It took a slight sigh and started to ask its question.

'What must you do to treat the elixir smallpox?'

'You should ask questions that would fit our background,'

'So, go back home right now coz none of the questions here have anything to do with conjuring tricks,'

Andy who was not insulted terribly this time looked to be satisfied.

Emily was standing at the end of the third corridor in front of an azure blue door discussing with a fussy speaking head.

'Oh, you got such dirty hands and legs! Step back, filthy girl! I'm busy. I gotta go!'

Then to make believe it was busy it looked around several times.

'I hafta go now,'

'That's Ms. Hiftoun's order!' said Emily.

'A black robe to hide from familiar eyes. A robe that takes orders from itself and its owner only' asked the fussy door unwillingly.

Andy was like a dog with two tails as he knew the answer to that question.

'Blanca! The Blanca transformation robe. I have seen it in the inventions museum,'

The fussy door was staring at Andy's mouth in disbelief. It started screaming. Lisa offered her dirty tissue to it.

'Here, let me clean your face, pretty boy,' said Lisa.

The wooden door took a sigh and fainted. It played the trick in order not to open the door. As it was pretending it had fainted, three pairs of enthusiastic eyes were gazing at it. It had to give up at last.

'Poor conjurers! You know nothing of magic. You haven't even entered the magic school yet!' said the head.

When they went in, Emily screamed with surprise. The place was supposed to be a room but it was, in fact, a big house with three bedrooms, a living room, and a study room. A thread was hanging from the lights to turn them on and off. The painting on the wall introduced the last masters of the Hiftoun House with sufficient explanation. On top of it was written, Wait for a new image every night at 12 sharp.

'Before anything read that book, "Informed". It's on the table. It's necessary to get familiar with the Hiftoun House. Everybody must read it,' said the fussy door with a commanding tone.

'This place is so spacious!' said Andy.

'You illiterate! The rooms here change according to situations. The more the people, the more the rooms and amenities. Only a speaking door is able to see these changes. Also put this in your head, idiot. The windows of all rooms open to the yard no matter which room you are in.

Happily, Andy stood by a window and checked out the jungle. Yellow 'don't enter' signs could be seen everywhere. He stood there for a while. He did not remember seeing such a view. If things went well, he could make use of the peace and calm in the house to make up for his school work. It seemed tough given the presence of the discourteous speaking door tough.

Andy had picked the western room that lay in a corner separately. On the wooden desk in the room was a graceful study lamp. The bed was by the window and a full-length mirror on the wall. His room even had a bathroom of its own but it had no books on the shelves. Andy complained about it and the fussy door humiliated him.

'You know, it's because conjurers are not allowed to read magic books,' said the door.

As it was getting dark, the race was starting. The trio was at the window watching fireworks in the woods. The " looked like black spots from a distance but their noise had filled the area. Everyone became silent with the arrival of Ms. Hiftoun. She stood at the podium. Her voice got amplified and heard all over the jungle with the help of magical funnels.

'Good night lovely "! Welcome to the Kashkool competitions! Most of you were expecting this moment like myself but before anything, I have to make a few points. Parents cannot engage in the games or else they will be expelled from the foggy jungle. You all know me well and you know that I'm serious. The next point is that the shortcuts are being guarded by beasts, I mean the gorgeous.

Loud cries filled the air. Child " were not old enough to fight the gorgeous. They were not able to disappear or fly, so they could hardly survive. Their parents had agreed to all the rules of the race and had nothing to object to.

'As you might have heard, there will be heavy fines for cheaters. To get hold of the map you have to use the caves under the hill. I hope you will not fancy playing tricks or else I'll have to bid you farewell now that you are alive. Very well. Here's the group's list. First is the Iknar group, then the coat-clad group, the long-eared group…'

Group fans raised their voice in support any time Ms. Hiftoun called a group name.

While Emily and Lisa were engrossed in the hue and cry of the " from behind the window, a black and ugly Jinn emerged in the lit area outside the house. It had hunted a giant red scorpion, dragging it on the ground. The trio distanced themselves from the window fearfully. The fussy door that was tired of the nightly tour had returned to the recess on top of the door exactly when this happened. Wooden heads were able to visit each other through magical walls and check out different parts of the house.

'Miserable cowards! You are safe in the house,' said the fussy door with a smirk.

It turned toward the corridor and spoke to a bent man who was carrying the food tray.

'If you are looking for a bunch of dummies, some here Eric,'

The frowning man emerged with the food tray.

'I'm not your servant, jerks! You hafta go to the canteen tomorrow. The eastern corridor, the third door!' said the man without any greetings.

He left the tray on the table hatefully and left.

They had charcoal burgers for dinner but with the fussy door around, they did not enjoy it.

'Don't leave the spoon on the table. It gets dirty! Why are you cleaning your hand with your pants, crazy boy? That's not the garbage can. It's for paper waste…oh, no! what are you doing? Don't make a noise when eating…'

An hour later, upon hearing Ms. Hiftoun's voice, the trio was standing at the window. She together with several mournful "emerged from the dark jungle. They were carrying the injured child Jinn with a suspending carriage. Ms. Hiftoun asked the "to bring her surgical powder. The pupils of their eyes were black and big as those of the injured Jinn. They were Iknar "with nail-looking pink teeth known to be very greedy. Iknar "had two black blades instead of foot fingers. They mostly lived in dark and damp valleys and were considered to be the fastest of all Jinns. Now their little kid was terribly injured and wailing.

Lisa and Emily left the window but Andy who kind of felt to be more courageous followed the "as far as the home entrance. He then felt great fatigue and felt like sleeping for many hours. Before mentioning his feeling, he went to his room, said goodnight and fell asleep.

The mail Room

Next morning the fussy door opened before Ms. Hiftoun knocked on it.

'It's kinda impolite but these are only conjurers so it's not worth knocking on the door,' said the fussy door happily.

The kids got up hastily and greeted her.

'Good morning, conjurers! It's good that you had the answer to the riddle,' said Ms. Hiftoun.

She then cast a look at the wooden door and continued.

'Junas, dear, you don't expect me to change the rules for your sake, do you? Your back luck per se is a big riddle…by the way; don't open the door without permission again! Even for me!'

Junas muttered something. Emily looked at it enthusiastically and started to speak.

'So, your name is Junas. How are you doing Junas?'

'Don't look at me like that, sewage cockroach!' retorted Junas angrily.

'The children of Glorite School are the first group of second graders who have reached this stage. Soon, we'll have many people here. Try to behave properly or else…' added Ms. Hiftoun.

She didn't continue to speak as it was sufficient to guess what she meant to say. Andy didn't know why but he was confident there was a kind heart behind that serious voice. Ms. Hiftoun warned that breakfast time was coming to an end and left.

Andy, Emily, and Lisa went down the foyer steps to have breakfast. The Glorite kids were standing in front of the jungle wall. Andy heard a girl speak.

'Ms. Hiftoun hears any should. All the creatures in the foggy jungle take her orders. They say she can cast a spell even when she's asleep. I heard an old witch say that,'

'They say she has been friends with the "since she was seven…' continued a boy with a triangular-shaped face.

Andy who had gotten to the canteen sooner, couldn't help hide his excitement. The sun was shining through colorful, polygonal windows creating a dreamy scene. Shortly afterward he took his eyes off the windows to state at the long tables in the hall on top of each of which were hanging dark clouds. Andy moved ahead curiously. Maybe if he stood on top of the table, he could touch the clouds but he thought otherwise.

'Is this real?' asked Emily surprisingly.

Even Andy who didn't know much about magic felt that he was standing in front of sophisticated magic. They looked at the end of the hall upon hearing the maid's voice.

'When seated, say that you are hungry,'

'When we are here, it means we're hungry,' murmured Emily.

Andy was still engrossed in the magical cloud and acted indifferently.

'I'm hungry,' said Andy.

Instantly, a tray of full breakfast got out of the dark cloud and was laid on the table. Andy looked in awe. He felt like repeating that statement hundred times more to see the cloud's reaction again and again but it did not work more than once. Lisa and Emily got their breakfast trays delivered by the clouds after saying that they were hungry. The breakfast included beans, eggs, turkey bacon, fried mushrooms, jam, butter…

Having eaten his breakfast, Andy announced contentedly that he is full. With that, the tray got detached from the table and went back to the cloud. Now Emily and Lisa were careful not to say anything until after they are done with the breakfast. However, as soon as it was eight o'clock, first they heard a tic-tac, then all the food on the tables got back to the clouds. Even the half bite slipped out of Lisa's hand and flew to the cloud. It was interesting to see Lisa's face when the bite slipped out of her hand. Lisa's face looked so funny when the bite flew out of her hand.

With the end of the breakfast time, frowning Patric arrived and told them to leave. He kept regretting the fact that conjurers had set foot in the Hiftoun House. On the way to the foyer, the children made fun of Patrick and laughed. They walked more quickly when they heard a girl scream from the other side of the foyer.

'…that must be the beastly gorgeous. I swear that's it!'

 Everyone turned toward the jungle wall. Inside the painted jungle, creatures like hyenas were standing. Their vertical and yellow pupils made them look like snakes. Ms. Hiftoun entered the foyer. When she made her way among the crowds to get to the wall, the Glorite kids made rude objections. They managed to get to the jungle wall which was impenetrable. There was a girl with an icy face.

'God help us! That must be Ms. Hiftoun! Who was protesting? Get yourself killed!' said the girl.

After sending the beast to other parts of the jungle, Ms. Hiftoun made it back home from the same route she had taken. Now, everybody was standing quietly. As soon as Ms. Hiftoun left, they cried in unison.

'Good day, Ms. Hiftoun!'

This emotional greeting did not manage to change any of her facial gestures. With the same dry and serious tone, she went on to respond. The Glorite pupils were scared to death. Some of them said that Ms. Hiftoun is making arrangements for punishment. Those who had uttered rude words doubted whether she could remember their faces.

After Lisa explained about the jungle wall, many just realized the presence of three strangers behind them. A tall and red-haired boy went ahead.

'Who the hell are you? Is your mom a maid here?' said the boy rudely.

'Being a maid is better than being a dummy. I know this place better than you do,' retorted Lisa angrily.

'Well, that's clear! Had I lived in that stupid house, I would have seen so many such stupid things!'

Just then the house started to shake. The doors started to squeak. Some of the windows opened and shut hard. People inside the painting that had been standing there motionless, were now trying in a threatening way to find a way out of the painting but to no avail. This time Andy was sure somebody there had waved to him the other day.

'Make a quick apology, Bill Foster! You've upset the house. You are getting everyone killed,' said a girl from among the crow.

Looking at the ceiling fearfully, Bill Foster found the house amazing.

'Not everyone deserves to go there. I have no right to,' he said.

Once again the dust settled in the house but some of the paintings were still shaking their heads as a sign of complaint. Now a voice that was trying to have Andy as the sole listener started whispering in his ears.

'The Hiftoun House is a nice place, isn't it?'

Andy turned around to face a round-faced woman with big white teeth smiling at him. He didn't have much on his mind to offer to the woman at that point. The woman displayed her big teeth and smiling face again and continued.

'I'm Angela Temple. I'm in charge of the Hiftoun Housetraining. You must be Andy Barnett. How are things, Andy?'

Andy tried not to hide his anxious look.

'Thanks, Ms. Temple! To be honest, I still don't know if it's been the right thing to send us on exile to this place,'

'Hush! Turn this threat to an opportunity. Your presence here is an experience that wouldn't repeat itself!'

'I'll try my best. Is…is there any monster around here? I think I heard a strange sound,'

'There's only one type of monster to be afraid of!' answered Ms. Temple thoughtfully.

'What monster?'

'I have to go now. Try to be happy.' she said as she pointed at one of the carpets hanging on the wall.

Andy cast a look. It read, "The most dangerous and hideous monster in the world is the inner monster!"

Andy then noticed a bespectacled boy with hazel eyes and a baby face standing there looking at him. He touched his pine color hair and turned to him.

'I'm George O'Neil. How do you do?'

'How do you do, George? Andy Barnett here,'

'Did you notice the home's reaction? I love this place! It's just amazing!'

'Right, but It's kinda scary too!'

George looked behind. Ms. Hiftoun had entered the foyer. Those who thought they deserve punishment looked pale but Ms. Hiftoun disregarded them and went past them. Then Ms. Temple arrived with a smile.

'Do you have the magic pen and the expandable notebook?'

'Yes, Ms. Temple,'

Everyone replied in unison.

'What about the "' correspondence book?'

'Yes, Ms. Temple,'

'Do you have a smile on your face and happiness in your heart?'

Their anxiety started to fade away. They started to smile.

'Now that you are still able to smile, I'll leave you to Ms. Hiftoun. Climb up the stairs at the end of the foyer. The "' building is not a bad place provided you abide by the regulations.' said Ms. Temple sarcastically.

Emily who had just realized that you have to go through the foyer to access the "' premises, was trembling with fear. Before long, everyone arrived in the round area while looking worried. Many were complaining why they had to go to the "' premises before the start of the joint course. They were all afraid but George O'Neil was different from anyone else. He had found Andy as the right person to befriend given his physique.

'Have you ever been to the "' building?' asked George.

'No, I just got here like you,'

George raised his voice a bit so others would hear it.

'Wild " have no rights to step into the Hiftoun House. Of course, it's not mentioned in any book why the Iknar " are regarded as domestic ". They somehow share many characteristics with wild "but they don't commit any offense. They even come to our defense. Based on the book "Familiarity with the "' premises" by Professor Atkinson, the "of the Hiftoun House do not belong to any of the wild species. The first law of section three of the joint book asserts that master "after a lapse of thirty years of cordial relations with humans receive their mastery certificates of the joint course. Also, all Jinn children are required to undergo courses on humans and appropriate mores,'

'If there was any threat, you'd never be invited here, idiot! You are dummy cowards! You're good for nothing!' said a speaking head from corridor number nine.

Andy expected the Glorite kids to be surprised about those comments but the second graders had already got to learn about speaking doors.

As Ms. Hiftoun emerged, silence prevailed all over the place. She told everyone to move to the first corridor and made an announcement after checking the children's attendance.

'As for the three saboteurs…'

Everybody started whispering and pointing at Lisa and Emily.

The old door started to speak to the door across from it.

'Fenite, look what type of people will make the future of the magicians!'

'Yeah, Woody! I don't see a bright prospect for the world of magic. It's been quite a while since no one has been able to answer even one of my riddles,'

Woody looked at the crowd.

'You, three. Did you manage to get yourself a room? Where did you stay overnight? On the floor?'

'You'd better ask Junas about it, dear Woody,' retorted Andy proudly.

Woody took a sigh.

'Poor Junas! Three conjurers beat him!'

By hearing the word conjurer, the Glorite kids turned surprisingly and spoke with one voice.

'Conjurers?'

The word was so belittling that Lisa blushed.

'Magic schools are negligent about the children's training. I've lowered the difficulty level of my questions, yet no one has been able to find an answer. So much for the function of the Council of Magic!'

It seemed as though Ms. Hiftoun was about to smile but she was resisting it. Woody meant to provoke the Glorite pupils.

'Why should three conjurers who are wet behind their ears stand next to second graders, Finit?' said Woody with a humiliating tone.

'But no one dares to make an objection to Ms. Hiftoun! Woody, are you hopeful these dummies can be of any use?'

Ms. Hiftoun finally wore the smile that she had been hiding by turning to the wall at the end of the corridor.

'One hundred homes and one home don't hide anything, gradually and steadily take us home,' she whispered into the wall's ears.

The wall collapsed like a curtain of sand. Sounds of exclamation were heard for a while. They were all excited! The "had an eight-story U-shaped building. It started from one side, then turned and ended on the other side.

The first floor belonged to little " who were going to school for the first time. Their commotion could be heard from behind the doors. Hearing a voice from the first floor, Andy raised his head. Two young "with half pink faces and funnel-looking ears were speaking humans' language.

'Is that her, Harrow? Ms. Hiftoun?'

'Yeah, it's her!'

'OMG! At last, she's here! I have my heart in my mouth!'

'Stop it, Hoopy! Don't act silly. She can turn you to ash!'

'Hello, Ms. Hiftoun! Here I am. Glad to see you. I'm one of your fans,'

'Enough, Hoopy! Stop bugging her before she turns you to ash!'

'Wow! How lucky I am! She looked at me. Ms. Hiftoun, I picked the course on humans out of my love for you. Can you sign on my face?'

'Stop that! Don't be an idiot!'

Andy was no longer able to comprehend their statements as they shifted to the "' language.

The higher floors were protected with small stone handrails with each floor having a corridor in the west as an entrance. Andy immediately realized that the seventh floor was the busiest of all. Then he mustered some courage and checked it out again. He couldn't believe that "had different races. He had been able to see two funnel-eared "with their half reddish faces and another one with a squeezed face.

The Glorite kids set off a little while after Ms. Hiftoun. George O'Neil was standing there indifferently introducing the "to Andy.

'This is the hoofed Jinn, the most resistance against spell…that one is the donkey-eared Jinn. It's called the wandering Jinn. It loves the sea and riding the whales…oh, look here! A child Iknar,'

The child Iknar was told to stand behind a classroom on the first floor as punishment for misconduct. Despite its young age, the Glorite pupils were scared of its nail teeth and blade feet. No one knew what the child was thinking about when suddenly they heard the sound of Ms. Hiftoun's magic.

"Akronaas!"

The child Jinn was removed from the ground and thrown onto the floor like a basketball. The poor Jinn looked so miserable! It looked lifeless but no such a thing had happened. It got up with tears in its eyes and looked at Ms. Hiftoun with half-closed eyes. The classroom door opened then and long reddish fingers emerged. A robust Jinni wearing a felt coat got out of the classroom. It had a lead color complexion. George looked at him in such a way as if he has run into a relative after a long time. He whispered into Andy's ears.

'Based on the book on civilized ", he must be the lead Jinn. They are great and respectable instructors,'

'Good day, Ms. Hiftoun! Congratulations on the new course!'

'Thanks, instructor Polo! This is going to be the toughest of all courses. Many schools are going to join us,'

She then looked at the child Jinn.

'No more misconduct, OK?'

'Sorry, but first graders don't understand the human language,'

'Oh, I totally forgot!'

Then she spoke the "' language.

'Ohay dalano himou. Ikoy namado,'

The child Jinn trembled a bit and then entered the classroom. It was going through such an agony that everyone felt bad.

Ms. Hiftoun went to another classroom out of which sounds of laughter came.

'Very ridiculous, Karbarou! Why should anyone laugh at these stupid jokes of stand-up comedians?'

The door opened immediately and Karbarou's happy voice was heard.

'My pupils are mercurial " and they must laugh, even out of fear of bad grades.'

Karbarou had a thin neck on top of which was a little round head. The mercurial Jinn was truly ludicrous. The kids could not imagine encountering a Jinni that would not somehow get them scared.

At the end of the first floor's corridor was circulating a mellow and clear whirlwind counterclockwise. The objects inside it were revolving slowly. The first thing that caught Andy's attention there was an old house the size of a book. It seemed to be The Hiftoun House. Nothing could be heard as though the whirlwind was happening in a distant world. Ms. Hiftoun had her back to the whirlwind.

'This is an internal transporter that is adopted from the magical mail chest. Does anyone know why the "' mails are delivered by the Jinn-born giant?'

Everyone stared at each other. Ms. Hiftoun looked dissatisfied.

'Just like you who just carry your books and know nothing about the content inside them. The Jinn-born giant has no idea about what it carries. Before its mental maturity, the Jinn-born giant is not able to locate distant routes. It only finds the destination through the mail chest. With the emergence of initial signs of perception i.e. at the age of thirty, the Jinn-born giant is removed from the mail carrier function… OK, now is anyone willing to prove their bravery? You just need to enter the whirlwind and utter mail room. Nothing to worry about! It's just an internal transporter and knows no place other than the "' building where there's only one mail room which is safe,'

Nobody volunteered to do so.

'So, I'm leaving. If the " need servants, you can assist them.' said Ms. Hiftoun.

Then she went inside the whirlwind, uttered the word mail room and disappeared. After she departed, they all stormed the whirlwind. At the thought of the whirlwind being hard of hearing, they yelled so loud while saying the mail room that part of their scream could be heard while they were in the mail room. As other rooms in the Hiftoun House, the mail room was only a name. It was in fact a huge storeroom from whose small windows shone the sunlight. There were numerous parcels and boxes on the tables and shelves. They were all standing in front of a wooden table expecting the shaky stack of envelopes to collapse but that would not happen. The paintings on the walls changed every five minutes. Elsewhere in the mail room, parcels and envelopes were being packed by magical ribbons to be sent. Colorful ribbons would detach themselves from the table and tie around the parcels. There was also a magical feather pen that was signing the letters. Ms. Hiftoun was leaning on a tall, wooden chest at the top of the little platform at the corner of the room.

'In case you faced questions regarding the mail room and nothing crossed your mind, you could blame yourself as we are going to start the course on the mail room right now,'

They took out their magical pens and expandable notebooks. Ms. Hiftoun talked about the mail room nonstop. Those who were using the old versions of magical pens could see smoke rising from their pens. They feared their pens may catch fire. Ms. Hiftoun spoke so much that all pens except the blue?? And oak pens started squeaking until the mail chest made a move. Ms. Hiftoun turned her head.

'We got a letter. Does anyone wish to receive the letter from the mailman to buy themselves some credit?'

Nobody volunteered.

'There's a little Jinn-born giant inside the chest called Gloufi. It is kind of edgy but has a kind heart. It's more good-looking than its relations. At least its parents boast of it so much,'

Everybody laughed but nobody volunteered. Andy was overwhelmed with the feeling that he must do something to prove himself. He couldn't help overcome this internal itch. When he pulled himself together, he realized he had raised his hand and was hearing words of praise by Ms. Hiftoun.

'Good boy! Step forward. It's great to have a brave person among us,'

Andy pointed at himself in disbelief. What had made him want to do such a stupid thing? Taken aback by his idiocy, Lisa and Emily expressed their feeling with their shocked looks. Andy was to change his mind but was not able to do so. They were all looking at him and Ms. Hiftoun's praise was making it harder to do. Before he could change his mind, she opened the chest door. They got surprised to see a long, red corridor inside the chest.

'Damn! It looked to be only two meters from outside!' said Emily with surprise.

Remorsefully, Andy cast a look at Emily and then stepped inside the chest slowly. When Ms. Hiftoun shut the chest door, many bets that he would return with cuts and bruises all over his body. Andy moved forward in the frightening and darkish corridor. Gloufi, the Jinn-born giant, was sitting on a stool with a dusty skin. With his big head and bad teeth, he was checking out the person who had gone there to get the letter. He looked like a slow-witted human who had undergone rapid growth. You could see his fat body sticking out of his short shirt from far away.

Despite the fact that Andy's brain was sending a barrage of alarm signals to him, he went to Gloufi. He did not expect to receive the letter without a wound after stretching out his hand but Gloufi was kind-hearted, unlike his ugly face and teeth. Itching for fresh air, Andy got the letter and ran out of the chest immediately throwing it in the room. The letter caught fire while going up displaying the image of an old magician. Everybody stopped speaking once the old magician started to speak.

'Hello, Ms. Hiftoun! The warehouse underneath the castle has been evacuated and the six-fingered "transferred to the ruins down the hill,'

The magician then turned to the children and bowed.

'Accept the felicitations of Captain Ericson. Congrats on the joint course! Farewell, dear ones!'

The fire was out and the letter was taken to the read letters' section. Before anybody said anything, the chest moved again. This time Gloufi got out of it. Screaming, the Glorite children pulled back but George was standing by Andy indifferently. Gloufi had a box that resembled a jewelry box which he wanted to present to Andy. He did so with stupid laughter and then got back to the chest.

'Gloufi is gone too. I think we just experienced the most perfect lesson on the mail room today.' said Ms. Hiftoun.

They were all gazing the box in Andy's hand whispering to each other. Having opened the box, Andy noticed the first person turning to him in surprise was the magical feather pen that signed the letters. Inside that nice box was a green stone with a galaxy spinning inside it. Ms. Hiftoun was surprised.

'I'm jealous of you! Gloufi never gifted me. What a gift! The galaxy jasper stone!'

She did not explain what the stone was used for. She just wanted Andy to put it to its best use and not to show that valuable gem to anyone since it would make humans' hearts go bad. She then announced the end of the class.

The flying book

Junas was so happy. He was telling the heads nearby proudly as to how he had gotten rid of the conjurers. He was however amazed to see Andy who had entered the third corridor.

'What the hell were these idiot "doing then? Conjurers cannot enter the "' building. Why are you in one piece, rats? That can't go on! I must take action. You're more thick-skinned than I had thought,' yelled Junas.

Junas who couldn't stand other heads smirking opened the door and turned toward inside only to see the Jasper stone e.

'No! That's impossible! What's goin' here? You have the galaxy jasper?' asked him with surprise.

'It wouldn't choose you. I mean it mustn't,' said Junas in despair.

'What do you mean it wouldn't choose?'

Junas laughed hysterically.

'I should've guessed that three novice conjurers wouldn't know anything about Jasper. Unlike you, Jasper has senses and picks its owner. Put yourself in its shoes. Would you accept a conjurer as your own if you are a galaxy jasper stone? It may even already have an owner,'

Having been able to displease them, Junas looked contended.

'Can you tell us something that would benefit us instead of looking like this?' asked Emily impatiently.

'You gotta communicate with it to see if it has an owner. If it has one, then…wait a sec! that's none of my business! How could I make myself teach you lessons, wet blankets? Your presence here is enough torture!'

'OMG! Look who's calling others a wet blanket!' said Lisa furiously.

'Come on Junas! How should we communicate with it?' asked Emily.

'I'm not sure if you deserve it but I may be able to help you. It's like a deal. To you, Jasper is as important as are other things to me,'

'Like what?'

Junas pointed to a small storeroom door in the room.

'There you can find my lovely tools. Stupid servants wouldn't clean them. I hate dust but looks like you are used to dirt.

Looking as if she had accepted his request Emily inquired, 'Couldn't you ask for this politely?'

Junas looked very surprised.

'But it was polite! You are so demanding!' answered Junas.

In the store, Junas kept a burnt lamp, a broken teapot, and an old calculator and some other stuff that were all good to be dispensed with. As Andy started dusting them, he forgot how many objects he had polished. Lisa was cleaning a baby pacifier.

'He's sort of nuts!' said her satirically.

Andy held a set of artificial teeth.

'Do you really like this?'

Junas pressed his teeth together several times.

'It sounds like this. It's so cool!'

'Yes, it is!' said Emily with a smirk.

Junas ignored it and mumbled something.

'None of your business, nosy girl!'

After an hour of incessant work, the three of them stood before Junas expectantly.

'Had you done so much to clean the house, I'd not have so many problems with you. Now, go to the library and get the Jasper book,'

'That's what you were going to tell us?' inquired Emily angrily.

'So, you were thinking that I'd lecture you for an hour?

'But it says in the wisdom book that going to the library is not allowed,'

Junas burst into laughter and fled. Andy felt he had taken a cold shower.

'I think he's fooled us!'

'How the hell could you volunteer? When the chest door opened, I was sure you would change your mind,' said Lisa.

'I jus' didn't realize what happened,'

'It was cool! Did you notice Bill Foster's face? He looked as if he was beaten up. Didn't anyone notice that? I did.'

She then looked at the hole on top of the door.

'Where does Junas go? How can anyone stand him?'

Emily was opening the wisdom book.

'Don't be mad at him. It says here these doors are called Pokouns who are notorious for being rude,'

Lisa was filled with hatred.

'So much for the disgusting invention! The Pokoun! What a silly name!'

Ms. Margaret, the Hiftoun House's chef announced the lunchtime with her magical bell. The trio remembered they will have to receive their food from magical clouds. That was entertaining! While leaving the room, thinking that it would hurt Junas, Lisa

140

kicked the door so hard she felt pain in her foot. With the bang on the door, the adjacent doors woke up and started to attack with insults…

'Stupid conjurer! Why do you kick the door? Would you do that to your dad's home's door? With these manners, you will never get anyone to marry you. What the hell is wrong with you? Your parents should have taught you some good manners instead of just feeding and clothing you…'

Lisa felt like responding but on second thought she feared they might want to hurt her.

When they went down the stairs, Ms. Melanie Notre Dame, Ms. Hiftoun's assistant, was speaking to an elderly man at the foyer's entrance. Emily turned to one of the maids who was busy cleaning.

'Excuse me, madam, have you heard of Jasper stone?'

The woman shook her head. Emily pointed at Ms. Notre Dame.

'What about that lady?'

'Ms. Notre Dame? Never approach her!' warned the woman.

'So, that's her! It's said in the book that she's got a hurting scream,'

'What the hell is hurting scream?' asked Andy.

'It's a magical scream that knocks the enemy unconscious!'

Ms. Notredam was seriously greeting the instructors who had shown up for the joint course. Some of them were only carrying a handbag. Some of them had big suitcases and some others carried evil eye beads and animal jaws.

Heedless of the spiritless welcoming ceremony, Andy went to the canteen straight away. Ms. Temple was blaming Glorite children.

'I just don't understand. How can you not know which piece belongs to which Jinn after studying the course on effective pieces?'

She changed to a mild tone.

'Of course, I didn't mean you, dear George!'

She then resumed scolding the kids.

'I won't allow anyone to defame magical schools. For long years Jinn masters have been envious of our pupils' talents but today we don't find a trace of that talent among you,'

She then moved toward the exit door angrily. She was happy to see Andy.

'How are you doing, Andy? Ms. Hiftoun was quite pleased with you. You now have galaxy jasper, right? That's just wonderful!'

'Thanks, Ms. Timpel, but I know nothing about it,'

'You must gain its ownership in any way possible,'

'But I don't know anything about it. The wisdom book has banned us from going to the library,'

'No, you're mistaken! That word has not used the word ban. It just says going to the library is not part of the curriculum,'

She sounded secretive.

'Ms. Hiftoun does apply punishment against conjurers but remembers you have not heard me say anything to you about it,'

Andy showed her the stone.

'Can you take a look at it?'

Ms. Timpel avoided taking the stone.

I know it may sound disappointing but the stone that Gloufi has gifted cannot be trusted. If it is cursed, then it had better harm you,'

She then started to laugh.

'By the way, I talked to Ms. Hiftoun and asked her to exempt you from going to class. She accepted that. Bye for now!'

Lisa was so happy.

'So, here's the go-ahead to go to the library! This Ms. Timpel is a gem!'

The joy of using the canteen and the mysterious clouds there distracted Andy from the jasper stone. He heard the Glorite pupils say the words I'm still hungry and receiving another tray full of edibles from the dark cloud. Still, Andy was already full and even returned what had remained of the plate of fish and chicken to the dark cloud.

After lunch, the trio learned the library route from directions on the building map. Then from the first corridor of the western corridor, they went past several corridors, junctions, and stairways. There was nobody there. Little by little, they started to think that they are lost. Finding the library was not that easy they had thought. They had reached the end of the house but had not been able to find the library yet. At last, Andy turned to a passageway in the north that had plunged into darkness. Pages of a large number of books were being turned there. He noticed the library sign there. It looked as though someone had erased the writing on the sign so nobody could find it.

'That must be it!'

'Are you sure? It seems weird!' said Emily.

'No but I can hear book pages being turned,'

Stepping into the ill-lit space down the passageway, Andy felt the ceiling was going higher and higher opening up a vast space before him. As he was curiously walking to the end of the corridor, he could hear the sound of books pages being turned louder and louder. He was now certain that it must be the library. He had reached a foggy area yet he was still curious when a flying book caught his eyes. It was less foggy there but still, he could hardly see things. Andy dodged a flying book.

'That's why it's not part of the curriculum,'

He then thought he could see the books storage down that foggy space. He was unsure though as he was not able to pay attention to that and at the same time be cautious not to be hit by flying books. Soon, a bunch of giant books went past the point where Andy was standing before. Lisa smirked.

'I hope there's a librarian here or else we won't be able to find the book in a month's time.'

Andy went forward in order to have a better view. He was lucky enough to locate a book which was flying in a little distance to the ground. He went after the book slowly. Emily was trying to get rid of a book that kept pecking at her head like a woodpecker.

'Where are you going, Andy?'

'That's it. I've found it!' said Andy excitedly.

The book screamed and flew away.

'Wait for me my dear book! Where are you going?' cried, Andy.

Andy started to run. So did Emily and Lisa. The book was reaching the wooden storages a large number of which could be seen there. They were holding millions of books. Each row was identified from the framework at its ends. Andy entered a row which was called dreamy books on top of one of whose storages were sitting the flying book. The books in that section were all asleep. Some of them were snoring quietly and some others loudly. Andy tried not to wake them up but he could not let go of the flying book. Emil and Lisa were silent after seeing all those sleeping books. The flying book was eying them from above thinking that Andy won't reach it. Like a mountaineer, Andy climbed the book storage. Several books slipped from under his feet. At impacting the floor, the books woke up with a yawn unable to fly or say anything. Emily and Lisa rushed to hug the books like infants and the books would fall asleep again with another yawn. Andy was up to the storage half way. Emily asked him quietly not to get himself killed for the book but Andy did not give up. Eventually, he reached the book. The book didn't expect that. It was kicking like a trapped animal one of whose legs was caught but to no avail. Andy climbed down happily and was disheartened when he noticed the book's cover.

'But this is not Jasper. The image kinda looks like it. Why doesn't it move? Is it dead?'

'Did you kill it?' asked Emily worriedly.

Andy moved the book like a corpse.

'Hey, get up! It's over! Are you alive? Get up and go!'

'It won't move coz I asked it to,' said a manly voice.

Without looking back, Lisa froze where she was standing. The voice belonged to a Jinni with a felt hat, tapering nose, triangular teeth and a robe like that of conjurers.

'Damn you, Junas!' cursed Andy.

The Jinn flushed.

'What? Did that stupid pokemon send you here?'

They had to forget about the idea of forgiveness with the hatred that was obvious in the Jinn's face upon hearing Junas' name.

'You are the jerk's friends, right?'

Before things got worse Emily turned to him.

'No, no, no! We are here on Ms. Timple's suggestion.'

The Jinn's facial features totally changed upon hearing her name.

'Ms. Timple? Very well. I'm Progue. The librarian of the "' library. I'll forgive you despite my hatred for that stupid pokemon. Things can change now. You can be happy to see me as finding what you're looking for is not possible without my help. Now, what is it that you are looking for?'

'Jasper,' answered Andy.

'There are several books on Jasper. Hope they'll prove to be useful,' said Progue.

It then looked up and mumbled something. In a strange incident, all the flying books went into suspension. Progue called somebody named Boroudi. The sound of a book flying toward them was heard and they just realized Boroudi was the book's name. Progue has picked a name for each book but how could he recall names of millions of books? Like a little bird which wouldn't land, the book sat on Progue's hand. He then summoned someone called Izas. He called several names and got eight books sitting on his hands. But, when he called Bilfu, nothing happened.

'Where are you, inspector Sari?' cried Progue.

A book arrived at high speed, just like a hunting bird.

'Go find Bilfu'

Inspector Sari left and returned with a wet book immediately.

'I don't think it's good for anything. Bilfu's contents are included in Boroudi too. Go dry yourself Bilfu,' said Progue disappointedly.

Bilfu looked embarrassed. With water dripping off its cover, it flew away. Progue muttered something and all the books resumed flying shattering the silence. Andy was surprised.

'Do you know the names of all the books?' asked Andy.

The feeling of pride was obvious on Progue's face.

'When the last librarian got retired, many were willing to replace him. But after a tough test, only three people remained. All of us knew the names and places of each book but the difference was that I had also picked nicknames for them. That made them choose me. OK now, follow me,'

Progue headed westward without explaining to them where he wanted to take them. He started to speak when silence prevailed gradually.

'It's not always this quiet but at exam times it must be as quiet. I will take you to the study hall since it's the only place where flying books don't fly away when opened,'

By the time they reached the study hall, Progue disappeared several times and anytime it came back, it looked so normal as though nothing had happened. Finally, they got to a big door.

'We'd better clarify certain things right now. You have no right to make a noise or disappear with no good reason,'

'Disappear and appear?' asked Andy.

'Oh, sorry! I forgot. OK, go in now,'

The study hall was hosting 11-year-old "who were sitting at round wooden tables reading big books. Gradually when they all notice the presence of three human beings among them, they started making noise. Progue said something in their language which sounded like a threat. Everybody got quiet when Progue started to speak.

Once you are done with the books, leave them outside of the hall. I have to go now.'

'But, what about us?' asked Lisa worriedly.

Progue smiled and disappeared.

Andy thought it's no use not being frightened, so he stopped thinking about the " and went to a table nearby and started to study. One hour later, he realized that nothing had been mentioned in those books regarding ways of communicating with the galaxy jasper. Most of them had just mentioned the use of Jasper only. Andy realized at that point that the owner of the stone will be able to store his thoughts in the stone and remove them from his own mind. The galaxy stone was a source of energy and would augment bravery and concentration. Andy wasn't interested to read about the stone's properties before being able to communicate with it. The explanations sounded boring but the more Lisa read the more she grew greedy. She said several times that if she realizes later on that the stone already had an owner, she wouldn't give it back. She then asked Andy in case such a thing happened, she would be happy to have the stone.

Closing the book, Andy took a glance at the " for the first time. They were making more noise compared to the time when the trio showed up. Some of them had closed their books. Now Andy was eying them in a different way. He was scared for no good reason as most of them looked fine. Some of them had horns or horrifying eyes and even squeezed faces though. Noticing a Jinni with white eyes and pale face looking greenish, Andy then took the sight of a human, a girl who was second to none in terms of beauty. Her black hair and wavy eyebrow were blacker than the night. On that white and beautiful face were eyes that resembled the stars shining in a lead-blue sky. When she cast a look at Andy with her infatuating smile, Andy blushed and looked down. When he looked up, he jumped up as the beautiful girl was standing right in front of him.

'Hi. How are you doing? What's your name?' asked her.

'I...I...I'm Andy,'

Lisa raised her head in surprise.

'What on earth are you doing here? Maybe you are friends with these eerie ", ha?' asked Lisa.

The girl's cheeks got red when she said she was a half breed Jinni.

Emily was embarrassed.

'Sorry! She didn't mean anything. What's your name?' asked Emily.

'Fentous,'

'Fentous. What a nice name! It's just as nice as yourself. You know what Fentous?'

'I'm sure you wanna know why I look like humans,'

'Not if it hurts you,'

'I'm half human. I have the body of humans and the skills of ". Among half breed " my twin sister and I totally possess human bodies. If we go back, maybe we prove to be relations,'

'It's hard to imagine,' mumbled Lisa.

'How old are you?' asked Emily in a friendly way.

'12. " enter the joint course at this age but human beings at age 14,'

149

'We are also 12. We are conjurers and are here for punishment,' said Andy.

Fentous was surprised.

'Wow! I can't believe it! I've always wanted to see a conjurer up close. I hear humans have to undergo conjuring courses before doing the magic school. But what do you do when you cannot perform magic? What exactly do you do?'

Lisa who didn't like to be called a conjurer replied.

'You have to be fully human to understand not half human,'

Fentous was offended but tried not to show it. To change the topic Andy pointed at a Jinni who was biting its nails out of anxiety.

'Why is it so scared?' asked Andy.

'One of the mercurial has told it that murderer "have attacked the village,'

'Have they really done that?'

'No way! You know, mercurial "would do or say anything to attract attention,'

'Where's the jungle?'

'Inside the jungle, not far from here. It's entrance exam day today. I hope I'll get a good mark,'

She pointed to a thick book she was holding.

'I've been studying for three months. It won't finish! Did you know that nobody is allowed to use magic in the Hiftoun House except the staffers there?'

Lisa smirked.

'But Progue performed magic. I saw that,'

'I mean humans' magic. "' magic can be performed in any place,'

Just then they heard a hammer being hit against a tin object. Concerned, the "jumped out of their position. Fentous stopped short of finishing her statement.

'Finally, the exam has started. See you later kids!' said the girl under stress.

'What if we don't wanna see ya?' muttered Lisa.

Andy knew that Lisa was jealous of Fentous' beauty. She had already told Andy that she would hate anyone who looked more beautiful than her.

It was time to leave the hall. As they had promised Prouge, they left the books outside of the study hall where they flew to their own sections.

Frowning Philip

Returning to the room, Andy, Emily, and Lisa behaved in such a way as though Junas was not present. Junas was just laughing.

'Oh, my God! What else should I do to make you believe that you are fools?'

'We got Ms. Timple's permission and went to the library,' said Lisa victoriously.

Junas's eyes got rounded.

'What? Ms. Timple? I can smell treason. Poor Ms. Hiftoun! I think you yourself can also be a spy,'

Lisa picked up a small flower pot at the side of the window angrily.

'No, no, no! We're not getting physical, OK?' said Junas.

'Look, Junas! We can be friends,' said Emily.

'How can we be friends when we have that blue-eyed spy among us? No one has ever harmed the pokouns,' said Junas anxiously.

He then thought quietly for a while.

'Well, actually there were a few cases. For instance, they chopped my uncle with an axe. My brother was also torn into pieces. My screaming cousin, Sonera who was not pretty at all, was also turned to torches. Of course, that wasn't too bad coz I didn't hafta marry her anymore. Wow! What a brilliant history! Throwing a flower pot is nothing in comparison. Anyway, leave it! She is a stupid girl! Can't do anything about it!' added Junas.

'We've cleaned your stuff, so we can be friends. Lisa will apologize to you, too. Isn't that right, Lisa?' said Emily emphatically.

'I'm Sorry, Mr. Junas!' said Lisa with hate.

'No problem, I forgive you. It's not worth being angry with you. Philip has the answer to the riddle. He is called the king of stones after all!' said Junas proudly.

'Philip?' asked Emily.

'The magician by the lake. If only Condoles wasn't there!'

'Who is Condoles?'

'The wandering phantom of the seventh corridor. The blood-sucking beast!'

George O'Neil who had just gotten out of his room in the third corridor heard his voice from the half-open door.

'He's lying! Condoles is the wandering phantom of the seventh corridor. She isn't that bad-tempered. She just hates disorder,'

'Get lost, nosy boy!' said Junas while laughing.

'Hey George, we saw a half breed Jinni,'

'Sorry, Andy! I gotta go. Ms. Timple has blown her top. I hafta take her some unending gypsum. I think she is going to teach the Jinn alphabet from scratch. If we do not reach the desired level before other schools, she will fire all of us. You're so lucky you don' have these idiots in your class. They are a disgrace! I made a mistake! I shouldn't have registered at the Glorite after admission at the School of Magic. I had to do it for my family.'

George went down the stairs making Junas happy.

'I hate all these school nerds! This idiot answered the poor Feron's riddle even after they opened the door for the Glorite pupils. Feron got depressed. Nobody had been able to find an answer to his riddle for at least ten years. It wasn't too bad though. It's not only me whose riddle has been solved.'

'Get to the main point, Junas,' said Emily anxiously.

Junas shut the door and lowered his voice.

'I will tell you the password to the seventh corridor. You must take care of the rest on your own. You hafta find the tears lake,'

'Then what?'

Junas burst into laughter.

'Wow! It's so enjoyable to deal with a bunch of conjurers! They know nothing about nowhere! I would've liked you to stay here, had you not been so filthy,'

Lisa was biting her lips with anger.

'Come on! Utter it out!'

'OK, OK! Easy does it, blue-eyed spy! The tears lake gets activated overnight only. It can move humans as far as twenty kilometers. You just need to enter it,'

'How are we supposed to get back then?'

'You hafta return from the same point of departure and utter the word tears lake,'

'I don't buy that!' said Andy in disbelief.

'No problem! I Jus' let you know the password for the seventh corridor and you decide.'

"A hall of magic, a hall of ", a hall of humans, a hall of phantoms"

That day everyone was speaking about a girl called Anna Stones who had entered the "' forbidden section. Anna looked as pale as chalk even after treatment. No one knew what had become of her. Anytime she recalled that she would scream. After several times she had stirred the situation in the foyer with her horrible screams, she was taken back to the clinic again.

Andy, Emily, and Lisa found the air in the eatery kind of heavy. Everybody was upset. George was also sitting in a corner in isolation.

'Anything wrong, George?' asked Andy.

George was sad.

'If Ms. Douglas wants to assess the Glorite kids' literacy level, it's got nothing to do with me! She didn't allow me to reply. Now they are all complaining why I didn't,'

'Ms. Timple must be pretty angry, right?' asked Andy.

'She doesn't know about it yet. But she will soon. By the way, I talked to her about the jasper stone. She said taking possession of the galaxy stone is just like getting your hands on a magical weapon. Not all books offer you the real way it could be put to use tough. It's sort of banned,'

'Didn't she say how you could communicate with it?'

'Yes, she did,'

'OK?'

'But you may be disappointed. She said the galaxy stone needs tons of power and concentration, which is outside of your ability. Sorry, Andy! I shouldn't have said this,'

'To be honest, it doesn't matter,'

'Really? I thought you'd do anything in order to own it. There's only one person who can make the stone speak but unfortunately, that person is not very well these days,'

'Who?'

'Philip Sander or frowning Philip. He lives with a fairy called Dimer Ill by the lake,'

Lisa who thought the topic of the discussion was really important, jumped in.

'Do you know anything about the tears lake?'

George eyed the Glorite pupil for a moment. They were whispering. He then continued haphazardly.

'The tears lake is a kind of latitudinal transformer that's given to Ms. Hiftoun by the phantoms. It's true that it's a lake but it doesn't make you wet,'

'So, Junas was not lying!' said Lisa mysteriously.

'What are you gonna do now?'

'Didn't you hear that Ms. Hiftoun's punishments are not exercised against conjurers?'

'You mean you believe they won't do anything to you just because you are a conjurer?' asked Emily.

There was a mysterious glare in Lisa's eyes.

'Communicating with the stone means entering the School of Magic without an exam!'

George forgets about his own problems and was surprised at what he had heard.

'If you go to the lake, you will be dismissed even from among the conjurers!' warned George.

'Even me and Andy?' asked Emily sadly.

'But in the wisdom book there's no mention of a ban on the seventh corridor,' said Lisa.

In an unbelievable move, Andy put the stone in Lisa's hands.

'Here! You can have the stone. Don' just put us in trouble!'

Lisa stared at the stone bewildered. She had never felt so delighted since meeting Andy.

'But the stone is yours, Andy,' said Emily surprisingly.

'I just told you. It doesn't matter anymore,'

Just then, Patrick Standman who was giving Andy the dagger's eyes went past them. Tired of his looks, Andy poured himself a bowl of soup and started to eat.

The following day the house saw the arrival of second graders who were coming from different schools. Andy had seen the arrival of new students from his room window several times. Now with the night falling, he was standing there reviewing the past. It was only three months ago when an invisible man and woman entered house number seven when he was turning around himself fearfully asking them to leave the house. He had gone through so many weird incidents in that period. He still recalled the burning cups and he was still overwhelmed with emotions when he remembered his look-alike. He had found no chance of meeting his look-alike but he knew that things had gone smoothly. He missed everything he had been deprived of. He missed Dias, his home, Eric... all of a sudden, he remembered that the house signs would change at twelve o'clock sharp. There were still two minutes left. Andy hurried out of the room. The sign by the window was displaying a magician called Tom Hoop.

…Tom Hoop, with the pseudonym 'the awake eye', was one of the greatest magicians when it came to discovering secret spells. He had located and nullified three hundred spells in an old warehouse.

Andy looked at the clock excitedly. There were only ten seconds left.

…Tom Hoop had developed resistance against spells after long years.

Five seconds left.

…Among his major discoveries was a mysterious spell on disorientation found in an old castle called…

The sign changed exactly at 12 o'clock displaying a man with a coat. He was sitting at a desk with a stack of thick books.

…Professor Fredric Hiftoun was a great magician of his time who had a special talent in building magical structures. The Hiftoun House is regarded as his masterpiece whose mystery still remains unknown for many after a lapse of a thousand years. His most outstanding work, how to cast a spell on our home, is still among the top priorities of magical engineers…

That night Andy dreamed that he was speaking to Dias book again. The book with its warning sentences was asking him to be cautious. It eventually flew away. Andy begged the book to go back but his dream was left unfinished when Junas started to shout and woke him up.

'Hey, wake up! We are doomed!'

Emily ran out of the room.

'What's wrong, Junas?'

'The blue-eyed is gone! She is going to find the tears lake,'

'You said it wasn't dangerous!'

'I should have made an arrangement with Condoles first. That's why I'm afraid. Go after her before it's too late!'

Andy and Emily rushed out.

'Farewell, poor conjurers!' muttered Junas viciously.

Andy was watching the foyer secretly. There was nobody there. On tiptoe, he walked to the end of the seventh corridor so that he wouldn't wake the pokouns. He then whispered the password into the wall's ears. On the other side of the wall, there was an amazing hall where an unusual and tranquilizing tune could be heard. Andy stopped Emily from moving further ahead. He showed her a sign that had a sun shining inside it like the real sun. Emily raised her head to be able to see the flower pots and suspending objects hanging overhead. Cautiously, she walked to a tall mirror but turned her back to it instantly.

'I don't wanna see what I'll look like in the future,'

Andy looked at the writing on the top corner of the mirror which read "the life mirror".

'Your future look?'

'That's what this mirror does. The more you stand here, the older it makes you see what you'll look like in the future. I don't wanna see that. No doubt, Lisa hasn't looked at it either,'

'Oh, we are here for Lisa then!'

A third person's voice was heard.

'That's right. You're after that greedy girl,

They both turned to the wall. It was the voice of a woman that was getting out of the wall like broken glass. After her body parts got connected together, she stood in the air. Condoles, the phantom of the seventh corridor, with azure blue pupils and reddish pink hair, was standing there like a boss. Her purple dress was so long that had covered her feet. Without taking steps, she moved forward. Emily gulped down her saliva.

'Good evening, dear phantom! You have a really tough job!'

Lisa, together with two young phantoms, emerged from a gold-studded door. One of them was holding her hand in front of her mouth and the other was hitting her head with a stick. Lisa got so happy at the sight of Andy and Emily that she stopped attempting to run away.

'She must be your friend, right?'

They both nodded.

'Well...' Andy started.

'You don't hafta explain anything. I can see behind the walls and hear everything. Did you not realize about that stupid pokoun's scheme? Junas knows better than anyone else that nothing remains hidden from my eyes. So, why should he send you here? Is it not because he wants to get you fired through me?'

The trio looked at each other. Junas had put them on one more time. Andy looked at Lisa like a culprit.

'I let you have the stone,'

'But as long as I haven't communicated with it, it doesn't belong to me,' said Lisa rudely.

Condoles extended her hand and clasped a lantern that was hanging in the air.

'Nothing in the Hiftoun House is as enjoyable as enraging that stupid pokoun. Follow the lantern to the lake.'

She then made some chocolate appear in her hands.

'Take these too. Dimer Ill likes them.'

Lisa looked at Andy and Emily in disbelief. They were still angry with her.

'I would go with him if I were you. If only you knew how precious that stone is!'

'But…' said Emily.

'Don't worry! My permission means you are safe from all forms of punishment provided you give Junas a hard time once you are back.'

The lantern produced some kind of noise and set off. They followed it into a dark corridor that would reach the wandering "' foyer at one end. Horrifying "with worn out clothes were sitting on wooden benches listening to the tune of a magical harpoon. Incense fragrance had filled the air. The "were leaning like human beings moving their heads to the tune. Suddenly, one of them raised its head.

'Looks like we got guests, kids!' said one of them viciously.

Lisa gulped down her saliva. The lantern was bad-tempered and impatient. It moved forward while making some squeaking noise. The Jinn turned to the lantern.

'Easy, girl! Why are you so anxious? You can pass.'

At that moment several long-eared "with a big tray of roasted lamb entered the foyer. There was ballyhoo as if it was marking the start of the wandering "' celebration. Andy had no interest whatsoever in that ritual. While going past the " following the lantern, he was thinking Ms. Hiftoun had done the right thing to allocate a separate place for wandering " as they were even more untidy, disorganized and poorly dressed compared to other types of ".

Andy looked behind several times before getting to the lake. A scary Jinni with a cracked and red face like magma had his eyes fixed on him. He looked dangerous and anytime he smiled, Andy was filled with horror.

The lantern eventually sat in the corner of the foyer. The lake was lying there, clear and devoid of any kind of impurity. Out of fear of the wandering ", they stepped into the lake without hesitation uttering its name. Before long, they felt something was removed from under their feet and immersed them in water. It felt as though they were being dragged to the deepest part of the lake. For moments, it was dark everywhere. The only thing they could hear was the sound of water. When Andy opened his eyes, he was breathing hard but he realized that it's over and he is just a few steps from the lake. Lisa was excited.

'No more of those ugly creatures! By the way, what was that fairy called?' asked Lisa.

'Dimer Ill or something like that,'

'It's not just Dimer Ill. It's smart Dimer Ill! Haven' they taught you how to mention a smart fairy's name? That's why Philip doesn't like you,' said someone sounding offended.

Then from the oak tree came a creature flying their way. It had a long skirt and milky wings standing in the air.

'If you stay up there, I'll get my neck broken. How am I supposed to talk to you this way?' complained about Emily.

Dimer Ill flew down a bit. It was a young and lovely girl.

'So, it's you, smart Dimer Ill! Where's Philip? Any idea?'

The fairy moved her long and black eyelashes.

'Before going to the lake, he said he had more important things to attend to,' said her while trying to change her voice to sound like Philip.

'Now, who should answer our questions?'

The fairy looked curious.

'What? Did you get questions? What about?'

'About magical stones,'

'Oh, so why don' you ask a smart fairy about it?'

'What do you know about stones?

Dimer Ill flew to a rock covered with algae by the lake and sat there.

'OK, let me think…uh…the history of stones. Oh, yes! I remember! The first magical stone that was discovered by magicians…'

'Only the galaxy jasper stone,' interrupted Lisa.

Dimer, who acted like a sprinter waiting for the race to start, moved her head quickly and continued.

'Oh, OK. Got it! Jasper stone is the first stone in the spirit-boosting stone family…'

Lisa showed her the stone.

'This is what I mean,' said Lisa.

The fairy who didn't know the answer blushed.

'I didn't know fairies can also feel embarrassed!' said Emily.

'It's not that! My cheeks jus' look rosy! You feel embarrassed when you are in the valley by the waterfall combing your hair when kids are peeking. They are so rude! They threw stones at me!'

'Yes, they are rude. Could you call Philip now? Do you care for some chocolate?'

Dimer Ill's eyes moved on the chocolate in Emily's hand. As soon as she got the chocolate, she flew up over the lake and called Philip with her piercing shriek. The water started to boil little by little and a man with a thick mustache and algae on his head got out fearfully.

'What's wrong Dimer Ill? What happened?'

Dimer Ill frowned.

'You gotta answer their questions right now or else I won't talk to you anymore, bad-tempered Philip!'

Philip cast an eye on the kids.

'When the hell are you going to leave me alone? Go back!'

He submerged in the water again. Emily showed another chocolate to Dimer Ill. The fairy instantly dived into the water and threw Philip to the coast. Philip was restless.

'OK, you win! But I will remember to get this kid a few boxes of chocolate next time. Ask me your questions but you must know before you do it that I hate you. I had been trying to kill pests under the lake the whole day. Now I have to answer questions of a few intruding kids who are adept at trickery,'

He then put his big glasses on and got surprised to see the galaxy jasper stone.

'The galaxy jasper!'

'We got it as a gift from the Jinn-born giant,' said Lisa shyly.

Removing the seaweed from his head, Philip continued.

'Let's go to the cabin. It's too cold out here. You said the Jinn-born giant? He must have found it on the ground somewhere,'

They headed for the cabin together with Philip and Dimer Ill. Enthusiastically, Philip examined the stone. Dimer Ill was not able to use her feet properly. She was moving on tiptoe with difficulty but seemed to enjoy it.

Philip's cabin with its hot wooden burner stood on the other side of the lake. They got to the cabin.

'They got delicious chocolate, so it must be important!' said Dimer Ill.

'For some chocolate, you mustn't violate my rules, cute girl!' said Philip.

Putting her hands on her face, Dimer Ill turned her back on Philip. She started singing a tune and caressing her new shoes. She didn't use shoes and didn't even know how to walk with shoes on, yet she enjoyed singing for her personal belongings.

'It was a rainy night, smiling, it was going to jump into the wilderness, a dark night, a crying fairy, had gone, out of the home, all alone. The terrible little giant, ugly and rude, threw at her, little stones. Dummy little giant, Bad little giant, go away, go away for good.'

Philip was thinking deeply. The children were looking at him hopefully. Philip was gazing at the stone. At times, he would move his head as a sign of confirming something that only he was cognizant of. He could sense the magical warmth of the stone and the incomprehensible range of colors that were being formed in his head but he was not able to penetrate into that depth. This was frustrating him. While studying an ancient scripture years ago, Philip got stuck in a black spell.

For long days he plunged into ecstasy and when he finally came to, he had lost his awe-inspiring knowledge of stones. Perhaps, feeling the warmth of the stone and seeing the vague colors would be regarded as a source of pride for others, but for Philip whose nickname was the king of stones, it would only bring embarrassment and frustration. Once he was a simple conjurer but he was able to sense the stones' warmth.

Philip was lost in past memories for a while, taking a deep and heart-rending sigh.

'I'm sorry to say this but this stone has an owner,'

Lisa's face showed that she had lost all hope.

'Why isn't much written about the galaxy stone?' asked Lisa disappointedly.

Philip had his back to the window facing the lake.

'If you were a criminal, you would know why. If you were captured, for instance, you could clear your memory as you had already stored it elsewhere. Then nobody would be able to draw confessions from you in any way,'

He then turned to Lisa.

'Don' worry! The owner may have died in which case the previous thoughts gradually get cleaned and the stone will be able to get itself a new owner,'

Walking to his old bookshelf, Philip took an old book.

'I can't teach you in this limited time but if you like you can learn ways of communicating with magical stones with the help of this book. You may be able to find a trace of its owner. You seem to be smart kids,'

'They are smart but not as smart as me,' said Dimmer Ill in protest.

'Definitely, nobody outsmarts my little girl. That's why they need to read books to become smart.'

Philip stopped speaking. Once again and for the last time he gazed at the galaxy jasper with his big eyes. The children bade farewell and returned to the wandering "' foyer through the same point they had found their way to the lake. Luckily, the " were gone. The lantern was asleep. It woke up and led them to the outside wall as it was nagging all along. Andy was certain that Condoles was watching them somewhere nearby. Without seeing her, he politely bade her farewell.

Junas was sleeping but as soon as the door was opened, he woke up with fear.

'Damn you! You must have a hundred lives! How the hell did you make it back, filthy worms? How could Condoles let go of you? She sniffs like a dog. I must tell Ms. Hiftoun that the phantom of the seventh corridor is so negligent and lazy that lets anyone go past it,'

'Conversely, she was pretty attentive but we promised we'd take her some pokoun burning wood if she let us go,'

Junas looked pale. His strong jujube-colored face looked like dirt and his olive pupils moved in his eyeballs quickly.

'You are not going to go back there again, so why should you care about what you have promised that stupid phantom?' asked Junas with a shaky voice.

Then looking frightened, he turned to Lisa.

'Was this lie that you told true?'

'Unfortunately, it was a lie,'

Emily showed him the old book.

'See what Philip has given us!'

Still feeling anxious, Junas was worried the fate of his relations may befall him. Lisa had managed to pinpoint his point of weakness incidentally. Junas suddenly started to open up his heart to them.

'They burned my aunties' husband before my eyes. The man who did that said he would make great burning wood. They took my friend to use him as columns of a field toilet. When I think of that, I feel terrible. They finally burned him. You won't listen to Condoles, will you?'

'Provided you promise not to insult us again,' said Andy.

'I've grown my wood with rudeness. Anytime I'm stressed out, I get ruder. Do you understand that, good-for-nothing conjurer? By the way, I knew that Philip would not be able to offer you any help,'

Andy gave him the dagger's eyes.

'But you said he was the king of stones,'

Junas burst into laughter.

'He used to be the king of stones. Now he's not even the king of asses,'

'I'm goin' to sleep so I could get rid of this jerk,' said Emily.

'See? You are rude too. This is intrinsic. You are just like me.'

The trio put heads together for a while and before Junas realized their sinister scheme, they pushed the dirty branches of the broom into his mouth.

Junas's olive eyes were fixated at one point.

'That's impossible! A dirty broom!'

Junas then fainted. The children felt proud of their victory.

'Long live the broom!' they cried.

The pokoun's objection

It was foggy but milder in temperature compared to the last days of November. Outside noise woke Andy up.

'Not that side. A bit higher,'

'Is it OK here?'

'Yes, go ahead.'

With caution, Andy opened the door. The maid was washing Junas's face. Noticing Andy, she greeted him with an open face.

'You shouldn't say hello to that jerk, Elena. So much for the agreement between pokouns and the Hiftoun House maids! Looks like you've forgotten that. So, listen! Enemy violence against my friend means my violence against my friend's enemy. My enemy's friendship with my friend means my friendship with the enemy...' protested Junas.

'I just acted so. Now that Andy and I are friends, why don't you make friends with him?' said Elena.

Junas gave the offer some thought.

'No, they may have written this part by mistake. You should misbehave toward him,'

Elena superficially frowned at Andy and tried to sound sarcastic.

'You have no right to bug Junas. He is the best pokoun in the world. Did you just realize what a brilliant personality you have beside you?' said Elena.

'Thanks, Elena. It suited him right. Do you think the dirty broom will harm my skin?' asked Junas.

'No,'

'It may have a deadly virus!'

'No. It's impossible!'

'Can a spell get into me through the broom?'

'No, Junas!'

'How confident are you about detergents being able to clean everything?'

'I'm sure,'

'Will you wash my face again?'

Elena did not take much heed of him. She took the bucket and the brush while winking at Andy.

'You have no right to disrespect the king of the pokouns,' said her emphatically.

'OK, sure! I didn't mean that,' said Andy.

'No, he's lying! It was intentional. Hey, where are you going? You weren't that mean to him!' objected Junas.

Andy eyed Junas.

'How does your face feel, dirty rat? Does it taste like a broom?' said Andy.

'I'm great, idiot! I took a great shower. Never been so clean! I smell brand new. I've reported what you did last night to the pokouns' guild. The complaint has been signed by the pokouns at the Hiftoun House and we will meet in court soon.'

Sleepy, Lisa left the room.

'You haven't found the right witnesses. Is it also mentioned in the complaint how rude you are?' asked Lisa.

'No one blames pokouns for being impolite. We cannot be anything but impolite!' ridiculed Junas.

Andy smirked, took his towel and after taking a hot shower, headed for the eatery hall. The magical cloud was really intriguing for newcomers. They paid more attention to the clouds rather than their meal.

'What's up, George?' inquired Andy.

'They've taken it too far! I'm a human not a Jinni!' complained George.

The Glorite pupils called George little Jinni given his knowledge of the ". Andy lost his appetite. He chewed the piece of beef he had in his mouth slowly. He was happy that the Glorite kids were not his classmates.

Magical funnels summoned everyone to the auditorium. It looked like a theater hall. The children had to climb down the stairs and go through doors decorated with inlaid work to reach it. Magical wooden chairs seemed rigid and dry but they were actually quite soft and comfortable. They made no noise when they were moved, either. Despite all the excitement over the start of the joint course, everybody was whispering to each other as Ms. Notre Dame was sitting with a frowning face. When Ms. Hiftoun arrived accompanied by a number of instructors, things changed and screams and yelling filled the air. Ms. Hiftoun was their heroin. In their cries was traced something like a proud feeling. With eager eyes they were watching a woman that had a high standing among the world magicians. Ms. Hiftoun was standing before students who had staggering interpretations of her on the back of their mind. At this magnificent juncture of time, they could not take their eyes off her. Ms. Hiftoun stood behind the podium.

'Welcome, respected guests! I hope you'll take many good things with you from here. Of course, I do not expect you to get familiar with the '" sophisticated world in a short period of time, but if you pay attention to the methodology applied by great instructors in this house, you will be able to defend yourself while encountering a vicious Jinni,'

Ms. Hiftoun gradually started to sound scary.

'We teach you how to face wild " who hide in the dark of the night within an invisible and black curtain.'

Suddenly, Ms. Hiftoun became silent and started gazing at a corner. Before long, a black-clad and tall Jinn emerged with old and wrinkled fingers, putting the fear of God into everyone. He had covered his face with a black cloth, seemingly to prevent further fright. Heedless of the tumultuous air in the salon, he reached Ms. Hiftoun, engaging in conversation with her for a while. Then with his wrinkled hands, he handed her a letter. The Glorite children asked George to say something.

'He's an acromansour, one of the most vicious of all ". I wonder why he's here.' said George surprisingly.

The acromansour vanished into thin air. Everybody was awaiting Ms. Hiftoun's remarks parts of which would definitely be related to that acromansour. Anything other than that would be unfair!

'You can be hopeful until your last day that some would abandon their treacherous and evil demeanor and change. It all depends on your determination and mindset. I dare say there is magic in thinking that is able to give out the most profound and latent layers of knowledge on nature and provide us with the best solutions. Thinking is magic without a name, magic that translates into getting stronger.'

Ms. Hiftoun brought an end to her speech at this point and left the auditorium. Afterward, Ms. Notre Dame stood at the podium and took up the helm seriously. She was the only person that could live long years without a single smile. The students gave her a round of applause but it was obvious it was out of duty lacking any trace of satisfaction. Behavior much colder than this could not influence her steely resolve. She started her stern speech by introducing the instructors of the joint course and reminding important hints. She also mentioned a few points regarding the intensive lessons.

After the welcoming ceremony, the students were led to the round space.

'Please be quiet! If each person even mumbles something, then it'll be difficult to control things,' ordered Ms. Timple.

The Pokouns were not happy having to let the pupils use the rooms without answering their riddles. The oldest pokoun, Woody, started to speak on their behalf.

'This is intolerable, Ms. Timple! I expected you to act fairly. How can a bunch of idiots avoid making the least effort to win a room without a serious test?'

All the pokouns supported Woody with their moans and groans being heard from all the corridors.

'...Well done, Woody! Defend our rights. These dummies must answer the riddles. They must be clean. I was looking for new riddles during the holidays. I got at least one million new riddles. Damn all the parasites!'

'Be quiet please! I know the rules better than you do,' commanded Ms. Timple.

'No, you don't. Rules are violated easily. Not even once have I had the chance them one single question...'

Ms. Timple got mad and started to yell.

'I told you to stop it! No more noise! If you cannot understand our sensitive situation, I should inform you that this is a very intensive course and we cannot keep the crowds behind doors for days. If you continue with this stupid game, I will have to ask Ms. Notre Dame to come back.' threatened Ms. Timple.

The sound that could be heard from the pokouns' side was not merely the voice of dissent, it was rather insulting remarks against the students standing in the round space in the stairs or inside the corridors waiting for the result.

Ms. Timple allocated the even corridors to girls and the odd ones to boys dividing each school among three rooms. The magical rooms turned into bigger houses with more amenities based on the number of people. Everyone was housed without any trouble despite the pokouns' dissatisfaction with the students' arrival. They felt they were stripped of their right. Yet, having consulted with their elder, Woody, they retreated to their roles satisfactorily. From then on, chaos prevailed. The pokouns would lock the doors and would go to meet each other keeping a large number of people waiting inside or outside of the rooms. Once they got back, they would simply make an apology and blame their forgetfulness for that. At times they pretended they were sleeping forcing the pupils to beg them to wake up. Some of them made believe they had a toothache or fell ill. Sometimes they even pretended to fight each other for a while to kill time and avoid opening the door. Things went on this way until nighttime when Ms. Notre Dame went up the stairs with a tin container putting fire to some wood in the middle of the round space. No conversation was held but the pokouns got the message very well and order was restored.

The nagging station

Andy, Emily and Lisa became indifferent to their stone ever since they heard Philip say it's got an owner. Lisa always carried the stone with her wherever she went to show it off.

For days, Andy followed a routine program. In the morning, he studied the conjuring lessons and in the evening, he went to visit George who stayed in one of the rooms of the third corridor. Inside that room there was a long corridor with numerous doors. George felt terribly lonely! Nobody would talk to him except when they wanted to make fun of him.

In the evening, mercurial "entertained others by funny moves in the yard. Mercurials were the only "that neither disappeared nor flew. In fact, they posed no threat to anyone. Some wicked students used them to carry their mail for them or contact friends in the area. The mercurial with letters in their hands ran to the most remote parts of the yard. They took so much pleasure out of performing standup comedy shows and went out of their way to make others laugh at their tasteless jokes.

One day when Andy was leaning on a tree at sunset, he saw Fentous pass by as she was lost in her thoughts. Fentous was the half breed beautiful Jinni who he had met at the library. After Andy called her with hesitation, Fentous turned to him looking very happy. This feeling emanated from the very same deep thoughts she had plunged into. Fentous regarded herself as a human and believed that her human soul dominates her Jinn spirit, so she thought she could live with humans. Like someone who has been

175

far away from their motherland for long years, she was fond of humans and showed extreme enthusiasm to listen to anything related to them. She was challenging some questions in her mind to which she had no answers when Andy called her. So, she thought it was a good idea to meet Andy at the same point on even days. Andy accepted the offer by all means. One of those days Fentoun started to speak.

How can humans do things without ever disappearing? Even "that are unable to disappear, can fly at least. Of course, the mercurial are only capable of camouflage.

'We travel using cars and aircraft which is not as speedy as the "' travels but it's better than nothing. We also have subways, a kind of train that moves underground,' replied Andy.

'I hear humans throw birthday parties. It must be so nice, mustn't it? Asked Fentous with overwhelming emotion.

'I couldn't imagine that'd be so interesting for you,'

'I wish I could live with humans!' said Fentous wistfully.

'Really?' asked Andy surprisingly.

'I'm more a human that has the "' abilities. None of the half breed " in the village are as similar to humans as my twin sister and I. we call this the end of change. I mean the next generation will not look like "at all,'

'How do the "disappear?'

'This is intrinsic. Of course, we must be ten years old first,'

'So, when will we be able to disappear and appear?'

'I'm not the one to answer this. Probably at the fourth grade, but I hope you'll use the method to disappear physically,' said Fentous with a smile.

'Is there any other way?'

'Yes, and that's too dangerous! It's called the soul disappearance. Your body falls to a side without any motion and your soul flies. The stronger you are, they farther away you'll be able to fly but your body may not be able to accept your soul in which case you'll head for the land of the dead pretty soon,'

The thought of that shook Andy. Fentous was ready to leave after wishing him a great day.

'The village, the village. I gotta concentrate on the village.' Andy thought.

Fentous disappeared and Andy praised her despite the fact that he knew she hadn't heard his words of admiration.

The next day when a chilly breeze was blowing, Ms. Timple asked Emily and Lisa to follow her to the "' building for inspection. The proposal could not be rejected after days of routine work. Ms. Timple led them to the seventh floor of the "' building through the whirlwind at the ground floor corridor. As soon as they stepped out of the whirlwind on the seventh floor's large corridor, darkness covered everywhere. Andy noticed several pairs of shining eyes in the dark gazing at him curiously. Lisa gulped down her saliva and put her hand on Emily's shoulder worriedly.

'That's no big deal, Mr. Kanouj,' said Ms. Timple.

First off, they heard some commotion and then light made a comeback. When Lisa realized that she had rested her hand on an ugly Jinn's shoulder the whole time, she nearly fainted. The Jinn's face looked even more surprised. It had a crushed face with yellow eyes and pale skin. The Jinn pulled its lips together as a sign of discontent and left. Mr. Kanouj was an old Jinni.

'What are these three people doing here, Ms. Timple?'

'I've recruited new maids, Mr. Kanouj,'

Lisa felt a bitter taste in the mouth by hearing it. She thought the Council of Magic might have condemned them to work as a maid in the Hiftoun House without them realizing it. If so, she had to sit in a corner and start sobbing her heart out. If her family heard the news that instead of studying to become a magician, she was treated like an offender, they would regard that as a disgrace and would make other children learn from it.

After days of living in the Hiftoun House, they were just realizing the reason for the seventh floor is so crowded and noisy. It was the "' marketplace with a myriad of stores. On top of a shop window you could read, "Fur coats for well-dressed "". It had all kinds of strange coats. Andy noticed a woman leaving a store of three-hundred-year-old vinegar with a jar. There was another store that had no name and sold all sorts of traps. The bookstore was packed. A little Jinni was running after a flying book. To avoid hitting the women who were standing in front of jewelry stores, Andy had to change course several times. Some were selling balloons and some others were shouting loudly to invite people to go to their stores...

They went past the busy parts of the market and then stopped at a point called "the nagging station". The "sitting on the bench there got so happy to see Ms. Timple. Ms. Timple left the expandable notebook and the blue beech pen to Andy, Emily and Lisa and turned to the crowd.

'My secretaries are ready to listen to you. Please observe order. I will return.' said Ms. Timple.

'Does that mean we will be left alone?' asked Emily quickly.

Ms. Timple points to a wooden desk.

'You have to listen to the "' nagging and put them all down. They have not been able to settle their problems in court and by counseling and have pinned all their hopes on us. Have a good day!' said Ms. Timple.

After she departed, a short Jinni summoned three people from the roster he was holding. A snobbish woman with a long chin and swollen skin sat on the other side of Andy's desk. Her elbow was covered with jewelry. Anytime she moved her hand, she distracted Andy.

'May I ask your name, Madam?' asked Andy politely.

'What can a gentleman have on his mind by asking my name? Has my beauty astounded you, too? Anywhere I go, men's eyes follow me,' said the Jinn with coquetry.

'I just have to write your name on top of the paper, that's it!' replied Andy sweetly.

The woman frowned.

'Lulia,'

'Can you please speak? I'll write it down,'

Lulia cleared her throat.

'I think they are not fit to marry me. A man who is able to perform the most accurate and farthest disappearances must ask my hand in marriage. At least he must be able to fly well. He must wear clothes made from fur, preferably deer fur from famous brands. He mustn't expect to have a child or let's say only one. He must also throw a huge wedding party!'

Andy thought she had an inferiority complex.

'I don't mind the age difference. He needs to be good-looking, like you,' said Lulia.

She took a quick glance at Andy, gulped down her saliva and went on.

'So, what about the age difference?' asked Andy.

'I'm only forty-seven,'

'Maybe this is not too much for " but it is for humans!'

'OK now. How rich are you honey?'

Andy was staring at her mouth in surprise.

'I have nothing except this pen and paper that I carry,'

'OK, OK, you just keep writing, good-for-nothing secretary,' said Lulia with hatred.

Andy staring taking notes again. Lulia started with her unusual conditions for marriage then she mentioned the inappropriate behaviors she had received. She then expatiated on her wish list that filled close to twenty-five pages of Andy's notebook.

Andy was looking at Lisa wistfully. There was an old and impatient Jinni in front of her with the tip of her jelly-looking nose moving up and down. She was speaking so slowly that Lisa had not finished even her second page yet. Emily also looked to have an easy job. She was mostly giving pet talk to a depressed Jinni than writing anything down. She had an extraordinary ability to imagine things and was thus able to put herself in the other party's shoes and sympathize with them.

For three hours Andy had been listening to the ". Some of them looked nervous and it was evident that even fifty pages wouldn't be enough for their complaints. Many were still waiting in line but luckily Ms. Timple got back and announced the end of the nagging ceremony. Andy jumped up so excitedly as though she hadn't met

Ms. Timple for such a long time. The ", however, were not happy to hear the ceremony was over.

'…I'm not even halfway finished yet…hey, when will it be my turn? Can somebody tell me why I feel I'm asleep when I'm awake? How should I know what my favorite color is?'

Disregarding them all, Ms. Timple set out.

'In fact, it's not up to anybody to solve their problems,' she said.

Andy felt pain in his wrist.

'So, why should we listen to them?' he asked.

'Because they need to be heard.'

Just then, a group of wrinkled little Jinnis arrived together with an old Jinni. Ms. Timple greeted them warmly.

'Good day, Mr. Hapuno!' said Ms. Timple.

'Good day, Ms. Timple! These three kids are really lion-hearted. I like them,'

'What's the matter with them?' asked Emily quietly.

Ms. Timple did not consider talking about their appearance to be an insult, so she responded.

'They were born like this. Interesting to know that they outlive all other Jinn races. I guess they could live close to two thousand and four hundred years,'

Emily was petrified for a second. Ms. Timple let the "' market and stepped into another corridor on the seventh floor. Opening and shutting several doors, she reached a cul-de-sac with no doors. She left her hand on the wall and mumbled something. A wooden door with outstanding pattern emerged. She said it was one of the doors of the house's storage and then opened it. They could see twilight behind the door with a faint and yellow moon shining on it. Andy noticed something darker passing by.

'It's me, dear Iknar!'

A coarse and weary voice was heard from inside the darkness.

'Oh, is it you? I feel bored at times,'

'There's no other way. You have to be on shift until new guards are recruited, my friend.'

Andy felt sorry for the iIknar Jinn who sounded sad. Ms. Timple asked them to wait outside the storage. Then she along with the iknar Jinn who was flying overhead went to the darker part of the storage with her shadow disappearing as she went forward. Andy, Emily and Lisa leaned on the corridor wall. When they got bored, they peeked through the open door and got staggered to see a small sunflower taking a nap inside the pot. It looked so real, they thought they could wake it up and talk to it. In her wild daydreams, Emily was imagining that if a sunflower can talk, then she can introduce it to her family as the weirdest friend of hers. She laughed at the idea. Lisa entered the storage quietly and turned to the sunflower.

'Wake up, lazy plant!'

The flower showed no reaction. Ms. Timple returned shortly afterward and got offended to realize they had entered the store without permission. She blamed all of them and told them out. The iknar Jinn that was about to shut the door seemed to be happy. It tried to wear a smile on its depressed and violent face while closing the door.

'It's very lonely, isn't it?' asked Andy sympathetically.

'Unfortunately, the admission of new guards has taken a bit too long, but I promise it will be done soon,'

'Andy, it's hard to explain certain things. So it understanding them. Anyway, I'm going to give you prizes now. So, hurry up!'

They went back to the "' marketplace again. It was kind of more crowded. Ms. Timple went to a store called Mr. Koloun's elixir store. She got back with three purple glasses.

'Here's the wages for your job at the nagging station. It's called the weightlessness elixir. It kills gravity. I hope you'll like it,'

'Is it not dangerous?' asked Andy.

Ms. Timple's face showed it was a stupid question. To make up for it, Andy gulped the elixir down ag a go and then stared at his feet in surprise. He felt he was detached from the ground whereas he feet were on the ground. With a leap, he got detached from the ground and then slowly went back to the previous position.

'Wow! That's awesome!'

Lisa and Emily looked at each other and then drank the elixir up. Lisa was screaming with joy drawing the "' attention. With one leap, she had reached the roof. Emily followed her. Now, the three of them passed by the "by jumping over their heads. Even instead of using the transporter whirlwind, they preferred to jump down the marble handrail of the seventh floor, landing in front of bewildered eyes of the second graders. Still, right after leaving the "' building, they fell on the ground with their faces. Ms. Timple arrived as the pokouns were laughing at them.

'It's your fault! I was going to tell you that the elixir works only in the "' building. But you gave me no chance to inform you.'

Shared Dream

One morning when Andy was climbing up the stairs at the foyer, he encountered a number of winged "that he had never seen. The "passed over his head hurriedly."

'They are all sitting in their rooms. Why should you be outside, idiot?' said the last one angrily.

'I was out for a walk. What's wrong?' asked Andy in surprise.

'Nothing, illiterate boy!' said the Jinn furiously.

Andy was looking around bewildered. There was no one there but Ms. Timple who was going up the stairs in a hurry.

"Good day, Ms. Timple! What's going on today? I had never seen winged ",

'What are you doing here, Andy? Didn't you hear the exit ban? Winged "are allergic to humans. Did you not notice that everybody stayed indoors so they could pass?'

Andy was no more curious why they had acted that way.

'What? They are allergic? Hell with them!' thought Andy.

Entering the round space, Ms. Timple asked the pokouns to issue the exit order as soon as possible.

'Move out, dummies! Hey, idiots, the exit order has been issued…' cried the pokouns.

Ms. Timple was announcing the plans loudly.

'The Wasgu pupils, this way. You need to get familiar with "of cold climates. Sea area kids should go to the basement classroom number ninety-three. Ms. Simpson is waiting for you. The Glorite and Kharaf pupils must attend the second floor of the "' building in twenty minutes for the joint course. The Araban children go to the storage…'

It was a different day for Andy as when he met Fentous, she was carrying a book called "The Magician Jinni". Andy realized Fentous was going to teach him about the "' magic.

'But, I'm a conjurer and have no right to perform magic,'

'Don't worry! This law applies to human magic not that of ". For you to have a Jinni's emotions, you have to imagine yourself present everywhere. Broaden your scope of vision in such a way that you could see the whole world before you. You must be able to overcome the sense of location.

'I've found the one who stole my book!' cried somebody suddenly.

Andy turned back fearfully. Fentous was embarrassed.

'That's my father! I didn't know the encrypted book alarms its owner,'

Andy greeted him politely and at the same time fearfully. Fentous was right in that in half breed Jinn families, their family was the most similar to humans. Her father only had ears that were somehow big. He frowned at Andy.

'Who the hell are you?'

'Andy Barnett,'

The angry face of the Jinn got happy suddenly.

'Oh, is that you? I'm Pharas. This girl tells me about you a hundred times a day,'

'He's only a friend, dad,' said Fentous shyly.

'Your mom was also a friend of mine,'

'What kind of a father are you?'

Pharas smiled and turned to Andy.

'Do you think you can marry my girl so easily? Of course, I have nothing against it. But, my first daughter asked my idea about marriage and I ruined the life of a poor boy. It's now my wife's turn to destroy someone else's life so we are even-steven. When I think of my lovely twins, I just realize my first son-in-law has not been that unlucky!'

Fentous was giggling quietly.

'Enough, daddy!'

'I was just kidding! Did you understand, good boy? I won't let go of this ugly face so easily,'

'You are very interesting, Mr. Pharas,' said Andy.

'It'll be even more interesting when they hand you upside down for using my book!'

He then disappeared and returned with a book called "The "' Linguistics" in a few seconds.

'No fool starts with that book. Here, take this, kid. You must first learn the "' alphabet so that you won't say anything that would harm you. Have a good day, little thieves!'

Andy took a sigh of relief when Mr. Pharas left. In Fentous' opinion, the "' linguistics was easy but when she started teaching it, she realized that Andy was flabbergasted. In their language, there were a number of letters that were not used so often. They were silent but if used in writing with certain methods, they could move the sentence and even make it disappear. There were some other extraordinary letters that were used only at nighttime. They were difficult to pronounce, yet Fentous admitted that she had no idea what they were good for.

Suddenly, Fentous looked back and then instantly wished Andy a good day and left. After several days of meetings with Fentous, Andy knew that this behavior relates to something customary in the "' households. They could call each other in short distances without a third person realizing it. Andy started heading for the Hiftoun House but no sooner had he set off than Fentous appeared again.

'Sorry, Andy! It was my mom. I had to go. She cannot stand waiting. You can keep this.'

She handed him the linguistics book and disappeared. The magical bell of Ms. Margaret announced the time for lunch. Before reaching the eatery hall, Andy read the book several times. He got there so late that made Lisa and Emily angry.

'Where the hell have you been? Were you out to see that girl again?' asked Lisa.

Ms. Timple's voice invited all to keep quiet. She was there to remind them of important educational points. To leave a bigger impact she repeated at the end of each warning that Ms. Notre Dame was not happy with them. She took the sight of Andy then.

'Oh, Andy. You act beyond a conjurer,'

Many people turned to Andy. They still didn't know that there is a conjurer among them, which was really amazing for them. Definitely, Ms. Timple did not realize how painful it could be to call somebody conjurer in the presence of everybody. Andy smiled but the fact of the matter was that he did not know for what he was being praised.

'Mr. Pharas told me everything. Learning the "' magic is not an easy task especially for a conjurer!' she added.

'Why didn't you tell us about it?' asked Lisa.

'I haven't learned anything yet, it's Fentous' father who can disappear and go anywhere he likes, not me,'

'So, he had come to visit his dear son-in-law,' said Lisa naughtily.

Andy did not say anything else. He started eating. Many were pointing at him and talking about him.

'They say his father was a Jinni!'

'No way, that's not possible! Ms. Timple didn't say that.'

'They won't publicize such things!'

'So, how do you know?'

That night Junas told Andy about those rumors happily.

'…Yes, that's right. They all say you are a Jinni. Some say you communicate with evil " and that's why you are restricted here so you wouldn't spy. I know you are nobody but they say interesting things about you,'

'Stop that, Junas!' commanded Andy impatiently.

'No, no, no, Wait! I'm not done yet. What's new with Fentous?'

Andy had no doubt that this one was leaked by Lisa. Junas wouldn't let go.

'You know what, boy? The "have their own traditions for nuptials especially if the bridegroom is not from among their race. For instance, on the wedding day you have to eat a plate of snails. The "then circle all around you, clap and ask you to dance. Of course, I hope your child won't look like you!'

When Junas left, it started to snow. The animals were moving under the trees hurriedly. The last time he looked outside the window, he noticed black and scary Jinn among the trees but he thought he might have made a mistake as he was not able to see anything after five minutes he kept staring at the same point. While sleeping, Andy once again dreamed of the black Jinn who was screaming wildly and passing through the woods. When he got tired of imagining those pictures of the black Jinn, he opened a new window to the world of dreams. He was taken to a lush and moon-lit jungle where a girl ran from among the trees hurriedly. The pale girl looked worried when she ran into Andy.

'Didn't you see my stone?'

Andy who unlike normal circumstances had no fear of that situation replied to her.

'Who on earth are you?'

'A lonely human who feels even lonelier after losing her stone,'

'Where did you lose it?'

'On the dark plain, the same night when the monster was roaring. I have to find it. It was a galaxy jasper stone,'

Andy took the Jasper out of his pocket.

'Is this it?'

Sighting the stone, the girl gave out mischievous laughter and walked toward Andy. Andy woke up scared. He looked out of the window hesitantly. It was dawn. Despite all the bad dreams he had of the black Jinn, he did not recall them and just remembered the girl. He believed he had met the owner of the stone. Now that he was thinking about the mysterious jungle in his dream, he was confident that he would never set foot in a place like that while awake. He was thinking of such things when suddenly he heard something.

'No, Lisa! You mustn't throw it!'

'But it may belong to the curser girl!'

'That's not true. It's a myth only!'

'How would you know? Maybe it was written based on reality,'

Hurriedly, Andy walked out. Lisa and Emily were fighting each other in front of a large window over the very same girl that Andy had met in his dream. That could not be normal! It became scarier when Andy told them about his dream.

'She will seek us!' said Lisa helplessly.

Emily was concerned.

'It doesn't belong to us. She will come to you only, Lisa!' she said devilishly.

Lisa was agitated.

'We should get rid of it. We must throw it away!'

Junas who was just back from his nightly stroll began making fun of them.

'You are a fool, are you not? Even if it has an owner, you can sell it at the magicians' black market at a high price,'

'Where the hell have you been since last night? Asked Emily.

'None of your business!'

'So, I'll let Ms. Hiftoun know that you disappear at night,'

'It's not mentioned in my job description that I have to stay close to you the whole night,'

'Leave this lunatic! Let's go tell Ms. Timple about it,' said Lisa impatiently.

'No one is awake at this time except roosters!'

At the breakfast table, everyone was happy to see an announcement posted on the bulletin board in the foyer about a visit to the Jinn fish lagoon. Many of them had already started bluffing about their ability to catch Jinn fish. Andy looked around the eatery hall but George was nowhere to be found. He wasn't there for breakfast as he had to help Ms. Timple to distribute disorienting incense among the Araban pupils. The incense was used to push cheating "away who were usually resting in the deepest crypts of the Hiftoun House. When Andy got back to the foyer, he found George among the crowd but lost track of him soon. Emily approached Ms. Timple.

'Good morning, Ms. Timple! We have just had a shared dream about the jasper stone!'

Ms. Timple had a lot on her plate at the time.

'Good morning, Miss Henderson! I really don't know much about stones but Ms. Hiftoun may be able to help you if she is not busy.'

Emily returned hopelessly.

'We should speak to Ms. Hiftoun,'

George's voice filled the foyer. He was announcing the plans loudly. When he caught sight of Andy, he waved at him.

'Hey, Andy! I'm picked as assistant to Ms. Timple!'

'Congrats, George!'

'You can ask me all your questions. I got the map of all corridors and classes see?'

'Do you happen to know where Ms. Hiftoun's office is?'

'Sure, I do.'

In the very center of the house, somewhere among the tall walls, in a yard with flowers all around and a blue sky overhead lay a detached cabin with wooden and painted windows with smoke going up the chimney. Gardening scissors could be heard from the yard that was brimmed with flowers and plants. When they entered the yard, Jinn who may have been a year older than them asked them a question rudely.

'What the hell are you doing here?'

The Jinni was s bony and had big eyes and around and tanned face, looking at them as though they had committed a wrong. It had buttoned up but still its clothes looked too big. The Jinn had opened his legs and arms so wide as though he was holding watermelons under his arms.

'We have to see Ms. Hiftoun,' said Andy.

With a tone that was devoid of any respect, the Jinni replied.

'Ms. Hiftoun reads books on Tuesdays. To meet her you have to get permission from Sultan,'

'Who is Sultan?' asked Emily surprisingly.

'It's me! Here! In front of you! Sultan Baniku!'

Andy smirked involuntarily. Baniku was hanging from the shed in front of the house.

'Now, politely make your request and I will see what I can do,'

Since they went to the Hiftoun House they hadn't met such a discourteous, rude and impertinent Jinni who thought he was very funny.

'No one can talk to Ms. Hiftoun without my consent. Even if she asks for it, it's me who decides whether the visit can be made or not. Now, tell me who you are,' continued Baniku.

Andy thought Ms. Hiftoun may not recognize his name.

'Tell her the conjurers are here to see you about something important,'

'What? Conjurer? Since when has Ms. Hiftoun's office accepted conjurers?' said Baniku in a humiliating tone.

Lisa took the Jinni from the leg and threw it on the ground.

'We only needed an ugly and skinny Jinni to insult the conjurers!'

Baniku got up indifferently and dusted his clothes.

'A conjurer touched me. I have to take a shower,'

Ms. Hiftoun put her head out of the window.

'What's going on here?'

'Nothing, I was just defending your prestige,' said Baniku.

'No need to do that. Come on in!'

'OK, it's up to you. You can let anybody get into your privacy,'

'Banikuuuu!' said Ms. Hiftoun with an alarming tone.

'I did it for you. I want to protect your dignity. I'm a sultan and you are Ms. Hiftoun only.'

Andy smirked one more time and entered the house. Ms. Hiftoun's cozy cabin was peaceful. On the walls pictures of previous directors could be seen. Andy just recognized professor Fredric Hiftoun, the main architect of the house. Ms. Hiftoun did not show that much reaction they expected of her too. She was reading the paper when sipping tea at the table.

'Good morning, Ms. Hiftoun!'

Ms. Hiftoun looked up for the first time after their arrival in the cabin.

'You said you wanted to talk to me. Go ahead, I'm listening,'

'We had a dream of the owner of the stone,' said Emily who had gone forward boldly.

'Well?' said Ms. Hiftoun without any reaction.

Emily expected her to be kinder to them. She was hopeless.

'She was asking for her stone,'

This time Ms. Hiftoun smiled.

'Well, nobody likes to lose their stone but I promise she won't be able to get out of the stone and hurt you,'

Ms. Hiftoun had just responded to the question they were embarrassed to ask. For an instant, Lisa thought Ms. Hiftoun had read her mind.

'By the way, stop bugging Junas!'

This issue had to do with Lisa directly, so she had to break her silence.

'He is always to blame even if we seem to be to blame,'

'It's natural of him to be like that, so he cannot be blamed,'

'Yes, that's right,' said Lisa humbly.

'Can we leave the stone here? We will feel more comfortable this way,' asked Andy.

Ms. Hiftoun paused a bit.

'Had I been a conjurer, I'd have made the stone communicate with me. Because that way I wouldn't need to pass the entrance exam. I know you've been to the lake. Junas told me all about it. I like your bravery and resolution but bravery without wisdom means suicide. By the way, the tears lake is a personal gift, it's not public. So do not repeat it. And keep the stone.'

The three looked at each other. They were not able to express honestly how embarrassed they were! So, they left the cabin with their heads down.

The Tenth Corridor

It was getting colder every day and snow had covered the whole jungle. Fentous who was used to the humans' lifestyle decided to send postal cards to Andy, Emily and Lisa to invite them to a party in "' café. The "normally used the simple letter to extend invitations so using a postal card was somehow special for Fentous.

The café, called courtesy café, was in the "' marketplace. When they arrived, there was nobody there but Fentous and her twin sisters. The twins had soft hair and funny little nose. Fentous waved for them from the back of the café. She was sitting in the area lit by colorful glasses. Her twin sisters could not speak humans' language. With their black and round eyes which were shining with joy, they saw the guests arrive. Fentous was delighted.

'This is the best café in the market. They care a lot about customers. At night you cannot find an empty seat here. In your opinion, have I been a good host so far in the eyes of humans?'

Andy and Emily looked at each other happily. Fentous should have learned more about humans. Human beings don't usually ask each other about the quality of their reception or at least they would wait and raise the issue at the end of the party. The twins were looking at Fentous happily. They were eager to know what she had told the humans. Fentous explained to them in their language and they nodded happily.

'Sorry, I forgot to make an introduction. These are my little sisters, Fana and Fanu. They will be four soon,' said Fentous shyly.

She sounded excited.

'I'm going to throw a birthday party for them. I'll get them a cake too!'

'That's cool! By the way, we didn't hear from you for a week, Fentous,'

'We had exams. I hear the owner of the stone came to your dream. That's how it is when there is an owner,'

'But, it could just as well have a new owner,' said Lisa angrily.

The twins gave Lisa the dagger's eye. They seemed to care so much about Fentous and couldn't stand any maltreatment. To make up for that, Emily touched Fana's cheeks. She turned to Emily happily and let her touch her hair too. She then nagged in the "' language.

Andy who was looking at the café's glass door looked down suddenly.

'I hope it hasn't noticed me,' said Andy.

'Who are you talking about?' asked Fentous.

'Lulia. That flirtatious woman!'

'What? How do you know her?'

We were at the nagging station. You cannot imagine how weird she is!'

'But you said nothing about it. Was Calima there too? A fat woman who thinks everybody is her child. Every day she collects several children from the market and takes them home. Inspector Lubanu then goes there to their rescue.'

'No, I haven't met Calima but I saw the strange storage,'

'Which storage?'

'The dark one which has an iknar Jinni guard it,'

'Oh, the tenth corridor storage,'

'But, we only have nine corridors. Where's the tenth one?'

'It's the invisible part of the Hiftoun House,'

'Have you seen it?'

'Of course not. No one is allowed to see it except special people,'

'You mean the jungle wall could be an entrance to the tenth corridor?'

'No, the tenth corridor has no visible sign,' added Fentous confidently,

A smiling Jinni greeted them.

'Would you like anything, respected guests?'

'Make sure they are clean, please!' said Lisa meticulously.

'Everything here is clean, madam. I'm professor Kingy and I'm pleased to see you in the courtesy café,'

Lisa pulled herself together and eyed the professor clandestinely. He was busy taking notes.

'Courtesy café offers the welcome elixir to the guests who come here for the first time; it's free, of course. I'll have it served soon.'

He then talked to the twins in their language and made them feel so happy. He promised to serve them strawberry ice-cream. Fentous looked at Lisa indifferently.

'Professor Kingy is a respectful and well-educated Jinn who has invented most of the elixirs. The café is called courtesy thanks to his respect and courtesy,'

Shortly afterward, the café's waitress emerged with a tray of welcome elixir and saffron ice cream. The welcome elixir was the best that Lisa had ever had. She wanted to order another one if her pride allowed her to. Andy thanked Fentous for the party.

'You mean I've passed?'

'It was great! You are a real human!' said Emily kindly.

This made Fentous overwhelmed with happy emotions. She told the twins about the big success. They too got happy and clapped for her.

Lisa was busy thinking about the tenth corridor.

'Is there really a tenth corridor?' asked her curiously.

'You may have gone past it but you know, it's invisible!'

Just then the café door opened and two people got in.

'Here's Mr. shy!' announced Fentous joyfully.

'Is he called shy?' asked Andy.

'Yes. Since he was born, he's felt shy. He's wanted to ask for a girl's hand in marriage since months ago but he is shy. Last time he was going to tell Biziru all about his research on phantoms but he was unable to finish. I wish I could help him!'

Emily looked mischievous.

'If you cannot do it, we can,' she said.

'How?'

'Come and you'll see.'

Shy and Biziru realized as they sat down that several pairs of eyes, standing around their table, were watching them eagerly. Biziru had small lips and a carbon pupil was shining in her silver eyelid. She belonged to the cat-eared " who had tanned skins but Mr. Shy was known for his azure blue complexion, oiled hair parted from the middle and a big mouth. Some blue veins were obvious on his face. He did not like to poke his nose in others' affairs but he also felt shy to make an objection.

'Excuse me! Can you tell me why you are here?' he asked shyly.

He looked down and blushed.

'Nothing. We are just here to let out your innermost feelings. How's that?'

'What feeling?' asked Mr. Shy with a shaky voice.

'Nothing, nothing!'

Lisa picked a flower from the vase on the table and gave it to Biziru.

'Have this for now and we will let you know soon,'

She was sweating in the forehead.

'Why should you give me a flower? What's going on here?' asked Biziru.

'Mr. Shy, will you tell her or shall we go ahead? If we go on like this, you must pay for elixir the whole evening. Of course, if she's ready to wait for you until the end of her life,'

Emily spoke into Mr. Shy's ears softly.

'I hear she has a suitor. She's going to get hitched one of these days!'

Shy felt embarrassed and was unable to look at Emily.

'Really?'

'Sure! They say it's a flying Jinn who's flown as far as the moon! When he disappears, he goes so far nobody could ever imagine! I hear his dad has given him storage full of magical tools. He's on easy street!'

Looking as though she felt like being nosy, Fentous was surprised to see how much interesting and useful information Emily had about ''. Shy's voice started to shake again.

'Are you sure?'

'Why should I lie? I know things you don't know. I heard Biziru's father say that she prefers men who are able to speak out their mind frankly. Now, it's up to you. That boy has a big mouth!'

Shy was so much under stress that he started to scream. All his body was shaking. Once again he looked at Emily. Suddenly, he stopped shaking and looked serious. Emily tried to give him some pep talk.

'Yes. That's it! You can, boy!'

Shy stared at Biziru's eyes.

'How can I wait for the morning to arrive in this sunset of loneliness when I know there's no hope of tomorrow to arrive? How am I supposed to shoulder that poetic dream if you are not here so I could gift it to you?'

Fentous looked at Emily in surprise.

'What have you done?'

Shy himself was also surprised.

'I appreciate it. Damn it! The beginning was just hard. I'm relieved!'

Then hurriedly he gave another flower to Biziru and went on.

'Will you marry me?'

Biziru's mouth was left wide open but Shy was not going to stop it.

'Have you found anything evil in me that made you give your heart to that rich boy?'

'What are you talking about?' asked Biziru.

'Oh, enough! Unlike him, I don't have much of worldly riches to attract your beautiful eyes but I have love in my heart that's unique! Let me be honest to you. Such love cannot be bought with the price of any expensive storage of magical tools,'

Shy rushed to the café door and stood there facing the market.

'I couldn't imagine him to be like that. What's he doing?'

'Oh, city dwellers! Do not put your love in the cage. In a land where love is incarcerated, brains rule. Get up and sip drops of love so that you are salvaged from worldly drunkenness! How could you ever call me Shy when I'm crying out my love bravely?'

Just then somebody tapped Shy on his shoulder.

'We are impressed, brave boy!'

It was Mr. Khojir, Biziru's father. Shy was speechless as he was gazing at Mr. Khojir's eyes with horror. He then pointed to the area inside the café.

'It was their fault!'

'Time we ran away! Mr. Khojir doesn't like such attitude!'

Andy started to run.

'It should have happened. He is relieved now!'

Taking the twins' hands, Fentous disappeared instantly. When Andy was escaping from the "' marketplace, he could still hear Mr. Shy apologizing. Mr. Khojir was turning around himself trying to find those who had collaborated with Shy in acting in such an unabashed way. The children ran away from the "' building. When they reached the first corridor, they heard the oldest pokoun of the house.

'What other mess have you made, minor conjurers?'

'You're right. We are minor conjurers and you are a big old man!' said Lisa hatefully while exiting the first corridor.

George was sitting by Junas in the third corridor listening to his cock and bull story. On orders of Ms. Timple, he had checked all the classrooms and deep storages all day and was just realizing what a tough responsibility he had undertaken.

'I've been looking for you for an hour!' said George as soon as he noticed Andy.

'How come?'

'Ms. Timple wants you to go to classroom forty-nine,'

'Where the hell is that?'

'Master Squart's place. A selfish instructor! I wish you tons of patience!'

'Why should we meet him?'

'It has to do with conjuring, I guess. He used to be a master conjurer. You'd better go now. He's been waiting for a long time.'

Instructor Squart's basement was down damp-patched and spiral stairs. It looked as if it was abandoned but that depressing atmosphere had not impacted the joyful instructor at all.

'Welcome, children! You think much of this place, I know. But, that's not true!' he said as he was greeting them warmly.

Without any interest, Lisa looked around. There was a nice and warm fire burning in the fireplace. Wind was blowing from inside an old chimney making the fire dance sideways. Instructor Squart who was wearing a thick pair of gloves, took out a nice yellow ball from inside a boiling pot.

'This is called the energizing ball!'

'What are we supposed to do, instructor?' inquired Andy.

Squart smiled.

'I hear you are exiled saboteurs. Still, you have to catch up with conjuring lessons. It's true that conjuring doesn't have much value but still it's necessary especially if it has something to do with the energizing ball. It's such a great pleasure for you to be able to have a skillful master teach you that lesson. And who' that skillful master?'

He then moved his neck a little and went on.

'Yes. That's right! Instructor Squart. We have time till the ball cools down to speak about our valuable tasks. Let me start with myself as I don't believe you have ever done anything extraordinary in your whole life,'

He didn't even ask them their names. Soon, he took a seat and asked them to do the same.

'I want to tell you memories which you cannot find anywhere. For instance, the saving of a prince. How's that? Do you like to hear about it? You must now think it's a great chance to listen to it. The prince had a spell on him. Who do you think saved him? You seem you've found the answer pretty quickly. Right! Instructor Squart,'

He then changed his tone to an informal one.

'Of course, they were involved too. A number of clairvoyants and novice fortune tellers that were not of much help!'

'I just thought I only hate Junas!' mumbled Lisa.

Having told the children a few selfish stories, Squart picked up the yellow ball and started to teach. Again, he spent most of the class time bragging about himself through exaggerated stories.

'I'm sure you enjoyed my company so much but it's enough for today. I'll see you tomorrow.' he said at the end of the class.

The trio looked at each other.

'You're pleased, aren't you? That was a surprise! One more time you can visit the great master Squart. Farewell.'

The following day, Fentous insisted she had to see Andy. She didn't find him in his room, so she rushed to the great foyer. Andy was sitting on a stone bench next to Emily and Lisa. He was staggered to see Fentous in the foyer. He got up like a spring. Fentous started to speak as soon as she arrived.

'Yesterday you did a fantastic job! Mr. Shy sent me here to thank you,'

'What's up?' asked Emily.

'After boxing Mr. Shy in the ears a few times, Mr. Khojir told him to act like a wise Jinni and speak out and Shy finally opened up his heart to him,'

Fentous smiled and then went on.

'He even told him about the lie you'd told about the far-flying rival. Mr. Khojir gave it a hearty laugh and eventually got to like Mr. Shy,'

Fentous started to sound excited again.

'Humans are really strange creatures. I'm one too. Half human, but I am one anyway. That means I'm also strange. That's cool!'

'But I was thinking that "are strange creatures,' said Andy.

Fentous looked back worriedly. Andy who knew what she was concerned about told her to take it easy and leave.

Most probably Fentous' mother who was an impatient woman had summoned her. After she left, Lisa felt her legs cannot take her all way down the spiral stairs to instructor Squart's basement. Having wrapped some cloth around his hand, Squart was sitting in a corner.

'Oh, you are here! I know that children don't like to see their hero like this but you know sometimes even heroes get injured. Don't worry! It's a minor burn. My reputation has brought me nothing but trouble. That's why I asked Ms. Hiftoun to allow me to be on my own in this basement. I feel comfortable here. Nobody can find me to take a photo with me. But, if you insist, I'll surely let you take one,'

Instructor Squart was not happy to see Andy disregard him.

'What's wrong, boy?'

Andy pointed to the end corner of the basement with hesitation.

'I know that flower has grown in the tenth corridor,'

'I brought it here for scientific purposes. What do you know about the tenth corridor?' said Squart worriedly.

Andy did not expect Squart to be taken aback so he also felt kind of agitated.

'Nothing. I just heard its name. That's it!'

'You won't say anything to Ms. Hiftoun, will you? I was going to take it back today. When I'm allowed to go to that place, then I have the right to take some of the stuff there for my research work,'

It was evident that Squart had embarked on thieving regardless of its scientific purpose.

'But this is thieving! Stealing something from a clandestine location?' said Emily.

Instructor Squart suddenly ran to the fire and pulled out a black stone without his gloves on.

'Oh, no! It was a very rare stone!' he said sadly as his hand was burning.

He then picked up his robe.

'I've burnt my hand again! Gotta go to the treatment room. Please don't touch anything till I come back.'

Squart departed as his moaning and groaning were fading away going up the stairs. That was the best chance for them to check out that unusual flower pot but it seemed as though Squart was really keen on scientific purposes as several more of such pots could be seen there. Squart's concern was understandable but Andy was thinking about more important issues. What were those flower pots good for? He looked around to see if he could find a trace of the tenth corridor. It was a mess! He was looking around so seriously as though he believed that there is an aperture to the tenth corridor. After a while, his quest proved to be futile.

Emily was staring at the seven color flower curiously. She bent over hesitantly and picked up a shining metal plate. There were lots of unknown words on the plate. There was something comprehensible on top of it, Instructor Squart!

'Squart is an unusual man. His stuff is also unusual,' said Emily.

All of a sudden, it became dark all over the place and nothing was left of the room. Andy felt he had lost his eyesight.

'What happened?' he asked nervously.

There was no way out of that horrifying darkness. The sound of fire could be heard in addition to something else, Lisa's scream. She was thinking she'd been entangled in a vicious curse. Emily was trying to calm her down. Only God knew how stressed out Lisa was! She just felt like running away but there was no way out. Suddenly, Andy thought he had seen something brilliant. Before he did anything out of curiosity, something more unusual happened. They opened their eyes in a big hall that didn't look like Squart's basement at all. In front of the heater that was burning with magical coal, there was a sign reading, The Tenth Corridor, Entrance to the Hiftoun House.

Emily turned around.

'Where are we?' she inquired curiously.

'The tenth floor! I think we have appeared in the control room,' replied Andy.

Andy was referring to the frames on the walls that informed the people about the area. In one of the frames, the students were entering the "' building. In the frame related to the seventh floor, Andy recognized the wandering "' hall but in the ill-lit frame of the ninth floor not much could be seen, yet Andy was able to locate something weird.

'How's that possible?'

He had seen Ms. Hiftoun down in the dump in a dull room but how was that possible while at the same time Ms. Hiftoun was crossing the great foyer?'

'Does Ms. Hiftoun have a look-alike?' wondered Emily.

'It's not possible to have a look-alike after the age 20. It must be her twin sister,' replied Lisa.

A bit further ahead were the boards for the tenth floor. The first one belonged to an observatory where astronomers with colorful turbans were watching the sky through gigantic telescopes. Emily checked many boards of the tenth floor which had occupied the whole wall.

'It's even more crowded than the Hiftoun House here!' said Emily.

'So we can ask about the exit and go back,' said Lisa.

Andy pointed at a wall painting.

'I don't think it's so easy to go back!' said Andy.

They could see their image on the wall. It looked more like a wanted advertisement to find criminals at large. Lisa lost hope of being forgiven and got mad.

'They have no right to treat us like offenders. We have to go to them and explain things. When Lisa opened the door down the hall, she didn't take any step further and stood still. Andy put his head out of the door and looked happy.

'Wow! Check the sleeping out! They are all awake!'

It was the place to grow flowers and plants that were always asleep outside the tenth corridor but they were all awake now whispering into each other's ears. Lisa looked pretty pale.

'Could you speak quietly, Andy? They're watching us,'

'Why? They are so funny!'

'Yes, especially the way they move around,'

'Wow! Look here! A pumpkin with a mouth!' said Emily excitedly.

Lisa had a lump in her throat that could have exploded any moment. She moved a moving ivy hanging from the ceiling with hatred.

'I don't wanna stay here to see these jerks go up and down my body!'

As she was screaming with hate, she stepped out of the greenhouse. She was screaming as the ivy was going to hug her lovingly. When she reached the end of the greenhouse, she felt differently. Her lips were moving but nothing could be heard. She was trying to warn Andy and Emily of potential danger. There was a conversation down the greenhouse corridor.

'I've also heard about a change of plan,'

Another voice responded.

'I was expecting this mess, dear Eliot!'

'Did you read today's news? The one who was selling fake elixirs has been arrested,'

'Yeah, I read it. He wasn't a magician. So many idiots around! Good day, instructor Martin!'

'Have a great day, dear Elliot!'

They could that conversation through a half-open door nearby. Andy looked serious again. He cautiously opened the door and took the sight of an ill-lit hall that resembled a coffee with wooden shelves and drawers all around.

'Where did they go? Did they disappear?'

She opened one of the drawers and saw a pokoun whose mouth had just been formed and mumbling. The same faint sound could be heard from several other drawers too.

'We should burn them all right now and save the others,'

'How easily you issue the death order of others?' exclaimed a voice.

That was the voice of a man who was smoking a pipe. He had a brown suit on with a blonde hair and beard. He emerged from one of the wooden rows. The man looked at his pocket watch.

I'm instructor Martin. I'm in charge of raising pokouns. Your faces show that you've come to this place without permission. The culprits' painting also verifies my claim,'

He pointed at a wall that was displaying the kids' pictures like culprits.

'We are not culprits. Do you understand?' said Lisa with a bad temper.

The man said nothing until after he puffed at the pipe for a long time.

'I would try to act more politely if I needed someone's help,'

'I'm sorry, sir! We came here from Mr. Squart's basement. We didn't mean to,' said Emily embarrassingly.

'So, you are in deep trouble! When Ms. Hiftoun is involved, you should look disheveled! I'll help you go back when I'm done with my work,'

He then got busy.

'What exactly is inside these drawers?' asked Andy.

'One of the most wonderful things you could ever get to see!'

'Pokouns are really wonderful creatures! Yeah!' said Lisa mockingly.

Instructor Martin seemed not to like Lisa yet he was a patient man. He pulled a drawer and went on speaking.

'I guess this one is hope-inspiring. One out of a hundred of them survive!'

'I think they are good for nothing!' commented Lisa.

'I don't expect you to understand the topic of our discussion, blue-eyed girl. After tens of magicians take pains to make a pokoun, things end up here, that's the waiting room. If you are lucky, you can have a speaking pokoun after six years,'

He then took a sigh and continued.

'This one did not take in the magic. I have to return it to the recycling unit. It's sad! I worked on it for three years. I was going to make a strong guard for wooden doors out of it. It's such a pity!' he said.

Lisa was not intending to surrender.

'So, you are not aware of the fact that it fears the fire!'

Instructor Martin smiled patiently.

'We do not treat this point of weakness on purpose so that they would obey us. This doesn't work when it comes to opening doors. They won't open any door unless they hear the answer to the riddle or on orders from their owners. Even fire won't work!'

Lisa showed off the Jasper stone that she was always carrying.

'In my opinion, this is something extraordinary, not that pokoun!' she boasted.

Instructor Martin took the sight of the stone in disbelief. Lisa thought she has impressed him so she looked at Andy in a meaningful way. Instructor Martin took the stone.

'Only a novice thief can steal from the death storage!' he said pessimistically.

He was flabbergasted. Soon, he shut the drawers and left angrily.

'Follow me,'

'Can you tell us what's happened?' inquired Andy.

Martin stopped and looked at him in a threatening way.

'You mean you don't know anything? Makes no difference anyway. Willy-nilly you've made a big mistake!'

Instructor Martin had flushed and was looking around worriedly. He led them to a room without an angle and shut the door. It was dark everywhere. Instructor Martin did not utter a word. It was apparent that he was still bamboozled. After a while, they could hear things in the darkness. It seemed they are going to find their way in a big foyer. Andy heard George's voice, as well as that of the two girls, talking to each other nearby. He was wondering how they would react if he appeared in front of them out of the blue. As optimistic as he was, he could not imagine a nice reaction. It was mischievous but he felt like checking their facial expressions when appearing in front of them. At the sight of Andy, the two girls started giving out a deafening scream. Everybody realized what had happened. One of the maids hurried outside and returned with Ms. Hiftoun. Instructor Martin started to speak without an introduction.

'Hello, Ms. Hiftoun. I realized these little thieves have Paramis's jasper stone, and that in the tenth corridor! Can you believe that?'

Ms. Hiftoun pushed the crowd and gazed at the stone Martin was holding.

'It's not the right time to speak about it. Let's go to my office.' Said Ms. Hiftoun after suppressing her fury.

Paramis

Like all days in late December, the sun went down in a jiffy giving rise to a long night. Andy, Lisa, and Emily were banned from leaving their room on orders of Ms. Hiftoun. Junas returned to the room happily.

'It's over! I hear that you are fired!'

Then he started making fun of them. Lisa was studying seriously. Anytime she was frustrated, she did that. Perhaps for her to become a great magician, it was necessary to get frustrated at times. After some futile anticipation and wild guess, intentional silence had prevailed in the room. It was required for the trio to take heed of certain facts that they had neglected out of childish games they had played. They needed to contemplate a little and focus on questions crossing their mind which needed to be addressed. Such questions as the reason for them to move about in the Hiftoun House freely in spite of the ban on the entry of conjurers. There were other things that required to be delved into such as the fact that Ms. Hiftoun who was familiar with the jasper stone made believe she had no idea about it. In his dreams, Andy had even ventured to blame Ms. Hiftoun and force her to explain everything honestly. He even felt like asking about the sad woman he had seen in the painting in the ninth corridor. Was she his twin sister? If so, Andy had to feel down in the dumps for her to be so upset. Who on earth was Paramis? Ms. Hiftoun hadn't told them anything about her despite the fact that she knew her.

Having drawn personal conclusions, Lisa closed her book angrily.

'I bet Ms. Hiftoun knows Paramis better than anybody else,'

There was a knock on the door. Andy opened the door behind which was standing to frown Patrick Stedman with the dinner tray.

'I have the prisoners' dinner. By the way, the pokoun administration has complained about you for attacking Junas.'

A familiar voice who they had been trying in absentia all that time started to speak.

'Never mind, Patrick! At times pokouns become intolerable. Send them a note and tell them the problem has been addressed,'

Surprised at seeing Ms. Hiftoun, Patrick left the dinner tray on the table sadly and left.

'I know that you may have fancied some thoughts that are unfair but you must know that you had been under protection until before heading for the tenth corridor. Don't worry! I'm not going to punish anyone. You will return to the Password tomorrow. I hope you will stop doing stupid things!'

Emily was emboldened at the sight of Ms. Hiftoun's smile.

'We'd like to know about Paramis,' asked Emily.

Ms. Hiftoun waved her index finger as a sign of warning and went on.

'I have told you whatever I had to tell you, Ms. Henderson.'

Following her departure, Andy had to answer the questions of his hungry stomach who had left the exam paper in front of him for a few minutes ago so that he would answer them. What must one do when hungry? What feels good when it's cold? Can the brain be friendly toward you in the absence of food?

The following day, many including George were looking forward to meeting the three unusual conjurers.

'Hey, guys! I have resigned from being Ms. Timple's assistant. I'm jealous of you. It's wonderful to visit the tenth corridor! Look at these people! They are all talking about you!' said George excitedly.

Lisa looked around the hall. Many were pointing at her and whispering. They could hear the word tenth corridor. All that time Lisa just wished she could find Bill Foster to be able to see his reaction to all this reputation they had gained. Now that she was pleased with the situation, it was a terrible idea to have to leave the Hiftoun House. At least to take some pleasure out of her fame she needed a week's time.

Andy took a glance at George cordially.

'We're going to leave this place today. You've been a great friend, George!'

George was not willing to hear that fact.

'You must be kidding me!'

'No, George! Last night Ms. Hiftoun told us about it,'

Sadly, George looked down. He was about to lose his only friend and become lonely again.

'I'm not leaving for good; I'll come to the Glorite to see you,'

Casting a look at the magical cloud for one last time, Andy uttered the statement I'm hungry in such a way as if he's lost that possibility forever.

On the way back to the room, they found the door shut. Junas happily hinted with his eyebrows that their place had been taken.

'So, what about the rules?' asked Andy.

'If we had good rules, Ms. Hiftoun wouldn't have shelved my complaint. Of course, I took full legal action as you are fired. You have no more room in this house. Also, I've asked this newcomer a question which is registered in the questions book. I asked him who the manager of the Hiftoun House was and he replied Ms. Hiftoun,'

Lisa kicked the door hard.

'Damn you! What kind of question was that? Come on! Open the door before I turn you to pokoun firewood,'

Junas burst into laughter in mockery.

'Ms. Notre Dame has said that based on rules no one is entitled to do such a thing!'

'If we had proper rules, Ms. Hiftoun would not have shelved your complaint,' said Lisa furiously.

Junas went pale in the face and felt he was no more assured. He opened the door and got away instantly. The three entered angrily but stood at the framework surprisingly.

'Don't you want a guest, kids?'

Eduardo was standing at the window. Unlike their expectation, he did not look scornful. It was refreshing for Andy to meet Eduardo just like the first time they met. This time it was different in that he knew him or maybe he believed that he knew him this time. Eduardo looked sharp and neat wearing a friendly smile. He acted in a way as though they had not been far from each other for quite a while. As though he had just said goodnight the other night. That's how he looked. No expression of surprise or missing on his face!

'Glad to see you! I guess you've had a wonderful time!'

'Yes, especially with this stupid pokoun!' said Lisa sarcastically.

'Where's Eric?' inquired Andy.

'No worries! He's fine,'

'How will we return? By that dilapidated motorbike again?' asked Lisa.

'Of course, not! You are no saboteurs anymore! Not conjurers either! As of next year, you can enter the Bartlin School of Magic,'

Any conjurer would feel so happy by hearing the news that they would jump out of their skin instantly but Emily was pessimistic.

'Bartlin? Without an exam?'

'That's a Council decision. With all you have done, you've proved to the Council that you deserve it!'

'What are you talking about?

'No conjurer has ever set foot at the hidden castle. Anyone who manages to open the recreating chest should be a smart third-grader, not a conjurer. One, who experiences the Hiftoun House, is no more an average conjurer!' explained Eduardo sweetly.

He then paused.

'One who makes the Jasper stone appear in his dream...'

Emily was confident Eduardo would finish his statements with this.

'Do you know who Paramis is?' she asked.

It was obvious that Eduardo was fully aware of the issue as he looked ashamed.

'Paramis or the death minstrel is the person you helped flee from the hidden castle,'

'So, it was all set up!' concluded Lisa angrily.

She then looked at the bamboozled faces of Emily and Andy.

'It was planned by the Council. Sometimes you may be able to prevent certain things but wisdom calls you not to. The Council felt it needed the stone more than I was worried about you. Of course, the Council did not achieve its goal but it wasn't the same for you. To gain the permit to enter the Bartlin and to experience staying in the Hiftoun House are not trivial issues!'

It was obvious that Eduardo was willing to go on speaking, however, he stopped to deal with an issue that was more interesting to him.

'Let me concentrate a little. So, it's a good thing that you've visited the tenth corridor. I'm proud of you. At least in this case,'

Eduardo then returned to the main topic of his talk.

'The stone was important due to the musician's thought treasure. The stone could have provided us with mind-blowing information but unfortunately, it goes into a defensive position in the face of people, who know Paramis,'

Andy was totally flabbergasted.

'But we had seen Paramis!' he said.

'I mean a deep knowledge and a magical one in nature, not just a one-time meeting. The galaxy jasper is an extraordinary stone. You just need to touch it and it will realize who is holding it. It can enter your mind and access all of those people who have already touched it and in case it finds a suspicious case, it shuts all ways of penetration,'

'So, why did it stay with us?' asked Lisa.

'Because it wasn't able to make heads or the tail of your stupid brains. I was kidding!'

'It wasn't a nice joke!' protested Lisa.

Eduardo was happy with the sarcastic remark. He then began to sound serious again.

'The Jinn-born giant was Ms. Hiftoun's great idea. The Jinn's brain does not record anything by the age of thirty. In fact, the stone would go to the Jinn-born giant and would find its way in a dark and information free world. At the mailing room, it was Ms. Hiftoun who didn't allow George, who was really fond of going to the mail chest, to raise his hand as a volunteer. It was Ms. Hiftoun who transferred George's bravery to Andy. Had you not been playful, you'd have realized that none of the members of the Hiftoun House was interested to hold the stone,'

Entangled in the clutches of a troubling feeling, Andy attempted to keep calm.

'Why is the minstrel so important?'

Looking at Andy's enthusiastic yet anxious eyes, Eduardo remained hesitant for a while. It was as though had he gone back to square one and was analyzing things for himself. There were a number of possibilities and speculations that he was not inclined to inform Andy about as he feared he might be scared.

'Nothing that's related to you,'

By saying that he just let the cat out of the bag but he tried to make up for it instantly.

'That murderer is a big threat for others. For years, Paramis had kept that quiet and nobody knew she had the stone. Do you know why? She didn't want anyone to get to know about her thoughts and ideas. The very same thoughts that she removed from her mind and transferred to the galaxy stone. In fact, finding the jasper galaxy stone sparked her first criminal incentive. An incentive called the ninth corridor,'

Emily was not able to see any link between the two.

'Why the ninth corridor?' she asked.

'Because it's where the black elixir is kept,'

'The black elixir?'

'" use this elixir to get rid of vicious " but in the case of human beings, it acts conversely and makes them stronger. Let's say, it turns them to the devil who has no boundaries and respect regarding the performance of banned magic. Of course, with iknars guarding the night corridor, it's a tough job to steal things from that place. Iknar " are able to see invisible individuals in addition to their speed and violence but still...'

Eduardo's pause stirred the situation for some time.

'...still, the minstrel managed to get in and steal a bottle of the elixir,'

'So, what the hell were the iknar "doing there?' asked Lisa hatefully.

'They are not to blame as Ms. Hiftoun's daughter was trusted and respected by all of the ",'

The three looked at each other. Lisa didn't realize that the pen had slipped her hand. They could not believe that the minstrel was Ms. Hiftoun's daughter. Eduardo continued to tell them the rest of the bitter story.

'Paramis had turned into a monster and would use disrespectful magic called the "death power" to claim the lives of a large number of people. From that day on, she was called the death minstrel but do you think she even cared? Never! That's because she was not happy with her previous nickname that was the magical painter. To be called the magical painter you have to uncover the secret of revelation frames but that was not what she was looking for. Her vicious heart yearned a vicious title. Bye the way, you must have seen the paintings of this treacherous painter in the tenth corridor, right?'

'Oh, those paintings on the wall...' said Andy in disbelief.

He then recalled something.

'There I saw Ms. Hiftoun's twin sister. She was badly depressed,'

'There's no twin sister, Andy. You have seen Ms. Hiftoun's mind,'

'Her mind?'

'It's called the sympathizing magic. After what Paramis did to the innocent people, Ms. Hiftoun had difficult times. Finally, she had to seek help from painful magic called the sympathizer magic to be able to transfer the sorrowful part of her mind to the magical room in the ninth corridor. OK, that's enough! Please get ready. I've promised Eric and Lili we'll be back home for dinner.'

When Junas got back to the room, they had already packed up. Junas was so happy to see it as though all the fires in the world had been put off.

'How are you doing, trouble-maker?' asked Eduardo.

'What do you think, stupid magician? You think you can insult Junas and go through this door contentedly?'

'I was joking, Junas! You are an interesting pokoun and really respectable!' said Eduardo with a smile.

Junas became happy.

'Really? Did you really mean it? Please tell me you were not lying. I accept criticism. I don't mind it if you disrespect me out of honesty,'

'Are you sure, Junas?'

'Of course not! What you already said sounded great. Don't make a mess of it. Let me have a good memory of you unlike these idiots,'

'You must be a real dummy to believe what he told you,' said Lisa.

'What matters is that he gave me a compliment. It doesn't matter how he really felt,'

'Don't worry, Junas! It was from the bottom of my heart. OK, time to hit the road! Farewell!

Junas opened the door.

'Hey, man. Why don't you stay here for a while? You know what? Come to me anytime you visit. Just don't bring these lunatics along. Are they your kids? If so, you must be very unlucky. May God bestow patience upon you! Hey, you have beautiful hair, your eyes...'

Two-blooded

At midnight somebody was taking strides out in the street. She was dressed in a cloak. Walking out in a winter night wearing a cloak was unusual. The mysterious passerby stepped into Password alley. Eduardo was standing there to help her go in without identification check. It was Kitty Reis. She was hiding something under her cloak.

'It was stupid but I had to do it. Here, Eduardo. Let's finish the job before they realize it. We should return it,'

She put some paper that resembled a newspaper on the table. Eduardo admired it.

'I couldn't trust anyone else. Of course, I knew nobody to be trusted by the Council either,'

From the deceased safe deposit boxes, Ms. Reis had picked up James Haris's notebook of prominence. The notebook comprised major moments of a magician's life. It was written with a drop of the blood of a magician donated before death. The information was written on magical paper with the magician having no role in the selection of what was going to be stored in that notebook. The notebook of prominence would be displayed with the blood of heirs only after the demise of the magician. The size of the notebook had to do directly with the number of extraordinary memories of the magician. Haris's notebook of prominence was the size of two pages of a newspaper.

Ms. Reis pulled out a glass with a streak of blood on it from her pocket. She had obtained the blood from James Harris's son in a complicated way. When the blood was dripping on the paper, it got up like a feather and opened up fully and was put on the table. On top of the paper, James Harris was pulling his magical robe

224

displaying his certificate of the Bartlin School. Eduardo was focusing on the section where James Harris went to the banned section of the library. At the bottom of the notebook of prominence was a marketplace where he had met with his lover for the first time. He looked the happiest in that market. His eyes were shining with love. On the left corner of the notebook was a circle with a vertical line dividing it into two black and white parts. The black and white circle was not comprehensible but James Harris must have been so attached to it for it to be registered in his notebook of prominence. The last major memory of his had to with the time when for the first time he had manipulated a secret memo of the Council of Magic by means of the penetrating magic. he was smiling viciously.

Eduardo cast an eye on Kitty Reis.

'It may be disheartening but anything related the penetrator must be sought at the Bartlin library. There is only one suspicious memory in which James Harris used the banned library once. He must have spent exciting moments there as you see that recorded in the notebook,'

Ms. Reis put the palm of her hand above the notebook of prominence and waved it. The paper got back to its original form like a snake that was turning and twisting in pain. Ms. Reis who was not going to undermine the pleasure of reading Haris's notebook of prominence placed it in its paper cover and went on.

'I think he was head over heels in love. Love of a lover who died at a young age and other memories that linger on for ages,'

'Isn't it unusual that his marriage is not recorded in the notebook of prominence?' asked Eduardo.

'Not at all, as he never managed to marry that girl. It's likely that the black and white circle related to the same issue. You know, while like love and black like a failure. I am aware of this. James Harris was in love with a woman called Amanda Blight who works in a café in the Geland market. I'll see you there tomorrow. I don't think to find Amanda Blight there would be hard. We must find a clue in any way possible.'

'But they were not that much involved in romance!' said Eduardo.

'Love is a complicated issue, Eduardo! There's no convincing reply when it comes to love. Anything you see on the surface has a story in its deep layers,'

'How can you be so sure about it?'

'I'm not sure but the only person who can help us is his love during his youth. I just hope she has a good memory.'

The next day at noon when they were standing in front of the door of an old café in the Geland market, a beggar who had covered his face completely was there but did not ask them for anything. Eduardo eyed the sign overhead. He had to ascertain they are not mistaken. Ms. Reis was hiding his long and unusual fingers under her cuffs. She wasn't embarrassed though, yet she didn't like to be a scene for sore eyes.

Lots of commotion at the old café. Some looked fashionable and some others looked different sitting at the tables. First, Eduardo thought they were magicians but after moments he realized they are a group of artists. There was an elderly waitress there.

'Would you like anything?'

'A hot drink that would take the cold away and make me warm. Makes no difference,' replied Eduardo.

'Does a lady by the name of Amanda Blight work here?' he asked quietly.

The woman let out her breath impatiently.

'I should have guessed you are magicians. You must be curious about James Haris again. I'm delighted no to ever marry him or else I had to keep tolerating people like you all my life,'

'What a surprise! We just want to know a little bit about him,' said Dr. Kitty.

Amanda took a look back and went on.

'Many magicians used to frequent here especially in the early days after James died but it's not that often now. I was not able to cope with James' unusual situation. He came back to me several times after we broke up. He said he was ready to put magic aside but he had this intrinsic thirst for magic and was unable to stay away from it for a long time,'

'Didn't James tell you about extraordinary magic?' inquired Eduardo.

'He would always make use of magic to make me happy. Any man in the café that would stare at me, would have the leg of his chair broken or his drink spilled all over his clothes or they could even see their pants drop down while getting up to walk. Of course, I did not want him to do such things but he always did,'

Eduardo showed the picture of the black and white circle to Amanda.

'Do you know anything about this circle?'

'He had a necklace with the same image. He said it belonged to his childhood,'

Eduardo realized that Amanda Blight was not happy with the conversation. He cast a glimpse at Dr. Kitty and felt she had the same opinion.

'Ms. Blight, you've been really kind! I know that you don't like visiting magicians but it was important to us as it's a matter of life and death.'

Hearing that sympathetic statement, Amanda tried to be more patient and think a bit deeper.

'He always preferred to confine himself to an isolated corner. At times he disappeared for a few days. He said he would go to the woods by the lake. I don't know where that is. It must be a pretty peaceful place,'

Eduardo suddenly got up. It was evident in his face that he had found a clue.

'Thank you so much! You've been such a great help! I just heard what I needed to hear.'

He bade her farewell and left the café. Ms. Reis took long steps to keep pace with him.

'What's up, Eduardo?'

'Two-blooded. He's been looking for two-blooded, dear Kitty,'

'How are you so sure?'

'The black and white circle and going to the woods. Important things just took shape in my mind a few seconds ago. In the woods by the lake lives a two-blooded. I already knew it. The white half circle belongs to the human face and the black part to their wild face. If we are lucky, then we may be able to get our hands on useful information,'

'You are so smart, Eduardo!'

'Thank you, dear Kitty!'

When the night fell, they reached the woods by the lake. There was water flowing under the trees for such a long distance. Eduardo put the wooden boat that was tied to an iron pole into the water and started to row. A thick fog was moving among the trees. The stars were twinkling from among the tree branches and the owls' shooting could be heard. Kitty Reis, who seldom frequented the woods, was much more excited than Eduardo who was born in such an area. Having looked all around for a while, Eduardo uttered some magic.

'Agreera Vakhiana,'

To Dr. Kitty's surprise, a tall and bulky tree that seemed to be a place for residence emerged from darkness. Eduardo was freaking out.

'I always thought it's useless magic,'

He then led the boat toward the tree. As the boat hit the tree roots there had wound up like a gigantic snake, the two got out of it. Slowly, Eduardo moved forward but he seemed to be worried. Maybe it was because of what he was expecting to see when he entered the house. They went in through a wooden door among the roots. It was an eerie and dreadful atmosphere.

Without seeing the two-blooded, Eduardo could sense its presence in the house, so he went forward with slow and cautious steps. He had images in his mind that discouraged him from the result of this adventurism. The two-blooded could have collaboration with the enemy. Dr. Kitty tried to show him a room at one corner of the house by body language. However, Eduardo could not hear the humming that Kitty was hearing. He was still taking steps with despair but when he looked beyond the half-open door and inside the room, he abandoned pessimism and moved forward so normally as though he had gone there to visit an old friend.

'So, you are here, dear friend! Sorry, I'm late!'

The two-blooded was sitting on a chair with an injured face. He was unable to stand. The right part of his face resembled the human face and the left part a dreadful animal. He was sneaking a peek at Eduardo.

'Who the hell are you?' he asked.

'In great likelihood, I'm looking for the bitter accident that you have had. I was going to knock on the door or make a cough to announce my presence but I guessed you were already aware of everything around you and would not regard this behavior of mine to be discourteous,'

The two-blooded showed them seats with his head and asked them to sit down. He was not in the mood for any introductory remarks, so he went straight down to business.

'I was sitting in this room when five rioters like you showed up without permission,'

Eduardo somehow blushed but tried to conceal it.

'They had come here to take my blood but I fought them. Apart from them, there was also another strange creature that wouldn't show itself. It had a horrible voice and spoke an unusual language. It said things the pressures of which I could feel and I started to faint little by little. When I came to, I realized I had lost lots of blood. At a glance, I noticed some of the roots had also dried up. It looked like the trace of that eerie creature with the horrible voice. It took the roots three days to come back to life and become fresh again,'

Eduardo had just realized an important secret and he tried to show it to Dr. Kitty with his look.

'Can you tell us about James Harris?'

The two-blooded eyes got round out of surprise. You could see concern and hatred in his face at the same time. His voice was also raised and sounded clearer.

'Do not mention his goddamn name here! He was a liar! A charlatan! He was the source of the misery I went through. He took advantage of my trust,'

'You have every right to be mad at him but he is dead. He died many years ago,'

'How did he die? I hope he had suffered tons of pain before giving up the ghost!'

'He was behind bars for long years. He committed suicide!'

The two-blooded tried to make believe that he was happy to hear the news, yet he was not able to suppress the agony he felt inside him. James Harris was his only human friend. He continued sadly.

'The first time I met him, I realized he is really smart! He always laughed and make fun of my strange face. He would laugh at the jokes that he told before anyone else. He used to say the two-blooded can never make itself an impact repellent halo because the wild part of his body would bore a hole inside the halo from within. Several times I didn't let him come to my house. He would sit on the roots and sing songs. Then I thought I couldn't stand his terrible voice so I'd open the door and let him in. We had great days together. He told me about his abortive love affair and bitter life. I also told him about others,'

'When was this friendship broken up?' asked Dr. Kitty.

'Since the day he told me he wanted to help me get rid of the wild part of my body. He said to do that he needed to take some of my blood. I fell for his lies. I hadn't heard of him for such a long time then. One day, he got back finally and gave me hope that he was going to succeed but he was lying. I realized that when he left his personal notebook here one day. His writing hurt me. The worst thing to happen in the world is to be taken advantage of by your friend. With the help of my blood, James had created magic that was able to change security texts. When he returned later, I didn't let him in anymore. The only request I had of him was not to tell anyone about it for fear that in future vicious magicians may not leave me alone,'

'So how did the rioters get to know about the secret?' asked Eduardo.

'Through his wife,'

'I've talked to his wife. She didn't have the slightest idea!' explained Dr. Kitty.

'I mean his first wife. He was embarrassed to tell anyone about her because she had joined the rioters.'

The wind was blowing softly. Night had fallen and the sky was glowing. They got in the boat and started rowing toward the coast.

'I don't why but I feel sorry for James Harris,' said Dr. Kitty.

'The mortal Jinni!' commented Eduardo.

'What?'

'You heard me right. The mortal Jinni. The one who leaves an unpleasant trace of himself behind is only a mortal Jinni. A highly dangerous and mischievous Jinni. Now I dare to say that the person that entered Eric's body in the Redicheh farm and forced Lisa to go to the museum of inventions was a mortal Jinni. It makes sense. They can live in others' bodies for a long time. But, the question is why the Jinni went out of its way to save the minstrel. I wish we could find a clue!'

Return to Self

Winter sunlight started shining on house number 7 at Mailman Street. Like other days, Andy had not heard of his friends. Just once after leaving the Hiftoun House, he had gone to the Password. He was looking at the two books laying on his table.

"The scattered waves in the galaxy" and "The seven skies and the supporting columns"

Eduardo had given him the two books and insisted that he study them carefully to find his way into the school. The books were so old that Andy thought there must be a mistake but before handing him the book, Eduardo had read them for a while and thus could not have made a mistake. Andy missed the house so much that he didn't feel like being too inquisitive about the books. On the way to the house, he was thinking he was going to be warmly welcomed but he just remembered that their family had never realized that he had left the house.

That day when he arrived home, his look-alike stepped out intrinsically so that Andy could go in. The first encounter was so exciting for Andy that he hesitated to greet his look-alike and ran inside the house. At the end of the day, he was so angry with him as he had just realized the look-alike had unwrapped all the gifts that William had brought him from his trips. Gradually the situation was getting worse. Anytime Andy asked a question about William's trip, he realized that the question had already been asked by his look-alike. So everyone was surprised to see he is asking the questions again. Anyway, having a look-alike had its own advantages too. For instance, he could find him somewhere nearby anytime he wished. There was this profound spiritual bond connecting them that made the look-alike come to him when Andy needed him. So, Andy would go to school anytime he wanted and he would not attend class anytime he didn't feel like it. He just had his look-alike do that.

On lonely days, Andy would keep busy reading the dials. The book became so mysterious and vague at times that would make him ponder for quite a while.

"Ancient gateways and hidden and under protection"

All of a sudden, Andy lost track of his thoughts and flew to his horrific world. An invisible woman would call his name from far away. Andy would remain motionless without even turning his face in any direction. He had been there. Torturous days were back again! The days when his room was host to invisible people. At that time, he was not familiar with magic yet. He was expelled from school. He was called crazy and abnormal. His loneliness was brimmed with fear and pessimism on those days. Yet, he could not conceal the fact that he was scared. He was dubious about what happened around him for a while. Scary and unusual dreams, as well as the writing in dias, could affirm the bad feeling he had. On top of all, the invisible screams were coming to him again. He was not able, to be honest to himself and he tried to protect the seeds of optimism that Eduardo had planted in his heart.

Everything started on Sunday when William had invited everyone for dinner. As always, William praised the roast beef and Flora's special sauce. Andy hadn't felt well since he had gotten up on the wrong side in the morning. He couldn't concentrate, so he moved a bit, drank some water and received the instant warning from Flora not to make noise while drinking water. He suddenly blew his top and hit the table. Nobody believed that Andy got furious at Flora's warning. In fact, the reason for that fury emanated from elsewhere. It was Dianna's behavior at that moment that had caused that emotion to overflow. Andy realized having uttered some good and bad angry remarks during that moment of fury when he was lost in himself. The abrupt change in his facial expressions resembled a miracle. No one was able to be furious in a jiffy and then looked around calmly and indifferently immediately afterward.

Having made a simple apology, Andy kept eating while immersing in his thoughts. He had somehow comprehended certain things but he didn't want to believe them. He had his own reasons for that and he just wanted to ignore them all. How similar was his deed to the old books Eduardo had given him! Was it possible that Eduardo had a special purpose by giving them to him?

Even when William was trying by means of jokes and humor to make peace between the children, Andy did not grasp his interesting jokes and headed to his room right after lunch, sat on his chair and sank back into his thoughts. He was a black hole talent, so, why shouldn't Eduardo tell him anything about it?

Andy analyzed everything from his own perspective. Despite the fact that he had managed to enter the realm of magic, yet he didn't know much about his intrinsic talent. Even after finding his way in the talents' castle, nobody had asked him to go there again. Andy turned with the sound of the dias pages flipping over. It looked as though the wind was blowing against the pages turning them. Andy was sure he hadn't uttered a word for dias to show a reaction when he was angry. Writing appeared on top of the book.

"The brilliant stone was glowing and that was the beginning of the path that I had never fancied in my mind. The wild horse of poverty and avarice had galloped much farther ahead of me. In the midst of altercation in my suffering mind, some involuntary force was leading me toward destruction."

That night I didn't have the slightest idea as to which bitter destiny was coming my way with its charming looks. My mind has been blown away by a craving for prosperity, which is making me run to it whereas I was heading for an ambush of evil power.

As I was returning home with weary steps and an agitated mind, I was about to see my heart get away from my chest. Lifeless wooden statues which I had made one day to earn a living had come to life and sneaking a peek at me. His whole body was trembling out of fear of the mishap. But I was only a lonely little boy."

The writing was sorrowful. It sounded as though someone who'd been left high and dry in the dark had spoken of a sad past and a painful eventuality.

Andy started to stare at the book inquisitively when it turned into a star-studded night. Suddenly, he felt he was plunging into the book and a second later he found himself in a night-hit land which was brimmed with stars. There, was standing a man atop a rock looking at the yellow man that had emerged from the Orient.

Things happened quite promptly. Andy was sitting on his chair in his room again when Dennis arrived and started to speak triumphantly.

'Hey, Andy! You did a great job today. Mum has been warning Diana about her behavior since soon. You will see that for yourself when you come for dinner. Even dad is picking on her for low grades at school. Everybody is looking for some excuse to bug her. I have my own criticisms too. It feels great! I think I have developed an inferiority complex. Come downstairs soon. Dad will show up soon. Dinner is ready.'

Of all the statements Dennis had made, Andy recalled one only. It's time for dinner! But he felt it was not past lunchtime much! He jumped up and looked out the window. It had gotten dark. Putting on his warm and soft pullover, he got ready to go downstairs. He had to contact the Password. He knew there must be a wall communication center on Calagan Street. He had to get out of the home so that his look-alike could come in and fill in for him. He would definitely show up when needed.

Having made up an excuse, he left the house. Unexpectedly, his look-alike was nowhere to be found. He could not wait any longer, so he set off but no sooner had he taken a few steps than he faced William.

'What are you doing here, boy? You just told me that you were going to your friend's birthday party,'

Andy just realized why his look-alike had made a delay.

'Yes. I'm on my way. I'm being late!' said Andy instantly.

Hurriedly, he walked to Calagan Street. Inside an old and abandoned alley way he found the communication center. There was commotion. So many people had gone there to communicate with official centers. All the ten booths were engaged. A leaning old man who had big eyes and was smoking a pipe ran to Andy.

'Is it urgent, boy?'

'Donno!' Maybe!'

The old man looked around furtively.

'Follow me if wanna do it more quickly,'

In a room at the back, stood an old communication wall. The old man opened the booth door.

'This place is mine. I do my urgent stuff here. You can do your communication thing here as I go for a spin.'

Upon the old man's departure, Andy closed the rusty door of the booth. The communication wall was a half-a-meter square resembling seaside sand. Andy placed his finger on the special spot and started thinking about the wall at the destination point. The sand panel turned white, which meant that communication had been established. With his finger, Andy began writing on the sand panel.

'Hi. I'm Andy Barnet,'

He kept looking at the panel waiting for Ms. Wagner's response. No reply! He pressed a green button to clean the panel so he could write again. He knew whatever he'd written had already been stored onto the wall.

'I'm in trouble! Everything's in a mess! Somebody answer me,'

Andy's heart was beating hard. There was no answer. He started to write again.

'There are so many things happening around me. I need to talk to you about dias. Somebody answer me.'

Andy was trying hard.

'I can hear things. It suddenly gets dark all over the place. Please answer me. I'm scared! As I'm writing, I can hear a strange sound. Commotion and screams!'

No answer! Andy stepped out of the booth. While leaving the communication center, his body was kind of trembling. He was walking but without being able to concentrate. He took notice of the sky. A cold wintery expanse was shining over his head with brilliant rays. A mild wind was blowing and folks were passing him by in a hurry. While he was walking home via Calagan Street, he heard someone.

'Where did you go all of a sudden?'

That was Hector, his classmate.

'Are you ready to go?'

'Where?'

'What's wrong with you? It's my birthday today,'

'Oh, I totally forgot!'

Andy was not thinking about having to accompany Hector to his house, he was rather worried his look-alike might show up any moment and ruin everything. He was really mad at him. The thought of William opening his gifts before him was making him even more furious.

The two took an empty street to Hector's house. Hector was speaking excitedly but Andy took no heed of that and was just worried in case his look-alike showed up, he would have to introduce him as his twin brother who had lived with his uncle for long years.

Andy was not happy with the waste of time at all. He had more important things to take care of. Suddenly, some force stopped him from moving while Hector was still raving about his birthday. Before Andy showed any reaction, he found the shoulders of his look-alike under Hector's hand. He was laughing at his words.

'How the hell did he show up?' Andy wondered.

A warm and mature voice replied.

'It wasn't very difficult to do Mr. Barnet; however, your negligence will go down in my notebook,'

Turning around, Andy saw an elderly man with big eyes and long ears standing by his side.

'Good night, sir! You're right. I should not have done this. I had promised Eduardo not to go out at nighttime,'

'I'm Nelson Spinner. I'm in charge of look-alikes who face misunderstanding. Your abrupt presence made him so anxious that he was not able to make a decision,'

'Why should my look-alike be here in the first place?' asked Andy sounding like a proprietor.

'It was Eduardo's suggestion. Sometimes your heart decides for you for things to be done without any reason. Perhaps it was because of the fact that that child was for years really expecting his friends to go to his birthday party. This was so important for Hector that it turned to a dream. A dream that started shining like a star in the sky inspiring Eduardo to take action. Did you know that Hector was adopted by a family and that he never met his own parents?'

Andy was taken aback.

'No, he never told anyone anything about it. I wish him happiness,' said Andy sadly.

'Tonight you gave that boy a present whose price was deducted from your personal account,'

'But, I have no personal account. Nobody has consulted me about this payment, either. I agree with what has been done though,'

'You already own a personal account. Any child whose name is registered in the first course on magic takes possession of a personal account. The account is deposited on the basis of your competency and great tasks that you do in the course of your scholastic period,'

'How much do I have in my account now?'

'Taking into account your penal fines in this calculation, it was almost the same amount you could get a birthday present with,'

Andy smirked and felt embarrassed to be regarded as a poor person among magicians. Suddenly, he got his act together and tried to look serious.

'Tonight, something weird happened to me. I have to inform Eduardo about it but no one answered me at the communication wall,'

'I'd be happy to hear it if it's not a secret,'

'You've done me a big favor tonight. I think I can trust you. Dias took me to a no man's land full of stars. Somebody was standing on a rock,'

That didn't matter much to Mr. Spinner.

'Did you see the owner of the book? He must have been the great Dias. You saw him because he wanted you to see him. You have extraordinary talents, Andy Barnet. There are many people, who would like to know what's going on in the world within you,'

Andy was astonished.

'What are you talking about, Mr. Spinner?'

'There they talk a lot about you. I mean at the Council of Magic. How can a boy come under the spotlight of the horror world since his childhood?'

Mr. Spinner was trying to somehow downplay facts while mentioning them to Andy.

'I'm sorry, dear Andy! I should speak more clearly. That night at the Tourin graveyard, it was the first time that the world took notice of the presence of an amazing little boy. They still remember that incident as a rare one. It's hard to believe how you survived a cursing wolf's attack. Of course, you must be indebted to the three poor magicians and that stubborn midget,'

Andy preferred to keep quiet so long as he was unable to make heads or tails of Mr. Spinner's words.

'I have a number of errands to run. Good night, Mr. Barnet.'

'But I have so many questions to ask you,'

With a smile coming from within a man overwhelmed with serenity and calm, Mr. Spinner replied.

'You don't need to ask. The right answers come your way when you need them. Soon, when your memories come to life, you won't take any pleasure out of receiving many of the answers as you don't need to know them any longer. I'm glad that I'm not assigned to answer your questions, otherwise, it would take so much energy to talk about certain facts.'

'But I cannot wait till then,'

Mr. Spinner had little regard for Andy's concerns. He entered the vapor-looking space behind him and vanished into thin air. Mr. Spinner left while Andy was begging loudly for him to come back. Before long, someone makes a sarcastic comment.

'Stop yelling! He must be home already!'

Andy spotted a little naughty girl with a freckled face.

'I'm Natalie Smith. What's your name?

'Andy Barnet. Are you a magician too?'

Natalie smiled bitterly while replying to his question.

'I just passed the conjuring course. I found no more chance to pursue it,'

Andy thought he was touching upon issues that are bothering Natalie. She might have been expelled for lack of skills or talent.

He then started to think that the same fate me befall him as well. What would he do then?

'What are you doing here?' asked the girl.

'I'm returning from the communication center. What are you doing here?'

'I live here. Let me show you my house,'

While taking slow steps, Andy told Natalie about the unusual things that had happened to him. Passersby looked at Andy who was talking to Natalie in a way as if they had seen a moron. The girl pointed at an old door that was left ajar.

'Here we are! That's it!'

Andy stepped into the yard. The lights were out and the glasses broke. It had the specter of an abandoned house. Andy looked around worriedly. Then he kneeled and picked up a letter. It had remained out there under the snow for at least three months.

'Dear Arthur, I just came to learn about the agony that has pulled up your heart's strings. I am really sorry about that. I contacted you several times and even came to your place only to realize that you were gone for good. I hope I will be able to see you again. I'm so sorry about your daughter, my good friend. Should you come back, please let me know…Aron.'

'Why did you not reply the letter?' inquired Andy.

'It doesn't matter!'

Andy felt he was frozen inside.

'Where are your parents?' he asked worriedly.

'They're gone! I live alone,'

She paused a little and then went on.

'OK, Andy. Good night!'

She went to a corner of the yard and into the ground all of a sudden. Andy ran after her and reached a tombstone with something written on it.

'This tombstone belongs to Natalie Smith, the daughter of Arthur and Helen'

Horror had filled Andy's eyes. He started to mumble worriedly.

'She is dead. Natalie is dead!'

He began to run away instantly. He fell down many times while escaping. The answers that Mr. Spinner had mentioned were coming his way. He remembered the memories of the Tourin cemetery, the songs of the poor Puliten and his childhood days on many occasions. They were so vivid and close that they seemed to have happened just the previous day. Now the spell that he had felt had encircled him for years was beginning to go away. His forgotten memories were coming back to life revengefully after years of homelessness.

Before reaching home, he heard a soothing voice that he really wished to hear at that sensitive moment.

'It was time, Andy. I knew that you had to experience such tough moments one day. You must be asking yourself what has happened,'

With eyes full of tears, he looked at Eduardo.

'She was dead. Natalie was dead. I was talking to her!'

'There are many people who wish to talk to the dead. This way, they don't have to shed tears while mourning for their bereaved ones. You are special, Andy! This can be both good and bad in the realm of magic. Spells lose their potency in the course of time and that's when you realize how special you are!' said Eduardo.

Horror and fear had not left Andy's eyes yet and his voice was still feeble and shaky.

'What has happened to me?'

'I can answer your questions but please do not ask me to do that. Let things happen in due time. What's for certain is that you must be proud of yourself. Very soon, many will come to you for interviews and photos and among them there could be famous people who have waited to meet you for such a long time!'

'Why should he matter to others?'

'For good reasons. One of them being the fact that you are an exquisite talent in the black hole. I think you've also realized it. As for the book I should apologize to you. They were kind of old, I mean a bit too old. But they were handy. They belonged to an old black hole when we were classmates. I knew you would need them sooner or later. There's something more important than the black hole. Much more important! You carry the insignia of life after death. Is this not reason enough for others to like to see you? To be honest, I also want to have your autograph,'

That was definitely not true. Eduardo said that to try and boost Andy's morale.

'What the hell is the insignia of life after death?'

'Look at your left hand!'

Instantly, Andy opened his hand. There were the lines that he had always dreamed about. The lines that resembled a book. Now that he was awake, he was able to see them. Eduardo continued to speak proudly.

'You own something that ancient scriptures have referred to with awe and astonishment. There were many people who believed it though. Spend the night away from all troubling fantasies and dreams. Just think of good things. By the way, get ready for next week,'

'Ready? For what?'

'It's to your benefit. That insignia is so precious that may make some people close their eyes on rules and come to meet you at a place where your family lives. You don't want this, do you? Next week I'll take you to the Council of Magic. They are all there. People who are craving for fame can be found everywhere. Many of them need to take photos with someone famous to sue that in their election campaign while running for the Council of Magic. Who can they find better than you? They will definitely make seductive proposals to you so you would promote them but I'll be pleased if you do not accept such humiliation. You'd better do that for a lofty cause,'

The Riddle Solver

As all nights, Frowning Philip told Dimer Ill her bedtime story before heading for the lake. He had just discovered a powerful pesticide to revive the plants on the lake's bed, so he was delightfully taking steps toward the coast where he came to a sudden halt. He had heard a faint sound which he suspected was not a usual one. Philip was looking all around himself with utmost care. Deep darkness had covered a vast expanse of land as far as the eye could see. The sound was faint yet audible and constant. Philip was not willing to accept that it may belong to a wicked and cursed creature.

Philip knew very well that in case that sound came from anywhere nearby, then its source would definitely be within eyesight, so he thought it came from afar. Apparently, the source of the sound had managed, by means of a magical procedure, to make his or her voice audible in remote areas.

Philip had turned pessimistic. The sound of the lake was like music to his ears. Never had he wished the sound of the lake to go away? He cast a look at the tree. Dimer Ill had fallen asleep, so the sound could not have come from that direction. This time, he checked out the lake. He suddenly came to a standstill. He felt something was approaching him. There was no sign or trace of it, yet, he was confident that he would come under an attack, not from the outside world but from the realm of his thoughts that may start flowing over him like floodwater any moment now. He was still looking around suspiciously, trying to listen to the faintest sounds he could hear so that he would show an appropriate reaction in the face of danger coming his way.

Philip was frightened. He went back to the cabin quietly. There was not much distance left when the world started going up and down like a clock pendulum. Unable to see objects standing motionless, Philip felt as though he was picked up by a giant who was turning him around his head up in the air. He fell down in front of the cabin. On all fours, he went to the chair. When the turning and tossing subsided, he took a seat. Involuntarily, he started thinking about the night when the three conjurers had gone there to meet him. He felt he had to start contemplating from that very point in time while the world around him was being plunged to darkness. Now, Philip was standing in the middle of a dark jungle with nobody around. Fearfully, he looked around to locate the person who had taken him there. Who could ask for Philip to remain all alone in a fall-stricken jungle? Taking steps, he realized there was no sound produced from the leaves under his feet. To make sure of this, he had to be patient and wait. He had to await something mysterious and significant.

Hearing the rustling sound that did not come from the movement of his feet, he turned back. Somewhere in the dark, a group was on the move. Before Philip could hide, they emerged from among the trees but none of them showed any reaction to his presence there. Philip was now sure that he had become invisible and taking steps within the memories of a wicked creature. A number of rioters together with a witch who had covered her face passed by him. Philip ran after them while trying to identify the woman. The woman stopped in front of two old trees. Her voice could hardly be heard. An ancient gateway opened up. Despite all he had put into oblivion, Philip was certain that the gateway was one of the fourteen gateways to enter the parallel world where nothing but darkness was there to be found. The witch pulled her robe and uncovered her face for Philip. It was Paramis, Ms. Hiftoun's cursed daughter. The minstrel was standing before the gateway, uttering a spell.

"Baberootsa quanta"

She then opened her fist releasing a brilliant powder toward the darkness encircling the gate. Soon afterward, Philip's eyes could not see anything for moments after that blinding light filled the space. Opening his eyes again, he realized he was standing in front of another ancient gateway on top of a snow-capped mountain. He could see the minstrel who had reached the gate accompanied by a group. Uttering the same unknown spell, she then let out the shining powder again.

After tons of memories from Paramis, Philip entered a lush and vast plain. This time, Paramis arrived together with a number of rioters and a chained prisoner. It was an elderly man with an aquiline nose and brown sunken eyes.

'Tell him what it is,' said the minstrel to the prisoner.

The man declined to answer.

'This is a big mistake! They will find you!' said the man unwillingly.

'Shut up!' shouted the minstrel.

The frightened man pointed at a vast hill nearby. Paramis moved in that direction without allowing anyone to accompany her. Philip was the only person who was able to go after her without being seen. On the way, he cursed her several times. In front of the hill, Paramis mumbled something. The lawn went to a side and an ancient gateway emerged.

"Babrootsa Quanta"

This was the last dream passing in front of Philip's eyes. He had returned to his cabin by the lake again. Incognizant of what had happened, he was well aware that he had managed to become the king of the stones once again.

He was not satisfied with gaining back his old powers as he could not sit in a corner idly by and get busy with the pests in the lake. He could not believe he was so content with the present job that would enable him to firmly reject the idea of becoming the king of stones again. He then recalled the fact that just moments ago he had experienced a great feat. He had managed to infiltrate into the galaxy jasper stone and he was aware of the reason for that pretty well. That night when the Jasper was taken to him, his mind was blank and devoid of any power or knowledge. That's why the stone put its trust in him. Philip could recall that night when he had seen incomprehensible strings and luminous rays. The luminous rays were the very strings of the minstrel's mind that he was not able to see with his power back. A wonderful secret had been uncovered for him. The ancient gateways were all cursed for which there was certainly a good reason. It was nothing appropriate in any way. Thinking of the issue, had Philip become indifferent toward the past agony and frustration.

'I have to go back. I must inform the Council of Magic. Get up, Philip! We should go as soon as possible. Things are happening. Important events. Get up, man! You are not meant for isolation. It's time everyone respected you! You are the king of the stone, man! It's time you did something!'

He kept thinking along the same lines while preparing himself to leave the cabin.

The Parallel World

Andy spent all the past few days feeling concerned. After his conversation with Natalie, he did not run into any other ghost but still he had not recovered his real power and was waiting to experience another even more bitter incident any time soon. In spite of the assurances that Eduardo had given him, he still could not accept the fact that no danger was threatening him. If Eduardo was confident that Andy had full security, then why had he asked him not to go out at night? What did the magicians that he encountered on the streets every day have to do with him in the first place? Anytime he stepped out, he realized that somebody was watching him. Sometimes he ran into them around a bend or inside a store. He would wear a meaningful smile and pass by them. At times, he would tell them sarcastically that they were acting like magicians. It was amusing for Andy to see them try to convince him that he was wrong about them. This, he thought was fair enough!

Fearfully, Andy woke up suddenly because of another nightmare. The clock showed twelve. Walking back and forth in his room, he thought of that nightmare. He had seen that unknown graveyard in his dreams once before. He could still recall the sounds from that graveyard at the foot of the dark and heat-stricken mountain. There were old graves and the sound he could hear in his ears would sink any heart. Involuntarily, he remembered the Tourin cemetery. The thought of meeting a number of ghosts in the Tourin cemetery was exactly what he was much afraid of. Was it possible for him to get to learn about the situation in the graves through his life after death insignia? No. That was a horrible idea! If so, he was really fond of ignoring this part of his skills or even maybe get rid of it if possible. He had lost most of his courage. The slightest sound from behind the window would freeze him with fear. Miss Spano's cat was sitting on the lamppost mewing as soon as seeing Andy, which was something he comprehended.

'What do you want? Why are you staring at an impatient cat like this? I'm sick and tired!'

'Nothing!' said Andy in surprise.

The cat got happy.

'Wow! Look here! I just realized it. You understand cats' language! Three-hundred years pass since the last time a human was able to understand cats' language. He was said to care so much for cats. Are you the same or good for nothing?'

'Well, I'm trying to be supportive of cats,'

'So, please tell Miss Dixon's stupid boy to leave me and my kittens alone. He is always bugging cats. He has no regard for animals' rights. You have written laws only as a keepsake and for the sake of show-off. What the hell do they teach you in those goddamn schools?'

Since the night he was told about his skills, this was the first time that Andy felt satisfied with possessing such a different personality. Having shut the window, he heard something clearly. He was certain it was from inside the room. He almost fainted when he turned. Had he not been caught by surprise that way, he would have been much more pleased to face this. Fentous, the beautiful Jinni he had met at the Hiftoun House, appeared in the room with some newspapers, cheese snacks, chocolate…

She was looking at Andy in such a way as though she couldn't believe she would be able to find him so soon. Andy started to speak slowly and at the same time excitedly.

'What are you doing here this time of day?'

Fentous was chewing a long gumdrop.

'Hey, Andy! I looked for you for so long! I thought maybe I'm not very good at appearing and disappearing. I appeared in ten homes before I found you here. I donno why they fainted anywhere I appeared! I just offered them to have some of these edibles, so why did they faint? Have some! They are cool! You have so many great edibles!'

The funny story Fentous was telling Andy left him gaping.

'Not all humans are magicians. Even if they are, seeing a stranger in the middle of their room in the heat of the night is scary. Don't "have anything called fear?'

Fentous offered him a big piece of chocolate one more time.

'Where did you take these?' asked Andy.

'I put a laced hat on and headed for the market. You can't imagine how many different kinds of edibles they have! It was written on a store sign that there was a big sale due to change of profession. I went in and took all of these,'

Andy laughed so loudly that he could no doubt be heard downstairs.

'When things are on sale, it means they are sold at lower prices. They are not free of charge!'

Fentous was still toying with her long gumdrop looking indifferent to his comments.

'You're right! It wasn't right to do. Leave it! He was to blame. He hadn't mentioned it clearly. I had read in a human's magazine that women are keen on going shopping sprees. I just realize how enjoyable it feels!'

Fentous was taking tons of pleasure from owning all of those colorful and delicious bags. Andy noticed the newspapers she was holding.

'You also have papers?'

'Actually, I came here for the same thing. This little yummy stuff made me forget all about it. I was thinking you've become so famous, that's why you behave like this. You are already famous among the "! My dad was going to come and meet you but he was too tired. You know, " get tired after repeated or long disappearances,'

In Andy's eyes, there was nothing worthy of being proud of his fame. It was more trouble than anything else. The papers followed other agendas more than merely introducing Andy. As Eduardo put it, papers were filled with electoral ambitions. Various people had made comments about Andy most of whom he had never met even once in his lifetime. However, things were different in celebrity papers and highly circulated ones. They were still sticking to their main mission and their news bore much resemblance with facts on the ground. Noticing the phrase which had introduced Ms. Wagner as Andy's program manager made him delighted. He was thinking how hard Ms. Wagner had tried to get the phrase to appear in the celebrity paper. Imagining that brought him tons of joy.

'…what do you know about the insignia of life after death? What kind of powers do black holes possess? Ms. Wagner, who claims is Andy's program manager, says Andy Barnet has managed to communicate with the book dias…'

Andy took an amiable look at Fentous.

'Have you heard of Emily, Lisa, and Eric?'

'When I got disappointed with finding you, I was going to the Password but there are so many security magicians there, you can't go in. then I thought, you don't have to still be in the Password. You must have gone back home after getting the certificate to get into the School of Magic to prepare yourselves,'

Knock, knock, knock! It was Flora. Andy turned anxiously toward Fentous when the door opened. Fortunately, she was gone but she had left the edibles on the table. It seemed that Flora had woken up suddenly as she had puffy eyes and felt annoyed.

'What the hell are you doing? What are all these?'

'I had a nightmare!'

'You must have dreamed of potato chips and cheeseballs!'

Upon Flora's departure, Fentous made a comeback while panting.

'Sorry, Andy! I didn't mean to put you to trouble. I will take these with me if you don't care for them. By the way, is that crazy sister of yours still bugging you? I can scare the hell out of her if you want me to,'

'No, no need for that! But please next time you are coming to meet me, please come during the day, not at night time!'

Fentous picked up even her half-finished gumdrop bag.

'OK, next time I'm here, we'll go shopping together. It's so cool! I know where to go.'

Fentous disappeared. She had taken with her everything except the newspapers.

One day, Andy got to realize an unusual thing. He took a sigh once his eyes met dias. How come he hadn't noticed it all that time? Most of the ambiguous statements that he had heard the book say in the past days had something to do with Andy and his strange dreams. He even remembered that the first time he had visited the book at the library, dias had spoken of shadows and dark passageways. The sentence that was taking shape in the book now was also another hard proof of Andy's claim.

"You'd better focus on love and affection should you wish to take possession of your black hole nature"

Andy was thinking deeply until there was a knock on the door and William entered.

'Andy…you know what, Andy…it's time you read your mother's memoir.'

Andy looked at him in disbelief. William had always been opposed to that request of his but now he was trying to avoid Andy's eyes when handing him Telma's memoir. William's behavior was unusually abnormal and it seemed that he had been forced by outside powers to do that. Andy took a glance at dias with hesitation. Could the book be behind all that? Andy's thirst to read his mother's memoir distracted him from any other topic. He was gaping when he took a glimpse of its prelude.

"It's me, Telma! The daughter of hearing and seeing. My body is on the earth but my mind up in the firmament. It's me, Telma! I hear the cry of the world. The galaxy whispers into my ears. I'm overwhelmed with observations that are hidden from the public eye. I'm brimmed with memories which if told, would have me looked upon as insane. It's me, Telma! The daughter of the galaxy, the daughter of the sun and the rain, the daughter of roaring thunders and blowing winds."

Two feelings were coming to life in Andy's soul simultaneously, astonishment and hope. So, her mother did resemble him. Andy gave dias the dagger's eye and went on to ask it with fear and hesitation.

'Who are you?'

The memoir's page was turned. Now, Andy was certain that dias had a role in William's decision. He started to read quickly.

"I was no more that little happy girl. Despair had filled me all over. That day, I was so weary I was leaning on a tree when a mysterious passerby showed up. He had a long robe on. I was scared at first sight but the man was so familiar with my mood that I felt we were the same as each other. He told me that I would get rid of that agony by focusing on positive thoughts that were devoid of any agitation and worries. The agony that was called the intrinsic black hole talent. The man left me with a brief smile, promising to come back with a special proposal.

I lived with worries for days. The two-faced people who smiled at me were incognizant of the fact that I was able to hear the things they were attributing to me while whispering to each other even tens of meters away. It was quite torturous but there were more important things for me…"

Knock, knock, knock. William came in hurriedly. He looked as if he had committed a sin.

'I'm sorry, son! You must give that back to me.'

He grabbed the memoir book and left instantly. Andy stared at dias. Why had it done that? Was it going to sympathize with Andy by making him remember his mother's memories or was in going to show him the way to get rid of his troubles? He was told to only think about good memories and to stay away from any source of concern.

On the following days, Andy was still thinking about his mother excitedly. He had the opportunity to decipher different aspects of the event. It seemed as though he had forgotten himself, which had helped him get rid of his woes to a great extent. Finally, after a lapse of several days, he met with Eduardo again and went on for a walk at the Calagan marketplace together.

'What do you know about my mother?' asked Andy with hesitation.

Looking as if he was talking about the crowded market, Eduardo answered him.

'She was a black hole talent by nature,'

Andy was surprised.

'You mean you knew she was a magician?'

'Your mother wasn't a magician,'

'But she had encountered a magician in the woods. She wrote about it in her memoir that I've read,'

'That man she has mentioned is Oliver Sawkit. I haven't met him for years but I know, for reasons we are unaware of, your mother did not show any sign of interest in becoming a magician. This is natural. There are many people who don't care about becoming one. By the way, do you care for some chocolate?'

It wasn't the right time to offer chocolate Andy thought.

'When do you think did my mom realize her talent?'

'Donno! Maybe during a fall evening or a snowy winter morning when she was passing through the jungle joyfully like all other little village girls. Perhaps she suddenly heard something, got startled or even frightened. Maybe, she never noticed anything the first time,'

'Why did she have no interest in magic?'

'I guess your mother kept secrets and avoided putting down certain things in her memoir. Considering her poetic emotions, I'm confident that she had no difficulty in finding the right words to express facts but she must have had a convincing reason for not doing so,'

Eduardo and Andy came to a stop simultaneously.

'We don't know what exactly has happened but we can guess that your mother didn't like the village folks to learn about her secret, that's why part of her life remains unknown. Perhaps if you find Oliver Sawkit one day, you can ask him about such things or maybe…'

'Maybe what?'

'Maybe one day when you get back all your power, you will be able to talk to your mother directly and ask her all your questions,'

'But, I may not be able to find her,'

Eduardo gave a pat on Andy's shoulder and went on.

'In this case, we will have to suffice to what we've already heard and our guesswork. I have to go now. I won't be around for a while. By the time I come back, I hope you will have learned a lot about yourself, even during nightmares and dreams.'

Eduardo spoke in such a way as though there was still an unresolved mystery remaining about Andy and that Andy had to brace for an unexpected thing to happen.

It was getting warmer and warmer day after day and people were turning to cold drinks and ice-cream more and more. Andy was also trying to enjoy himself by indulging in such things. One spring evening, he came across three familiar faces with laced hats and colorful dresses on standing by a billboard. At the sight of Fana and Fanu, Fentous's twin sisters, Andy felt like a dog with tails. He got so happy he felt he never suffered any pain in his whole life! They had managed to learn the human's dress code so well.

Fana and Fanu had their long hair sticking out of their hat. They ran to Andy and uttered the most basic human words that they had learned. Fanu had a childish tone.

'Andy, ice-cream, yummy!'

'Andy, gumdrop, stretches!' said Fana.

'How's my dress? Do I look good?' asked Fentous.

It was such a blessing that Fentous was able to go and freely meet Andy without any restrictions. She could fill his lonely and uneventful days. Fentous had said that Eduardo had asked her to meet him less often and not to tell anybody about his living quarters. Andy was not surprised. His life had become so strange that such issues did not seem to matter at all. He bought the twin sisters ice-creams four times. At the end of the day, they had eaten so much they had a bump on their small bellies. Fana and Fanu stood in front of huge billboards on the street staring at the images in them in astonishment. Their eyes followed cars down the street. The two held Andy's hand worriedly while crossing the street.

Andy and Fentous sat in a park near the house at the end of the day. Andy was unhappy.

'Nobody gives me a reply. They seem to have forsaken me. I haven't met Eduardo for a month. Can you bring me some newspapers?'

'Sure, I'll bring you some tomorrow,'

Delighted and satisfied, Andy took a glance at Fentous. It seemed his thoughts had been transferred to her mind.

'No need to thank me for that. You would do the same thing for me, wouldn't you?'

The day was coming to an end and the sun was about to set. The warm temperature that had filled the homes was little by little turning cool. Unlike many people, William did not show much reaction to cold and hot weather much. He was sitting on the couch skimming through the tourism magazine packages for hot days of the year. He was planning a summer vacation for the family. In the kitchen, Flora was nagging as the ventilation system had suddenly broken. Diana was thinking of redecorating the house just like she did every spring. As usual, William would ask her not to move his couch elsewhere. It was under the window facing the street where he was able to see the lawn outside.

That night when Andy was walking back and forth in his room, pages of dias started to be turned. Deadlines for purchases are coming to an end.

This had nothing to do with black holes and their possible hazards. It rather had to do with some kind of danger. Andy heard some faint sound. Looking for it, he stared at the book. All of a sudden, he was taken inside it where he set foot to an unknown land.

Under the star-studded sky, in the wondrous whispers of the night when a breeze was touching that plain, a man with dark blue clothes on, was standing there with his back to Andy. He was aware of Andy's presence, so he turned his head over his shoulder. His face looked violent bearing signs of agony he had undergone in his life. He gazed at Andy with his black and penetrating eyes.

'It's time to go! They are coming. Run away! Save yourself!'

The world around Andy disappeared and he found himself back in his room. The book was shut and went up like smoke and then out of sight.

Andy was staring at the point where the book had disappeared. Dias was gone! However, it had left its last warning in his soul in such an effective way that he wouldn't let it down. Andy was startled when he heard little rocks hitting the window glass. Out on the street were standing Eduardo and Andy's look-alike. He realized he had to accept a compulsory substitution. They had gone to him after days of loneliness. Andy still felt worried in spite of all optimism. He got dressed quickly and left the house on tip-toe. He started to speak as soon as he saw his look-alike.

'Where the hell have you been? You're so irresponsible!'

'I know what's made you mad. You've nagged to me since I opened William's present. You are a beggar!'

Eduardo coughed to announce his presence. Andy turned to him.

'You will excuse me but your look-alike makes decisions according to your manners. He would do things that you would do. He cannot decide on his own,'

He then patted the look-alike on his shoulder and sent him to the house. It looked as though Andy was supposed to stay the night outside the home. He was concerned.

'Dias took me to its land but it then disappeared for good!'

Eduardo seemed to be busy thinking about something more important.

'I need to go. It's not safe here anymore,'

Andy was filled with worry.

'I know I have to go but I don't know where to. Dias also told me to go,'

Eduardo took no heed of dias acting indifferently again.

'I want you to be brave. I know it's hard but we have no other way. If you stay here, they will come to you much sooner than you could expect. They would even go to your family. You have to go!'

'Who is coming? I don't know them!'

'But they know you very well. They are the ones, who've been after you since you were a child,'

'Are we going to the Password?'

'Put such a place out your mind! I have to send you somewhere else for which I may get fired from the Council of Magic but your life matters to me the most,'

Andy looked at Eduardo and went on with hesitation.

'It's the parallel world, right?'

He then became depressingly silent. Eduardo tried to sympathize with him.

'Gateways have been laid under a spell. The Council was always seeking an excuse to keep you for its own sake. Now it is in no hurry to cleanse the gateways under the pretext of the spell being solely for the sake of detecting you and the fact that it's not dangerous for others. We don't have much time to wait for the gateways to be secure again,'

'So, what are we gonna do now?'

'Wait here. An old yellow car will come here to pick you up. Get in the car. Do not make any hesitation, Andy. Trust me!'

In the silence of the street, Eduardo walked into the dark of the night. Soon afterward, an old yellow car showed up as it was signaling Andy with its lights. It was in a hurry. The car stopped next to Andy with an abrupt break. The driver was a young man with a sense of humor. He had a baseball cap on.

'Hey, young boy! What are you waiting for? Hop in and we'll have a great ride together!' the man told Andy immediately.

'Where are you taking me?' asked Andy.

'To the place Eduardo has ordered me to take you,'

'And where is that?'

'The same place that Eduardo has ordered me to take you,'

'Why don't you tell me about it?'

The car door opened with a squeak. Apparently, it hadn't been oiled for a while. Andy got in. His safety belt was buckled on its own and the car set out at an incredible speed. It left the city in a short time. The young chauffeur who was laughing his heart out, knew the road like the back of his hand. He took a side dirt road and left the obstacles behind in such a way as if they had never existed. The car made long jumps over multiple ditches. Andy was glued to his seat all the time without uttering even a single word for fear he may distract the reckless driver.

Scattered snippets of knowledge were gradually storming Andy's mind. The driver had opted for deflection; yet, Andy knew that they were on their way to the Tourin village. The car was racing on the jungle path toward the lake. Andy was looking at the delighted and frantic face of the driver.

'You are driving to the lake!'

'It's at least thirty meters deep!' he said happily.

The driver moved his cap a bit, pulled the car windows up and jumped right into the lake. Startled, Andy started to scream out of fear and put his hands on his face. When he opened his eyes, he found the car moving under the water like a submarine. Schools of fish were staring at him from behind the car window. The driver was elated.

'Stupid fish, the lake doesn't belong to you. Show me your proof if it belongs to you. Come on! Bring me your ownership papers and I will get out of here.' raved the driver.

Andy was ignorant of the events under the water. All of his senses were focused on the destination about which he knew nothing. In the darkness under the water, he had an opportunity to embark on a bit of guesswork. The driver distracted him several times by asking him to check out the fish.

He was just paying attention to his own notes and multiple signs on his map.

'Yes, that's it!'

He then got out of the water and drove onto the jungle path again. At the sight of light that was visible in the dark of the woods, Andy felt he was frozen with horror. It was the Tourin village. The situation changed for Andy in a scary way. Good moments were pulling back. The stars were getting farther and farther and the world in his heart was being drawn into darkness.

Before the car entered the cemetery premises, Andy had noticed some people moving around the graves. Now that they were getting closer, he couldn't see anybody there. He was pleased that his power had not been fully restored yet. He was well aware of the fact that they are dead people whom the driver is unable to see. At that moment, the abandoned house in the graveyard, looked in his eyes to go higher and higher like a deadly and haunted tower. The driver came to a stop at the graveyard.

'We are a bit too early but it's better than arriving late. Get out of the car and wait,' announced the driver gladly.

'All by myself?'

'Yes, that's what Eduardo told me,'

He then checked the time and went on.

'In five minutes' time, somebody will come after you. An old midget. Listen to whatever he says. Get out now. The next passenger is waiting for me.'

The last thing among the community of the people who were alive was the noise of the speeding yellow car that was distancing from the cemetery at an unbelievably high speed. Andy preferred to visit her mom if he was supposed to visit a ghost. As he was walking slowly to his mother's grave, he could hear some chirping sound that came from moving branches. He reached the lilac tree and sat there. He tried not to look at other parts of the graveyard as far as possible especially the abandoned house about which he had heard such horrifying stories.

The midget was late but Andy was beginning to muster up some courage. Most definitely, he had to brace for worse days. He got up to his feet and started to watch the graveyard. Silence prevailed and the frightening dark jungle was not doing anything against him. Everything seemed to be normal.

'Oh, I'm sorry to be late!'

He heard some noise and then the voice of an old man. Andy turned fearfully. The midget didn't seem to care about frightening others.

'You must be Andy Barnet. You've grown up a lot since the first time we met,' said the midget joyfully.

Checking out the midget's size, Andy was wondering whether he had been behind his forgetfulness all those years. He then remembered that the midget had saved his life once and he ought to be polite to him.

'Hasn't anyone taught you to greet others?' complained the midget.

Hurriedly, Andy greeted him and then made an apology.

'To be honest, I was kind of scared. I have no idea what's going to happen. You know…it's…'

The midget didn't seem to be impressed.

'What is there that frightens you here? Are you scared of that cursing wolf that's looking for you? Oh, come on, kid! Don't underestimate me. Should it come your way, I'll do something to it that it would prefer to get lost for good,'

Andy felt relieved somehow despite the midget's exaggerated tone.

'Now, what are we supposed to do? I'm ready,'

'It's great that you are prepared. They have cast a spell on the gateways so we will have to make use of the midgets' way. It's somehow difficult and worrisome but we have no other choice,'

'Difficult and worrisome?'

'I have to help you pass through my own personal gate. I know where I am going to end up in but I'm not sure where you will. I just hope that you will end up in a safe and secure place,'

'What if the Council of Magic puts you to trouble for doing that?'

With a wet face that looked as if it was spitted on, the midget replied.

'What? Trouble? We are hated enough. This won't change anything any further. You can be assured about that, young man!'

He then stood on the gravestone so he could put his hand on Andy's shoulder.

'Birara shavna mitalda!'

A bit farther away, a yellow and blue flame started to burn. Among the flames was a tiny metal gate on the other side of which was nothing but darkness. When the midget leaned on the gateway, Andy realized that the fire at the gate was harmless.

'Wherever you may end up in, just take shelter in a safe place before acting curiously!'

Andy moved his head worriedly.

'Does it hurt?'

'It doesn't hurt me. I hope it'll be the same for you too. I'll come after you once you're gone. By the way, my name's Parco. You can also look for Stubborn, my nickname, if you wanna find me,'

He then went on explaining without looking at Andy.

'Look, Andy! You are going to the parallel world illegally. If you should face any creature while moving through, if anyone asks you any questions, you'd better just keep quiet. Silence is the best answer because you won't be harmed this way. The only thing is you may just end up in some distant location. Anyway, go now!'

'What kind of creature do you mean? Human being?'

'Go now! You are being late!'

Andy was filled with worry. With shaky steps, he got to the gateway. He looked back for the last time. He then took a glimpse of Parco, the pig-headed midget who was looking at him confidently.

Andy passed through the gateway. The last thing he heard from the world behind him was the voice of a woman who called him a son. He, however, had no chance to return. The world had plunged into darkness and the fire at the gateway was going out. Andy had set foot to the parallel world.

About the Author,

Abolfazl Haji Mohammadi

(1986 /Gorgan-Iran)

Abolfazl Haji Mohammadi is a novice novelist, and this is the second book of his. As an ambitious writer, he tries to address readers in the in the global arena. That is why the characters of his stories do not belong to any specific territory. He uses the genre of imagination and fantasy to narrate his fictions.

Haji Mohammadi currently lives at his birthplace in Gorgan, Golestan Province and is working on the compilation of the second volume of the present work.

www.ingramcontent.com/pod-product-compliance
Lightning Source LLC
Chambersburg PA
CBHW070852250626
47159CB00003B/1039